BEAR

AF089473

BEAR

KIRI LIGHTFOOT

AUCKLAND · SYDNEY · MELBOURNE · LONDON

First published in 2025

Text © Kiri Lightfoot, 2025
Illustrations © Pippa Keel Situ, 2025

All rights reserved. No part of this book may be reproduced or transmitted in any form or by any means, electronic or mechanical, including photocopying, recording or by any information storage and retrieval system, without prior permission in writing from the publisher.

Allen & Unwin
Level 2, 10 College Hill, Freemans Bay
Auckland 1011, New Zealand
Phone: (64 9) 377 3800
Email: auckland@allenandunwin.com
Web: www.allenandunwin.co.nz

83 Alexander Street
Crows Nest NSW 2065, Australia
Phone: (61 2) 8425 0100

EU Authorised Representative: Easy Access System Europe, Mustamäe tee 50, 10621 Tallinn, Estonia, gpsr.requests@easproject.com

A catalogue record for this book is available from the National Library of New Zealand.

ISBN 978 1 991006 93 6
Design by Kate Barraclough
Set in Adobe Caslon Pro
Printed and bound by CPI (UK) Ltd, Croydon CR0 4YY

10 9 8 7 6 5 4 3

To Ben and Anahera

WHO AM I?
I AM YOUR LIVING NIGHTMARE
I FOLLOW YOU, ALWAYS CLOSE BEHIND
YOU CAN SENSE ME, SMELL ME, HEAR ME GROWL
DO YOU FEEL MY BREATH HOT AGAINST YOU?
I AM A TEST
YOU WILL FAIL
IT IS TIME TO SURRENDER
THIS IS THE BEGINNING OF THE END OF YOU.

1.

I'm hiding in the tree again.

Nearly fourteen years old, one hundred and seventy-three centimetres tall and I'm halfway up a tree in my front garden. It is not one of my proudest moments, but I really don't want to go inside.

I thought I would have grown out of climbing trees by now, but up here I feel as if I don't really exist. No one can see me and nothing can get me. And that's fine by me. Because I don't want to exist. Not like this.

I don't want to have these bad thoughts.

Do you want to know another bad thought? There is this darkness inside my house. Someone will soon be dead. Gone. Lost. Destroyed. It's not me, not yet . . . It's someone else. I can feel it. And sometimes when I feel things, they come true. They do. It's a real worry.

Do you know what's worse? I think I want him to die. This is a horrible thing to admit, but I actually do. The waiting for him to die is driving me insane and the house feels like it has a dark cloud over it, darker than normal. I can't live like this, that's why I'm hiding in a tree. You would too. You would hide.

I wonder if he knows he is dying? What would it feel like to know that? Would it be awful or would it be okay? Would the *knowing* mean you just accept it, maybe even welcome it? I mean, the scary part of living is wondering when, isn't it? When will it be my turn to die? When will this all be over? Or maybe I'm the only one who thinks like this. But when it's your turn and you know it . . . you just wait, right? You stop fighting. And wait.

Or . . . Do you never stop fighting?

Or . . . Does it depend on whether you've got anything to fight for?

Oh man. These are the kind of thoughts you have while on a branch looking at leaves and hoping no one sees you. Intense ones. I know you can't answer these questions for me, by the way. I know that's not why you're here. I just save these thoughts for when I'm up in this tree so that I don't have them in the middle of a science lesson and yell in front of the class: 'Why the hell ARE we even here? Who cares about this nonsense?'

So this is me, Jasper Robinson-Woods, up a tree: not going inside, not facing the reality that someone is dying inside my house and I don't like my life. Plus I can't find the remote which means I can't watch television, so what else would I do?

He is my goldfish, by the way, the dying someone. He is not a human... Sorry, I probably should have said that earlier. But he is a *someone* nonetheless. It still means death is in the house. It feels just the same, you know, the same as when it's a person. I know that feeling too. It's not nice.

So yeah, I'm pretty sure my fish is probably most definitely going to die any day now. Or he is terminally depressed. But either way, he's not good. Not. Good. At. All. He is always down on the bottom of the tank, hardly moving, just drifting around aimlessly. I think it's only a matter of time. Poor fish.

If anyone sees me up this tree I have a plan, by the way. I'm going to tell them I'm saving the neighbour's cat. My neighbours don't have cats, so this plan won't work if one of the neighbours finds me. When whoever sees me (not a neighbour) asks where the imaginary cat has gone, I'll say it got down from the tree, but I got stuck. Yes, stuck as a result of being so caring and community-spirited. Plausible? I think it will do. It's a plan I worked out ages ago. I haven't had to use it yet. Still hiding. Like a ninja.

I'm going to have to go inside eventually. My mother will be wondering where I am. Her car is in the driveway. She must have finished work early for once, she's not usually home until late. I'm just not sure if I can face her right now.

I look at my watch. It's 4.44 p.m. I love it when you check your watch exactly at a cool-looking time like that. 4.44. It's a sign. I should go inside, it's already nearly 4.45. I also need to go to the toilet, urgently actually. *Right, Jasper, don't think about watery things. Don't think of waterfalls, water cascading down rocks, a slow-leaking tap, that kind of thing.*

Drip, drip, drip.

Dammit! What the hell is wrong with me? Now I'm thinking of ALL of those things, all at once.

It's impossible to tell yourself NOT to do something. Have you noticed that? Do not think about an elephant. Did you just think about one?

I tell myself not to do things all the time and it never works.

Don't be angry.
Don't be sad.

Don't make an absolute dick of yourself.
It backfires and I do all of those things. Hourly.

JASPER ROBINSON-WOODS. DON'T BE YOU, OK?

I can hear Mum in the kitchen. The kettle is boiling and she's moving stuff around in the cupboards. She's probably trying to find crackers: she would have missed lunch again. The smoke alarm starts beeping so now she's obviously started cooking dinner. She isn't the best cook. I can hear her muttering and using the pointy end of the mop to try to mute the alarm.

It finally stops and she says something to herself, something sweary. She has probably sent me about ten text messages but my phone battery is dead. DEAD. Not a surprise when she only lets me have a cheap cruddy phone, any decent apps are SO slow on it and by the way she DEFINITELY won't let me have any social media. Great way for me to make friends at the new school, Mum. Thanks.

Where are you, Jasper?

Right outside, Mum, right outside the window! Hiding in a tree like the lovely weirdo you raised. Proud?

I wait until the road is clear and jump down, looking around to confirm I'm not spotted. I grab my school bag which I hid behind Mum's rose bush. Seeing it reminds me of school and I feel like my heart skips a beat. I'm pretty sure it's because I hate school but could it actually be an undiagnosed heart tremor? Can thirteen-year-olds have heart attacks? And can you die from stress? I will add these to the list of things to google later.

I walk up the front steps jiggling my keys loudly before entering to attract attention. Mum appears, still in her scrubs from work. Did I tell you she is a dental hygienist? Well, she is. I know — terrifying. I live with someone obsessed with dental care. There are never lollies in the house. Plenty of toothpaste though, and copious amounts of floss (which I tell her I use but don't).

She walks towards me, tying up her brown curls into a bun on top of her head, her forehead full of frown.

'Jasper! Why is your phone off?'

'Battery died,' I say as I go into my room, throwing my bag on the bed.

It died. DEAD.

'What's for dinner?' I ask, changing the subject quickly

and rushing to the toilet.

'Make sure you charge it for tomorrow,' she says from outside the bathroom door. 'Jasper?'

'Yes, Mum. I will.'

'Why did it take you so long to get home?' She is still outside the door. Just because she's home early she somehow suddenly cares where I spend my afternoons. 'Where were you?'

'Nowhere,' I say, opening the door. She's standing right there. Still frowning.

'What's wrong, Jasper?' I see through her dark-rimmed glasses that her eyes are darting around my face at record speed, looking for answers.

'What's wrong with *you*?' I say and go back into my room, shutting the door behind me. She finally walks away.

And then silence.

Silence.

Except for the bubbles of the fish-tank filter.

Blub, blub, blub.

I look into the tank. He is there. Still alive. Not dead.

Not.

Dead.

I thought he would die today. I thought I would come home to him floating at the top of the tank, or sucked right next to the water filter. That would have been okay, it

would have. Like I said, I've kind of been willing it to happen. I just can't cope with the waiting. The waiting to die bit is torture. Poor Han Solo (that's my

fish), poor little thing. I called him Han Solo after the dude from *Star Wars*, member of the Rebel Alliance . . . that Han Solo. Yes, I named my goldfish after that hero even though his life was going to be swimming around an awful, dirty fish tank and amounting to absolutely nothing. It seems unfair now.

Have you ever thought about what it would be like to be a goldfish? What an awful existence. Swimming around a boring, glass prison looking out at a dirty bedroom with an ugly face staring at you now and then (but mostly ignoring you). I can't believe I allowed this imprisonment to happen. I am a terrible human.

I don't know why I thought having a fish would be fun. I wanted a pet and this was the only one I was allowed. Mum gave in, probably thinking — *He is an only child, he needs a friend.* Now I'm pleading for the universe to kill the sick fish friend because I'm so disturbed watching him die.

Everything might get better if he dies.
Maybe I'll sleep again.

I haven't slept for twenty-eight days.

Twenty-eight days.

That's a long time not to have slept.

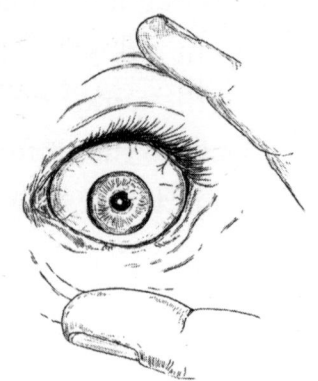

I suppose I must have slept a little bit. No one can go without a wink of sleep for twenty-eight days, can they? Sleep always wins. Knocks you out in a mathematics class or something. All I know is that for twenty-eight days every morning it feels like I haven't had any of that proper sleep, where your mind goes somewhere else and your body fully relaxes. Deep sleep. When you don't have that, you feel like you are forever moving around in a dream. You don't know what's real anymore.

The other day I googled *longest time someone has stayed awake*. Supposedly in 1965, some seventeen-year-old in America set a world record for a science-fair experiment. He lasted two hundred and sixty-four hours, or eleven days. Either I have set a new record with twenty-eight days or I am sleeping without knowing it. Apparently, lack of sleep affects 'motivation, perception and concentration'. Yep, I have problems with all of those.

What did people do before Google? I contemplate googling it.

I haven't told my mother about the not-sleeping. I haven't even told her about Han Solo being sick. Because I might cry. She will think I'm crying because I'm so attached to him. Sorry, Han Solo, I just don't like watching things die.

And if he dies, who will be next?

I've had to have one eye open at night. Just in case. For twenty-eight days.

Maybe it will all be okay if he just dies.

The nightmare might stop. The real reason I can't sleep: I

started having this nightmare, again. Twenty-eight days ago. You wouldn't sleep, either, if you saw what my nightmare is. Who He is.

Even worse: something weird has happened. I had the nightmare ... while I was awake.

WHO AM I?
I AM YOUR NIGHTMARE
I AM BACK
THE DARKNESS HAS RETURNED AND YOU WILL SOON KNOW WHY
YOU ARE NOTHING, JASPER
YOU DESERVE NOTHING
I WILL DESTROY YOU FOR GOOD
IT IS TIME TO SURRENDER

2.

'I left the pasta boiling and now the pot is burnt. Another one.'

My mother is standing by my door with her handbag over her shoulder. She's out of her work clothes now, wearing jeans and a knitted sweater. It's an ugly mustard colour and it doesn't suit her.

'I'm really hungry, Mum,' I say in my most *'don't deprive your growing child'* voice. I'm going to have to make eggs, again. This happens a lot and perfect eggs are the only thing I have totally mastered. With a mum who is always at work, I eat a lot of poached eggs.

'And we don't have any eggs,' she says.

NO EGGS!

'I thought I could go and pick up a pizza? I need to chat about something.'

A pizza chat. About 'something'. These pizza chats never end well. We had pizza when Mum told me my grandmother was sick. I didn't even eat the pizza in the end because . . . Well, I just couldn't.

'No salami,' I say, remembering my new thing.

'Ham?'

'No ham. Or bacon. I'm going vegan,' I state proudly. I read an article online, all about how processed meats are carcinogenic, etc. There have been studies.

'So you want a *vegan* pizza? Is there such a thing?' She looks baffled.

'Vegetarian for now. Or prawns, or chicken.' I'm not sure what would arrive if I ordered a vegan pizza. Could be risky.

'You know chicken is not vegan, right?' Mum says, looking concerned.

'Yeah, like I said I'm not there *yet*.'

'But you're not vegetarian yet either?'

'Are you even listening?' I yell it, and I probably shouldn't have but she asks too many questions sometimes.

'Don't shout at me!' she shouts back, then puts a hand on her chest to calm herself. 'I'm just confused, but I'll work it out.' She sighs loudly and snatches her keys from her bag and walks out. I'm an inconvenience. As usual.

I hear her start the car in the driveway and I listen as the sound of the engine fades down the street. And I am alone.

Alone.

Apart from my dying fish.

Thoughts are worse when you are alone. It's why the tree is there. I mean, it was there before I existed, but it's why I sit in it. To avoid coming inside and being alone.

I lie on my bed and try not to think about how hungry I am. I particularly don't like it in my room at the moment. There is too much history here, the room I have lived in for my whole life. Perhaps that's the problem — that I've lived here my entire life, before everything was different. I still remember the before: the before everything got so complicated. My height on each birthday is written on the door frame; there are glow-in-the-dark stars on the ceiling and there are lots of little holes from pins that held up posters over the years. All still here, all the little holes.

I've got the same bed that I've had since I was five. The same bed where Dad used to sit at the end and make up adventure stories while I fell asleep. When he lived here. And Nana used to be in here too, doing puzzles on the floor and playing Scrabble while Mum was working. Now that history is like a shadow.

My stomach rumbles loudly. I'm so deeply hungry. I bet Mum gets the wrong pizza too. What will I do if it has ham on it? I think I will have to eat it, I'm that hungry. Or I could just take it off. That's fine, I reckon ham residue is okay for now.

I am thinking seriously about becoming vegan though, or at least vegetarian. My dad is vegetarian. I'm not doing it to be like him. I one hundred percent don't want to be like him. No. Way.

But cheese isn't vegan, is it? I do like cheese. And yoghurt. And milk. Vegan would be tricky, now I think of it. But I don't have enough hobbies at the moment and it could be my new 'thing', you see.

It has a ring to it . . .

That still works.

In more pressing matters, I wonder what this pizza chat is about. I hope it's not more bad news, I don't think I can handle it. I do think I know what it's about... or more *who* it's about.

Manly Steve.

This guy! This manly, manly guy is my mother's boyfriend, or whatever you are supposed to call him. They aren't married and he doesn't live with us or anything. He is her businessman boyfriend and I call him Manly Steve — not to his face, just when I'm talking about how much I despise him and everything he stands for.

You can probably figure out why I call him Manly Steve from my great drawing. I mean, compared to my actual dad, most men are quite 'manly' but Manly Steve is really manly. He has chest hair, facial hair, hair on his legs, hair on his back, even hair in his nose and ears and on his fingers. I didn't know we were supposed to be that hairy without actually being gorillas.

Maybe Mum does want to marry him? Maybe that's what she wants to talk about. She wants to marry this monkey man! Errggh. Maybe she will take his name. Heisner. Ha. She might want *me* to take it too. She can't make me do that, can she? I have been researching changing my name but there was nothing about that on the website. I have spent hours contemplating a new name but maybe I won't even get a choice about it. Mum will just force it upon me in an effort to play

'CHILDREN CAN ALSO BE LEGALLY FORCED TO CHANGE THEIR NAME IF THEIR MOTHERS BELIEVE IT'S IN THE BEST INTERESTS OF THEIR HAIRY, MANLY, BUSINESSMAN BOYFRIENDS.'

Happy Families with Manly Steve.

Jasper Heisner-Robinson-Woods. Or Jasper Heisner. Oh shit balls. Maybe Mum is going to make me change my name to Jasper bloody Heisner! It sounds like when you sneeze and stuff actually comes out your mouth and lands on the floor — one of those sneezes.

"Heisner family"

He is an idiot. A big, hairy idiot and he annoys me. Everything about him annoys me. His face annoys me, his dumb businesses annoy me (yes, he has a few of them and I don't really know what they are, something about packaging and shipping). His 'important calls' about 'important packages' annoy me. His fancy European car annoys me and how much he loves it even though it's ugly, it takes up too much room in the driveway and smells like fly spray. His disgusting public displays of affection with my mother annoy me.

HE ANNOYS ME.

But most of all, he doesn't like me. Not even slightly. He makes that pretty obvious, so if this chat involves him it is deeply worrying.

Also worrying is how long this pizza is taking. I am so

hungry I feel ill. I usually eat twelve bowls of cereal and a loaf of bread after school but today I was too busy in a tree avoiding the front door. My stomach acid is possibly eating my stomach lining now. This could damage my delicate gut. I had a lot of antibiotics as a child and I'm still recovering. Can you permanently damage your stomach by being hungry? I will google that too.

I leave my bedroom, gently closing the door behind me, to keep the *death* inside. I walk down the hallway to the kitchen and grab a piece of bread from the freezer. As I put it in the toaster, I notice the pantry door is closed, but the light is on inside. I didn't think that was possible because the light goes off when the door is closed ... unless ... Is there something inside the pantry? Someone?

I listen just outside, for the sound of breath. But I hear nothing. Just the toast starting to sizzle. I don't open the pantry door, just in case. The toast pops.

POP!

AHHHH! My heart jumps. I'm a little on edge. I have to be alert at the moment.

Toast with butter will have to do. I eat quickly, staring at the pantry door. Not weird at all. Out of the corner of my eye, I notice a pair of Manly Steve's running shoes at the back door. Can't he keep his shoes at his own house?

It pisses me off that when he is here he always tells me to 'Take your shoes off and put them at the front door.'

In my own house! He invents new rules all of a sudden and Mum just lets him, pretending we always do things that way. When we don't. She wears her shoes inside all the time. I mean, I approve. I read an article about the amount of germs we can bring inside on our shoes ... so I'm all for it. But I don't like Steve telling me what to do. And on top of that, now *his* shoes are sitting at the back door, *inside*. Big dirty, manly, stinky shoes too. Imagine the germs he's brought inside with those hairy toe-holders.

The hypocrisy of it all. He just invents a new rule and then breaks it. He makes me so angry. He always has. Before I even met him.

I eat another piece of buttery toast and remember the lost remote.

I'd better try to find it. Watching television now will stop me from eating four more bits of toast and getting too full for pizza. I take the cushions off the couch and wedge my hands down in between the cracks at the back. There are lots of crumbs and a broken pen but no remote. I lie on the carpet and look underneath the couch. No remote — but I find two dollars. Score. I pull the curtains out from the wall and look behind them, no luck. I collapse onto the couch, defeated.

Where the hell is it? Life is not worth living without a working television because watching endless YouTube clips just depresses me. This sucks. And where the hell are my mother and my pizza?

What if there has been a terrible car accident? Or the pizza place has been held up by a gunman? Maybe a tornado is ripping through Auckland destroying everything in its path and I'm just here looking for the remote while there is devastation all around me?

I don't hear any sirens or anything but like I told you, death follows me around. I have to worry like this. How likely is an alien invasion in New Zealand? It could be that. A UFO may be hovering over the pizza place ready to take Mum to some planet somewhere. Lucky her, it might be better than this dying one.

But then I hear a sound and it's not particularly extra-terrestrial. It's the sound of Mum's keys at the front door. She walks down the hall, spotting me on the couch.

'Oh, you're in here.'

'I'm looking for the remote. It's gone.' I say, putting my hand back behind the couch cushions.

She walks into the kitchen, putting the pizza boxes on the table. 'It's on top of the bookshelf. Steven put it up there.'

Ha! Sabotage! Why didn't I guess that Manly Steve was involved in the remote's unexpected and untimely disappearance? I sigh loudly and as I stand I mutter 'typical'. Mum looks over to me, glaring, always sensitive when it comes to her precious Manly Steve. She does seem strange though, stranger than usual. I'm starting to think she does have a 'bad news' look on her face.

'Jasper . . .' she says, as she hands me a plate.

Here we go. What is it? Hit me with the bad news. I'm as ready as I'll ever be. Who is dying?

'I got one ham and one completely meat-free option for you, in case while I was out you decided you definitely were vegetarian.'

Oh.

'But it has cheese, Mum? I said *vegan*.'

'What?' She slams her plate on the table. 'No, you said . . .'

'Just joking . . . calm down.' I open the pizza box. 'Ugh, is that courgette? Gross.'

'If you want to be vegetarian you'll need to eat vegetables.' She doesn't look happy.

'Okay, so what's the deal?' I ask, flicking the courgette off the pizza.

'What's the deal with you?' She watches me, eyes wide.

'What?' We both just stare at each other. There is no deal! This is weird. Her eyes don't usually go that wide. 'You're freaking me out — what's wrong?'

'Nothing, everything's great,' she says, taking a bite of her cancer pizza.

I suppose this is good. No one is dying, yet (except Han Solo).

'I need to talk to you about Steven, actually,' she says, pointing to the chair. 'Sit down.'

So I was right . . . Manly Steve is involved. They're getting married. My new last name is Heisner. Yes, I need to sit for this.

'Can I eat? I'm starving,' I say, although I'm not because

the toast has filled me up. I'm just not in the mood for this conversation.

Mum slides the pizza boxes towards me and I inadvertently grab a piece of the ham pizza and start gobbling. Whoops.

'Steven is spending a lot of time here,' she says, charging on anyway.

'I've noticed,' I say, staring at the stinky shoes. Is that toe jam I smell?

'I can hardly go to his house with you here ...'

'Sorry for being alive,' I say, mid-mouthful.

'I don't mean that, but he is here a lot and it seems silly to have his house empty.'

'And?' This pizza tastes weird. Maybe I can taste the carcinogens?

'So to save his time travelling back and forwards,' she stands and walks to the cupboard and grabs a glass, 'and to save on the cost of petrol ...'

'Yeah, what?' She is talking a lot; this is the biggest conversation we've had all year.

She stares at her empty glass. 'Long-term we need to consider, or reconsider ...'

This is starting to feel very bizarre. 'You're not getting married, are you? That would be weird, Mum.' I just say it. *Speed this up!*

'No, Jasper, I don't want to get married again.'

'Thank god! And you don't want Manly Steve to move in with us?' I ask. Surely not.

'I do. We do. That's what I'm trying to tell you.' Her eyes

jump to my face as she looks for a reaction. 'We could rent his place out, you see?'

I put my pizza down. I don't know where to look, what to say. Why would he want to live here with us? With me? I don't see how that would work. I hear a strange sound in one ear. A long, drawn-out note. It changes pitch and turns high-pitched, piercing.

'Jasper? We're just talking about it but please don't call him Manly Steve. I hate that.' She does hate that.

She continues to look at me, trying to read my face. Or can she see the sound drilling into my skull?

'Are you okay with it, in theory?' she finally asks.

In theory? No! The high-pitched sound moves through my veins deeper, deeper inside the channels of my brain. Can she see it? The sound moving?

'Jasper. Are you okay, love?'

Okay? Okay? Am I okay? No. I am not okay.

'No!' I shout. 'I'm shit actually, and I hate the idea, in *theory*, and I hate Manly Steve, so why would I want to live with him when I hate him so much?'

I stand up, the chair falling away behind me.

THUD.

Mum stands as well. 'Jasper. Don't . . .'

'And can you move his shoes? They stink.' I storm out of the room but briefly walk back in, avoiding my mother's eyes while I grab one of the pizzas (I don't want to waste food). I stamp down the hallway.

'Do not eat that in your room,' Mum says firmly, but I push

open my door and slam it behind me.

BANG.

I will eat it in my room. I will!

I sit at the edge of the bed and jam another piece of pizza into my mouth, even though I'm not hungry at all and it's the diseased pizza. I stare across at the fish tank, Han Solo is wonkily lying near the bottom of the tank.

'Just hurry up and die, you stupid fish,' I say, throwing the pizza box at the fish tank, pizza flying.

I don't want Manly Steve to be here all the time.

Why would he want to live with us? I annoy him with my very existence. Why would he want to be reminded of that every day?

Wrong. It's just wrong.

I should have known he'd want to move in, though. He was already trying to make it his house anyway, putting his shoes at the back door, like a dog pissing on everything so everyone knows it's been there.

The only room in the house that will just be mine is my room, the death room, and I hate it in here.

Maybe I could go and live with my dad? I could call

him and tell him there's been a terrible development in my mother's love life and it is time I came to live with him.

HA! Not gonna happen! Mum would never allow that. Dad doesn't want me anyway. He has made that pretty clear with his giant, black-hole-sized absence in my life.

He doesn't want me.

HELLO JASPER
CAN YOU HEAR ME?
DO YOU KNOW ME?
I KNOW YOU
I KNOW YOUR SECRETS
YOU CAN'T HIDE FROM ME
I CAN SEE YOU. TRULY SEE YOU.
I WILL DESTROY YOU
IT IS TIME TO SURRENDER

3.

I feel queasy.

I've eaten too many carbs too quickly, and it's all so salty. I now need water — a whole jug full, but water is in the kitchen and Mum is in the kitchen. Do I call it quits and go back out? Or do I commit to making a dramatic statement and leave her stewing, regretting all of this?

Salt thirst can't kill me, can it? No, I don't think it can overnight. I'm just going to get in bed and pretend to sleep, I'm not even going to brush my teeth. My mother will HATE that. It's the ultimate revenge against a dental hygienist.

I flick off the light and lie in bed, clothes still on. I stare at the ceiling in the darkness, but my heart is racing. I hear footsteps and a click as the hall light goes off. Mum is going to bed; she's not going to even say goodnight. That's just rude (says the one who just dramatically exited the pizza conversation, taking the pizza with him).

Now there is darkness. Not even any light creeping in under the closed door.

Total darkness.

I am supposed to go to sleep now. But I know I won't. I can't. Twenty-eight days since I've slept and after today, I know there will be no sleep.

Twenty-eight days since the nightmare came back and Han Solo started to get sick.

Twenty-eight days.

I close my eyes tight.

I know the nightmare is close. I don't even need to be asleep for it to come, I know that now. It is only a matter of time. So I just wait, in the dark.

Can I ask you something, while I wait for Him to arrive?

What are you scared of? At night, what is it that haunts you in the darkness? Is there anything that comes to you in your dreams to turn them into nightmares?

I know mine. He's been there for a long time.

A grizzly bear.

Him.

A bear is looking for me, hunting me, trying to destroy me. Claws ready. Razor-sharp teeth ready. A low growl. I've had this nightmare too many times to count. Again and again. When I was younger, in this room, when Mum tucked me into bed at night, turned off the lights and said goodnight, that's when I first met Him. The darkness brought Him here: I would see the darkness, really *see* it; what it was, what it could be — the unknown — the inevitable.

And now He's back.

Just like I thought I'd grown out of hiding in trees or believing in monsters under beds and trolls under bridges, I thought I had grown out of this bear too. He was gone. But He's back to haunt me again. He's been here for twenty-eight days. He wants to destroy me and I can't sleep in case He tries.

My nightmare starts with a dream. Just a normal dream about anything. School. Home. Sometimes I am at my Nana and Poppa's old house. But then I hear His hot breath, that's what comes first and that's when I know it's not a dream anymore. I listen as the sound turns to growls, behind the curtains, under the bed, beneath the floorboards. Wherever my dream is, wherever I am, He appears. He will be sniffing me out, following my scent, hunting me down in the corners of my mind. I hold my breath, as if that will help and I try to find somewhere to hide — in a wardrobe, in a kitchen cupboard, anywhere. But He can smell me anyway, the droplets of sweat on my forehead.

Once he's spotted me I run, run as fast as I can — anywhere, everywhere. But my legs are heavy, stuck in setting concrete. I can never run fast enough. I can never get away. No noise comes out of my mouth. There's no one to help.

He always gets to me.

That's when I wake. I jolt awake before I'm eaten alive, my heart jumping from my chest.

When I was little this is when I would scream: a crying boy. Mum would come, but could never calm my fears. She didn't know what it was I was scared of, I couldn't put Him into words. There were no words. I knew, even then, He wasn't just a bear from a nightmare; I knew He was far more than that. Perhaps I even knew we would meet again.

I don't scream anymore. What is the point? Who would come?

He appears eventually. Of course He does. In the dark, while Mum brushes her teeth and thinks about her boyfriend and I lie in bed waiting.

I sense Him coming, like a feeling brewing in my body. A bear sixth sense bubbling away, first in my stomach, then moving to the tip of each limb. Shivery panic races through my veins and the hairs on my arm lift. I'm on alert. My heart pumps hard in my chest and my fingers shake inside their skin.

I hear His breath first, a low raspy note coming and going, almost wheezing.

My world begins to swirl around me in the darkness.

I want to be invisible.

I close my eyes but it's dark in there too. In fact, I don't know if my eyes are open or shut — I can't tell the difference.

Not tonight.

Please.

Not tonight.

Why won't you leave me alone?

Why are you here?

Tick. Tick. Tick.

Then He shows His face.

I turn to see Him; I can just make out His shape in the dark. He is on His back legs ready to pounce, saliva dripping from His mouth, teeth snarling.

Who are you?

WHO AM I?
WHY DO YOU NOT SEE ME FOR WHO I AM?
THERE IS NO POINT IN HIDING FROM ME
PRETENDING I DON'T EXIST
I ALWAYS FIND YOU
I WILL DESTROY YOU, JASPER
PIECE BY PIECE
INCH BY INCH.
IT IS TIME TO SURRENDER
THIS IS THE BEGINNING OF THE END OF YOU

4.

There is a new hole in my wall, up by my bed.

The floor is covered in pizza. The smell of old cheese and oily bread wafts in the air. I feel sick immediately. I don't know how to start cleaning up this mess. I gag as I pick up a dry, crusted piece of pizza from my pillow and throw it across the room into the open pizza box.

My body feels heavy, unrested. It is hard to move, so I pull myself slowly out of bed and stand with a rush of blood to the head.

SWOOSH.

Here we go again.

I need to cover the hole. There are others too. One day I'm going to have to deal with them properly, but not right now. I move a football poster over the top, pushing the pins into the wall. I don't even like Liverpool Football Club now and

Fábio Aurélio doesn't even play for them anymore, but I need it to conceal the damage, so the poster stays.

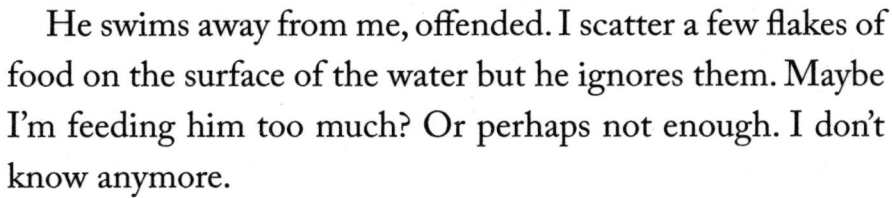

I check the fish tank. Han Solo is staring at me with a cold, evil stare, but a still-alive stare.

'Morning,' I sigh. 'Will it be today, Han Solo? Will you die today?'

He swims away from me, offended. I scatter a few flakes of food on the surface of the water but he ignores them. Maybe I'm feeding him too much? Or perhaps not enough. I don't know anymore.

There is a green slime starting to take over the fish tank walls. A green, sludgy, thick slime.

'You awake?' Mum's voice comes through the door; she doesn't enter, just shuffles around out there.

'Yeah,' I reply.

'I'm leaving now. What was that crashing last night?' she adds, quietly.

Crashing?

'Nothing. I just . . . changed my room around.' I stand, looking for evidence to hide but she doesn't come in.

'Okay, bye.' I hear footsteps down the hall, then the front door slamming. She doesn't rush in to say, 'Manly Steve won't move in if you don't want him to.' There is no, 'I love you so much. I just want you to be happy.'

For a moment I think I see green fish slime on my walls.

But I blink. And it disappears.

I move around the house, lethargic, shoulders hunched, contemplating not going to school at all.

But I do. What the hell else am I going to do today? Clean fish slime off the walls? I'd rather be out of the house.

I get dressed, choosing whichever T-shirt is on the top of the drawer then grabbing my cap and bag, without thinking what I need inside it. I shut the door and drag myself towards school. My walking is slow though and I feel like I am pulling myself through mud and heavy air, brain detached from body. Is it the lack of sleep? Or is this a strange disorder I have — that causes a lack of sleep? And hallucinations? Maybe something is seriously wrong with me.

While I'm walking I use my phone to google 'Can you catch diseases from goldfish?' I just hope I haven't caught something from Han Solo because there is seriously something wrong with him too. Is it a coincidence? Maybe that can happen when a fish is sick — you can catch it too. I feel like I'm hanging at the bottom of the tank moving through thick slime.

Sometimes when I move the fish stuff around inside the tank I don't wash my hands properly. Mum warned me about this. Maybe I'm going to die of some rare disease that normally only goldfish get. What a way to go.

I find a site. 'Like all animals, fish may carry germs that make people sick.' Oh shit balls. 'These germs can contaminate the water in which fish live. Although fish and aquarium water can spread germs to people . . .' Shit. Shit. Shit.

'. . . illness due to keeping fish is rare.' Oh, okay, better news. But I'm bound to be that rare case: wouldn't be surprised. So much to worry about.

Like I said, death follows me around.

OBITUARY: Jasper Robinson-Woods, died age thirteen-and-a-half of algae-disease-itis. He fought hard, but it really was his fault — he didn't wash his hands properly. Son of David and Michelle. No friends except a fish that died of the same thing.

5.

I have no idea how long it takes me to get to school, but it is a long time.

School is quiet when I arrive. Everyone is in class.

I am late: surprise, surprise. Another visit to the dean. It's not the start to the school day I need. *Swallow me up world, just get it over and done with. We all know it's going to happen anyway.*

I nearly stayed in bed this morning, I was so close to deciding I just couldn't be bothered with school. But I chose to come, to push through because I have to, because it is expected of me. I showed up! I think this deserves some sort of recognition. The dean doesn't see it this way.

'Hello, Jasper. Again.'

She looks at her computer, then back at me, over thick-rimmed glasses. She's wearing a skivvy under a shirt, which should never be done.

'I'm looking at your file and this is the eleventh time you have been late so far this term. Can you tell me why?'

'Nah,' I say, dropping down into the seat opposite her. This could take a while.

'I see you live about a hundred metres from school. What is that, a three-minute walk?'

'Depends how fast you walk.' It's true; I have a valid point.

'Why are you late today?' she asks, not interested in my logic.

'The bell rang before I got here. I don't think it likes me.'

She's not impressed by this attempt at humour. Her forehead wrinkles into a frown.

'*Why* are you late, Jasper?'

'I probably don't leave the house in time, Miss. Maybe our clock is wrong.'

Still not impressed. She takes a sip of tea from a mug on her desk. The mug reads 'WORLD'S BEST TEACHER'.

She looks at me over her glasses again. This time they have steam residue from the warm tea air. 'Can you start doing that? Leaving earlier? And check your clock.' She passes me a late slip.

'I'll go straight home and do that today,' I say, with false enthusiasm.

'Fabulous!' she says, with even more false enthusiasm. What a strange conversation.

'Nice mug,' I say as I stand to leave. Maybe she can share some of the 'world's-best-teacher' vibes with me. She rolls her eyes. I find this rude — I'm not allowed to do that to teachers and have had many detentions for doing so — but she can do it to me? It could have been worse, though. I got no detention and no huge lecture.

The rest of the day does get worse, however. I forgot to do my science homework last night due to the pizza chats, or to send a book report in (which I already had an extension for). I also forgot to study for the maths test, which I forgot was happening today and I forgot lunch, lunch money and my PE gear.

As I walk home, stomach rumbling, I think about whether Manly Steve has moved in yet. Will I be coming home to more of his fancy appliances, like the giant coffee machine he brought over last week? I should have known that was the start of it all.

I walk like a detached zombie. Gazing ahead but dazed, lost in thought, I pass a group of boys from school sitting on the grass by the bus stop.

'What the hell are you looking at, Weirdo?'

Doh. One of them is Leo Fulham. My least favourite person.

'Nothing.'

'Nothing? Are you calling me *nothing* because you were fully staring at me?' He stands and walks towards me.

'I was thinking about something else. I wasn't even looking. Well, I probably was *looking* but not like properly registering what I was seeing.'

'What the hell are you talking about, you nut bar?' Leo takes another step forward, spitting chewing gum from his mouth. All I can think is . . . RUN!

So I run. I run as fast as I can past the bus stop. I look back to see him shaking his head. Well, that's going to help my weirdo status . . .

I hear behind me: 'That guy is such a loser. Always has been. LOSER!'

But I can't deal with him. I have known Leo Fulham since primary school and I have no idea why he picks on me constantly. I'm the one who saw him piss his pants in year two. Maybe I should remind him of that one day.

As I arrive home, heart still racing, I throw my bag off and climb into the tree.

I pull myself up to the first branch. I usually go higher but today this will do. Maybe I don't even care anymore if someone sees me. I'm too tired to care.

It is uncomfortable. My knees are leaning against a sharp branch and I immediately get a sore neck because I'm tilting it to one side to stop it hitting the branch above. It was a lot easier when I was younger and smaller. It felt so big, this tree. It's not so big anymore. I should really stop coming up here. What the hell *am* I actually doing up here?

I hear a cough and look both ways along the street. Our neighbour, Mr Schultz, is coming out his garden gate with Princess, his chocolate cavoodle. I pull myself up onto the next branch. Stealth ninja once again. I watch as they make their way towards our house, completely oblivious to me. They are off for their afternoon poo-on-everyone's-garden stroll (the dog, not the owner). Mum hates Princess the cavoodle (Princess Poo, we call her) and she doesn't care much for Mr Schultz either, though she wouldn't admit to that one — she's far too polite for that. I can't tell you how many times Mum has had to scoop up dog poo because Mr Schultz is too lazy to bring a pooper-scooper on his afternoon strolls. Lazy knob.

Mr Schultz walks, head lowered, back crunched forward. He is pulling Princess along against her will: Princess is desperate to sniff but is yanked onward. This is when I have to be particularly stealthy in my tree hiding, when there is a passer-by. I slow my breathing and try hard not to move an inch. I am a ninja.

Princess Poo comes right in front of the house, onto our property — sniffing around on the grass and . . . no . . . she is not. ARGH! Yes, she is! Caught in the act. Princess does a poo on the grass in front of our house. Mr Schultz looks up and down the street to see if anyone notices and then just walks off, leaving the warm, stinking princessy-poo on our lawn. Disgusting. *Mr Schultz, how do you sleep at night?* For a moment I want to yell: 'I am watching you, Schultz!' But I can't, I can't blow my cover.

Stealth ninja.

Mr Schultz walks away. Princess prances. The street is quiet once again.

I am getting bored now. And I can smell dog excrement wafting towards me.

SO BOOOORRRREEEEEEEEDDDDDDDD.

My dad used to say, *'Only boring people say they are bored.'* Well, I am boring then. Borrrrrring!

He'd probably still say it.

If I ever saw him.

I should go inside. I should be one of those normal kids who just walks home from school and goes into their house. Because I am hungry and I have loads of homework (today's and yesterday's). But more importantly, I am hungry. And uncomfortable. In fact, now my feet feel tingly. (The left more than the right — is this a bad sign? I will google it later.)

Think of something else, Jasper. Something different from your tingling foot, Jasper.

Okay, so have I told you about my name? I don't like it. I want to get rid of it. Jasper Jonathan Robinson-Woods. I know. It's a long name ... definitely too long. I don't mind the Jasper bit but I don't believe in double-barrelled surnames: they make me angry (angry with my parents). Why couldn't my pathetic parents make a decision about which last name I should have? Why does it have to be 50/50? Life can't always be 50/50, sometimes you have to make a decision and stick to it. Their inability to make this decision left me with a long name that I hate with a passion. They let me down from day one.

I pull a small branch off the tree and break it up into as many pieces as I can. It hurts the palm of my hand and one of my fingers starts to bleed but that feels good. I use one of the broken branches to dig as hard as I can into the side of the tree, to make my mark, to hurt the tree too. And it just feels better.

That's how much I hate my name.

J̶A̶S̶P̶E̶R̶ JONATHAN ROBINSON—WOODS (SUCKS)

So . . . I figure I could just ditch one of the surnames, not based on which parent I like best (Mum) but purely based on which sounds cooler, or less uncool.

Jasper Robinson. Now he sounds so boring.

Jasper Woods. He sounds kind of cooler, I like the woods, trees and stuff (I'm up one, right?) but when you go from Robinson-Woods it feels like a big jump to just Woods. I would have more time on my hands though — writing a long name takes ages. But is it too boring? Too small? Is he just an invisible guy, this Jasper Woods, insignificant, in the background?

He doesn't have much to say, this Jasper Woods, does he?

And choosing my dad's name? I don't think I can do it, not after everything that's happened.

So the other option: think of a new last name. You have to pay to change your name legally so if I'm going to the expense why not get a *new* one, a fresh start and a new me? It could be just what I need. I have investigated all this, by the way, I'm that serious about it, I have googled it. Google told me that you have to be eighteen to change your name unless you are getting married or have permission from your parents. I'm not ready for marriage.

You can have only one name if you want, no last name, like Madonna or Prince. I could just be *Jasper*. But you have to write a letter of explanation when you apply and that sounds like a hassle. I can't even finish my book report.

Jasper Hendrickson.

Jasper Montgomery.

Jasper McDonaldson.

Jasper Montague.

Jasper McDermott.

No, no, no. Boring. Boring. Boring.

I'll cross off any surnames that are first names as well. Jasper Henry, Jasper James, Jasper Thomas, Jasper Edward, etc. Not only are they confusing but also I have unintentionally listed off trains from *Thomas the Tank Engine*.

Am I overthinking this? I tend to do that. Jasper Robinson-Over-Thinker. But how do you think LESS when there's so much stuff to think about? Do you know what I mean? Like life decisions? Like what am I even doing?

Oh god... My heart skips a beat. What AM I even doing?

I have a cramp in my left leg now and a strange tingling in my hands too! Could this be the start of a problem with my brain? Like a tumour? It's just I can feel the tingling moving down my leg. An electric-shock feeling... I don't like it. Pins and needles feeling, but not pins and needles, different.

Worse. My eyes are fuzzy too now. All this and the weird heart stuff — maybe something is seriously wrong with me.

Of course there is something wrong with me.

I already know this.

6.

Being in the tree is stressing me out today.

I jump down and rush inside. It's not doing what it's supposed to do — hide me from my reality. I go straight to my room and to Han Solo's fish tank. He is lying on his side again. Is he dead?

I think he is. He's not moving. This is okay... It is. This bit will finally be all over. I tap the side of the glass but he has a burst of crooked, dying fish energy.

'Oh, you're alive.'

The clock is still ticking.

I collapse onto my bed and remember about Manly Steve. I haven't noticed anything new in the house. Yet.

Why now? Why this week of all the weeks does Mum think she should move in with her dickhead boyfriend? I wish she'd never met him. I wish he'd never gone to her

dental practice. If he'd chosen another dental hygienist my life would be very different right now. He used to be one of Mum's patients, if I've not made that clear. That's how they met — brought together because of a root canal or something equally revolting. How do you fall in love with someone when you have seen the inside of their mouth? That's just disgusting. Insides of mouths are foul.

Isn't it against the law to have relations with a patient anyway? Mum claims he was no longer one when they had their first date but it should still be illegal. Sometimes I imagine Mum leaning over Manly Steve while she cleans his manly teeth and his eyes wander around my mum, admiring her. Sometimes I imagine even grosser stuff like him taking off those glasses you wear at the dental clinic and sitting up and kissing her, there in the dentist's chair...Yuck!

When Mum finally gets home we

have dinner in front of the television and don't talk about Manly Steve. I thought she would bring it up again, or he'd be here — but she doesn't and he isn't. Mum seems tired. We sit and watch *Friends* reruns although neither of us laughs, even at the funny bits like when Joey's fridge breaks and he says, 'So I had to eat everything.'

When it finishes I get up to leave. 'I'm going to bed.'

'Goodnight,' Mum replies. That's it — she doesn't even bring it up then.

I brush my teeth, check my phone and remember I haven't done my homework again. Whoops. Maybe Mum will knock on my door soon. Surely she will want to discuss this more, her boyfriend moving in. Maybe she's changed her mind. This is good. I may have guilted her out of it.

I climb into bed, shoving the piles of clothes off it.

I was ten when Mum and Manly Steve had that first 'date'. Three years ago. And only three years before they met, Dad left. This is happening too fast for me. Can't she just wait until I move out? Is that too much to ask?

That date was not just Mum's first date with Manly Steve, it was her first date since divorcing my father. It was probably her first date ever because apparently my father never asked her out, they just fell into their strange relationship. I don't ask much about this because it grosses me out. Although once she over-shared and told me she thought she and Dad were going to just be a one-night stand but ended up staying together ten years. I had to have a chat with her about boundaries after that.

How can I stop Manly Steve from moving in? Maybe I could pay some sort of mafia man to 'get rid of' him? Nah. I don't have any money to pay (unless $41.20 is enough). Besides, we would get caught. I've watched those police forensic documentaries and they always find the bad guys, there's CCTV everywhere. I would find prison life difficult too. If high school feels hard, prison would be a disaster.

I could move out and go flatting. Again, highly unrealistic. I can't live on just eggs and cereal. Or pay rent. I could demand my mother break up with Manly Steve and put me first for once in her life. Would that work?

Highly unlikely.

I lie in bed looking at the ceiling.

Here we are again.

Night time.

I hear Mum put the dishwasher on and brush her teeth, then check that all the doors are locked, then double-check they're locked. Is that where I get it from?

Come on, Jasper. Sleep!

TICK. TICK. TICK.

I still remember that first date. Mum was getting ready to go out, putting on a dress she'd never worn and make-up I didn't know she had. I didn't like it. It had just been us since Dad left. Just me and Mum and my nana too. How could she desert me to have dinner with a near stranger with dental problems? What kind of parent does that?

Nana was in hospital again. She was really sick at that same time. I'd never had a babysitter because it was usually her who came around if Mum was working late. But she couldn't look after me this time.

Mum went on the date. I think she knew her mother was dying. I knew it too, and I didn't understand why she would start dating someone then but maybe she knew she was going to be lonely soon. Wasn't I enough?

Nana never came out of the hospital. She died three weeks later and my world fell apart all over again. I lost another person I couldn't live without. But I don't want to think about all that. I don't want to remember her smile, her homemade gingernuts in the pantry and how she would listen so intently to everything I said like it was the most important thing, like I had something to say.

He came a lot then. The nightmare came a lot. There was a void — a deep void — and I didn't know how you were supposed to keep going when there was such an empty space left behind when someone you love died.

And when Nana was gone, Manly Steve started staying over at our house. Those nights I couldn't call out for Mum if the nightmare came. Manly Steve didn't want her coming into my room after dark. He said at my age I shouldn't need her anymore, I shouldn't be scared of the dark. It was time I grew up.

It's still time I grew up.

I feel like I'm just drifting off to actual sleep when He comes. The nightmare comes.

Again.

I am in a near dream. Or is it a memory? I am with my

nana, we're sitting in the garden at the unit where she lived before she died.

'You will be okay, Jasper,' she is saying, in her soft, warm voice. 'Everything will be okay.'

But then He comes. He comes from inside the unit. He tears out at such a speed we both don't know what hits us. Thunderous footsteps.

He goes for her first this time.

He goes for Nana.

She looks to me just before He gets her.

HELLO JASPER
DO YOU REMEMBER ME?
I REMEMBER YOU
I REMEMBER YOU TOO WELL
I'VE COME BACK TO SHOW YOU WHAT YOU'VE ALWAYS KNOWN
WHEN WILL YOU SURRENDER?

7.

Another sleepless night.

When I finally get out of bed I see Mum is still home and hasn't been up. I knock on her door.

'What's wrong, Mum?' I say to her closed door.

'I've had to call in sick. I have a stupid cold. Sorry, I should have woken you, now you're going to be late...'

'It's fine.'

I rush to school, but I'm late anyway. Mum rings the school to say she is unwell and it's her fault I'm late. The dean doesn't question it this time.

'Hope your mum feels better.'

'Thanks.' Turns out she does have a heart.

As I leave her office I go past the reception and another student is getting a late slip. She's in my art class, one of the nicer students. For some reason, the receptionist likes her too because she isn't giving her the frosty treatment I get whenever I'm late and she isn't sent to the dean. She looks up and smiles at me as I pass but it only lasts a millisecond.

'Name, love?' asks the receptionist.

'Nina Frankton-Forbes.'

Nina Frankton-what? Nina *Frankton-Forbes*. I didn't know that was her name. I chuckle all the way to class (just in my head, not out loud ... that would be weird). Nina Frankton-Forbes becomes the only person I know my age with a double-barrelled name. Someone else in the world has mean parents. And Frankton-Forbes, that's up there with Robinson-Woods.

The day doesn't go as badly as I thought it would. The whole Nina Frankton-Forbes thing helps a little, plus I found out I passed last week's algebra test, only *just* but I passed and did not expect to. We also had a relief teacher for English who didn't seem to know what he was supposed to do. He talked about water polo because his kids play and he thinks we all should.

'It's brutal! People get swum over and hit in the head.'

No thanks.

I saw her a few times around school, Nina. Once crossing paths on the way to PE (not my favourite class) and once on the field at lunch. I don't sit there, that's where you go if you've got friends and I seem to be struggling in that department at present. I did have one friend, Finn: we went to the same intermediate school, but his parents decided private school education was what he needed. So he left and now he has a bunch of new private school friends and does fencing. Weird.

Anyway, I normally go behind the science block at lunch. It's quiet there. I put earphones in my phone and listen to podcasts about films from the nineties. I'm like a grandpa sometimes. Except my poppa wouldn't know about podcasts. I did find myself saying Nina's name a lot, *Nina Frankton-Forbes*, just in my thoughts, not out loud, again that would be weird. It would just pop into my head throughout the day.

Then there was art class. I accidentally knocked all the paintbrushes over with my bag as I was leaving and instead of laughing, like the rest of the class, Nina stopped and helped me pick them up.

'Thank you,' I said as she handed me the last paintbrush.

'All good,' she replied and rushed to catch up with her friends.

I can't believe she has a double-barrelled name too. There is some kind of relief that I'm not the only one. I wonder if she would like Jasper Black as my new name, though — would she think that was a cool name? I kinda like that one at the moment. It's on my list of top contenders.

Maybe she would actually prefer Jasper Robinson-Woods because we would have something in common, some kind of shared pain. That could change things. But thank you, Nina Frankton-Forbes. Learning your full name today somehow made my day a little easier.

Thank you very much.

8.

I need a moment to hide from the noise.

It was a good day, but a noisy day in my head. Mum is home in bed so I won't be long in the tree, or she'll start stressing.

There have been other trees but there's something about this one. I used to climb trees for fun, but mostly trees are for hiding in. There was one at primary school, I went there if anyone was calling me names. That happened a bit. They were often younger than me but that didn't make them any less scary. I'd stay there after the bell rang; just in case anyone was hiding around the corner.

My teacher would usually find me there after roll call. I never told her exactly who I was hiding from, but there was Leo Fulham who called me Weirdo and Cole Mathews who called me Crazy-head. She once told me I would never amount to anything if I always hid when life got hard. Hearing that made me hide more.

The first time I hid in *this* tree I'd just turned seven. Mum had just thrown a plate at Dad and it had smashed into the microwave and landed in pieces on the floor. I was in my room listening to all of this. There was a loud BANG that made me flinch. Like a cymbal crashing or fireworks bursting, there was the sound of ceramic exploding, which was followed by a short silence. Then Dad yelled at Mum, saying he'd had enough of her 'unhelpful bullshit'. I still remember that. I don't think I even knew what bullshit meant but it was a rage that didn't seem to belong to him. I'd seen him be sad, but I hadn't seen him really angry and that did scare me. I didn't like that man, that angry dad. It's not a nice feeling when you don't recognise your own parent.

Then he drove off in a rage and didn't look back. I ran after him but there was no point, he didn't stop. Why didn't he want to take me with him? His car sped off around the corner, tyres screeching. Instead of going back inside, I climbed this tree. I didn't know what else to do. I watched the car disappear down the road.

I was up here for seventeen minutes. I know this because Nana had given me a digital watch for my birthday the day before and I'd spent most of that day timing things using the stopwatch setting. When Dad left, I set the timer. I remember: seventeen minutes it got to.

17:00

'Jasper! Where are you? You're scaring me, Jasper.'

Mum was panicking. She even called Nana to see if I had gone to her house. About ten minutes later there was the sound of Nana's car arriving in the driveway. I could hear her shoes hit the pavement and her car door slam, then her running up the pathway just underneath the tree. I was that close to her, I could hear the worry in her steps — her seven-year-old grandson, missing. And she loved me, she really did. I remember that feeling, of being loved by her.

I listened as they frantically tried to decide what to do. Should they call the police? Should they drive around the block?

'Where's David?' Nana asked.

'He's gone,' Mum replied. 'We had a fight. It's over, I can't live with that man anymore. And now they are both gone.'

'Did David take him?'

'No. He drove off alone.'

Alone. Without me.

I heard Mum's tears. I hated hearing her cry. I still do. That's when I got down from the tree and walked inside. I stopped the stopwatch.

17:00.

On the dot. I timed it that way.

Then I heard relief.

'Oh thank goodness!' Nana pulled me into her. 'Don't do that to me . . . Don't you ever do that to me again.'

Nana brought her hand to her heart and sighed a deep sigh. I remember that sigh. I didn't like Nana worrying about me either, she'd never done anything to hurt me. Never. Mum told me later it was the longest ten minutes of her life. She wasn't timing it — she didn't know it had been longer.

I didn't see my dad for a long time. He disappeared for a bit. It's okay though. I stayed here with Mum, waiting, waiting for nothing. Mum didn't ask where I had been, where I had hidden. It didn't matter to her. But what I discovered that day is that this tree is a place where I can hide from the world, like the one at school. A place where I can hear the world as it continues without me. Like I said, I don't exist when I'm up here.

For my birthday that year, I got a hiding place and a digital watch. And my parents' divorce.

Happy birthday, Jasper.

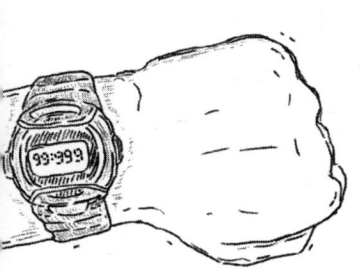

I don't have that digital watch anymore, with the stopwatch setting. I cracked the screen by throwing it at the microwave one time. Sometimes I throw things, just to see if they will break.

It broke.

If I'd never stopped that timer I wonder how long the screen would say it had been now, how long has Dad been gone?

Mum stays in bed all evening. I make canned spaghetti on toast and watch *Seinfeld*, falling asleep on the couch at

midnight. I sleep. A deep couch-sleep but I think that counts as sleep. I shuffle to my bedroom like a zombie. It's so hard to move, I feel an overwhelming body exhaustion. My eyes are still half-closed as I walk but I make it to my room and before I start to worry whether I'll sleep again, or ever, I do.

I actually sleep.

The sleep drought is over! I wasn't sure if it would ever end.

I wake — thinking maybe this means Han Solo is dead. Is that why I slept? And why did He not come, the nightmare? Maybe He came for Han Solo instead.

But Han Solo isn't dead.

Once I'm up close to the fish tank I see his slow swim up against the slime. It has grown more, it covers all sides of the tank now and is a thicker, darker green. It is beginning to grow on the little castle in the middle of his tank as well. The castle he ignores. Why the heck would a fish want a castle?

But I slept! I'm still tired, almost more tired, but I know I have slept. My body knows it. It still needs more, though: it's hard to even motivate myself out of the room.

Mum is feeling better and makes me avocado on toast and a salad wrap for lunch. I even get to school on time.

But.

There's a but.

Today doesn't go well. It doesn't go well at all.

WHO AM I?
YOU CAN'T HIDE FROM ME, JASPER
I WILL FIND YOU
WHEREVER YOU GO
WHEREVER YOU HIDE
I AM YOUR SHADOW AND YOU CAN'T HIDE FROM YOUR SHADOW
I WILL DESTROY YOU
FROM THE INSIDE OUT
IT IS TIME TO SURRENDER

9.

There is an incident at school.

The nightmare . . . It didn't come last night. Instead, it came to school.

The bear found me in the light of day — while I was wide awake.

It was during PE, my least favourite of all my least favourite classes. I wasn't enjoying it at all; I never do, but today we were playing basketball in the gymnasium, doing a warm-up thing where you throw a ball to someone and run to take their place in a circle and they move to the middle and throw it in another direction or something. I didn't understand. And there were balls everywhere. And people moving at speed. I got jumbled up over the order of the throwing and the moving and the ball receiving.

I'm not into ball sports. I never kicked a ball around the

garden or threw a ball at the beach; that was something other kids did with their dads. I didn't get to do that stuff. How could I when my dad wasn't even around? I was watching those families from my beach towel while Mum read a book and ignored me because it was her weekend and she needed to do something for herself. I didn't even want to be at the beach. I don't like beaches.

Mum wasn't a kick-a-ball-around Mum either. She did force me to play football one year but I was so useless, happy to sub off. So yeah, not a ball-sports dude. 'The incident' is my parents' fault. I blame them.

I don't think we should force kids to play sports if they don't want to. It's just humiliating. They should teach this at teachers' training college. And after dropping the ball a bunch of times and feeling like an idiot, I told the PE teacher this.

'I'm not gonna do it. I suck at this and kids shouldn't be forced into sports,' I said and walked away.

Her response was that I 'had to' come back and I 'had to' participate in the activity, that everyone else was 'giving it a go' and so should I. That's what school is for apparently, 'giving it a go'. Whoopdee flippin' do.

'No, it's not,' I replied. 'School is not for learning sports. School is for learning stuff to help us get a job and I don't want a job involving balls.'

The class snickered at that.

Plus, I don't have to do anything I don't want to (I mean, I don't, do I?). Isn't that in the Bill of Rights or something? If not, it should be. Clearly, my PE teacher deeply believes in the whole 'giving it a go' school of thought though, because she got so mad at me that she made me go and sit on the bleachers at the far end of the gymnasium — so I could think about why I should believe in it too.

I don't know why she had to send me away when I was leaving in the first place. But . . . The lights weren't working up that end of the gymnasium. It was dark. You know how I feel about the dark. And I was in a shitty mood too — not just because my rights had been cruelly dismissed but because everyone had laughed at me while I walked away. I think even the teacher did. I hate being laughed at; I really hate that.

I was so pissed off.

That's when He came. He turned up, in the dark of the bleachers.

First I heard Him underneath me, under the bleachers. I closed my eyes and willed Him away. I told myself He wasn't there — it was my imagination. I wasn't asleep, it was the middle of the day, how could I have a nightmare? I wasn't asleep, was I?

I pinched my arm. It hurt.

I wasn't asleep.

My heart began to beat loudly in my ears.

DOFF. DOFF. DOFF.

It couldn't be Him ... Not at school. But I heard the low, recognisable growl and I knew He was there. And He was angry. He was sniffing around, pacing under the bleachers, pushing His back against the bars. Next He started to scratch at the floor and I could hear Him right below me. He knew exactly where I was, He was just messing with me. I couldn't stay there with Him — He would destroy me.

I had to move. I had to get out of the darkness. I couldn't be alone in that moment. So I ran. And I knew I wasn't asleep, because I could run. I ran back to the light, back to the other end of the gym, to my class. I stood there, against the wall, watching, trying to get my breath back and calm down.

I looked back to the darkness. The bear had stayed in the dark.

'Did I ask you to return? Or does this mean you are ready to participate?' the teacher asked. She threw a basketball to me but I didn't put my hands out to catch it. It just bounced against the wall and dribbled next to me. Everyone laughed again.

'What are you going to do, Jasper?' she asked, staring at the ball.

More laughter. Much more laughter.

I saw the ball at my feet. I picked it up, heart still racing, thoughts red with anger. More sniggers.

I threw the ball hard against the gymnasium wall.

I didn't know I even had the strength, but it turns out I do. It turns out I *can* throw a ball — because the ball hit the wall

hard then rebounded and like slow motion it flew across the stadium, to the rest of the class, where it hit a girl in the face. Really hard.

BANG!

She had to go to the school nurse because her nose was bleeding so much and I had to go to my friend the dean to repeat the details of the 'incident'.

'What happened, Jasper?' she asked. 'Why are you here?'

'I was trying to tell Ms Freedman I shouldn't have to play basketball. I warned her and she didn't listen. But somehow it's still all *my* fault.'

THANKS A LOT, JASPER

Why don't adults listen properly? Why doesn't what I think and say have any meaning to them? Why do they always think they know what's best for me? And I'm the bad guy again.

Bad guy.

Bad Jasper.

The dean just stared at me blankly.

'I didn't want to hurt her,' I said quietly. 'I hardly even know who she is. I didn't throw it AT her, her head was in the way . . .'

The dean just stared at me more. Then sighed.

It was His fault too. Why did He have to come to school? Why did He have to find me there? But I couldn't say that bit.

What happens now that a nightmare is following me to school?

Where do things go from here?

I have a detention after school and an email has been sent to my mother. Mum didn't answer her phone when the dean rang her. She wants Mum to go in at some time to discuss 'the incident'. To discuss me. What a problem I am.

HAVENSIDE HIGH SCHOOL

From: Dumb Angry Teachers
To: Angry Mum

Dear Mrs Robinson,
Your son Jasper is a nuisance and has a problem with his temper. In all honesty, he is destined for nothing. Please arrange the removal of him from our school immediately so we can all get on with our lives.
Kindest of regards,
School staff, students and the wider community

Mum can add this email to the others she's received over my school career. 'Jasper threw a chair against the wall', 'Jasper ripped a schoolbook', and 'Jasper pushed a desk over'.

I don't know why they don't just say it.

'Jasper is NOT OKAY!'

I don't see Mum when I get home, post detention.

It's her late night at the dental surgery. Convenient timing. I make myself eggs on toast now there are eggs in the house. There's no way I can be vegan, I live on eggs. I make sure I'm in bed before she gets home.

I'm lying there staring at the ceiling when she comes to check on me. I pretend to be asleep so she leaves.

My sleep isn't great. It's non-existent. I restart the no-sleep tally.

I stare at the ceiling and imagine inevitable conversations with my mother. In one of the imagined conversations, she tells me she's read the email and I've been expelled from school. She's sending me to boarding school in the middle of nowhere: Hamilton or somewhere. I practise pleading for her not to make me go, making my case.

'I will do better. I won't throw basketballs. I won't lose my temper. I will be normal. Normal Jasper. Good Jasper.'

I tell her I'm changing my name and it's all going to get better. I won't be Jasper Robinson-Woods anymore.

I imagine telling her about Him.

'There's a bear, Mum. It follows me around. It's not my fault. I'm a good kid, I just don't know how to get rid of this nightmare!'

Him.

I don't understand. How did He come while I was awake and at school, in broad daylight? How can a nightmare come to life? How can it follow me to school? I know that's what you're thinking, but it's true. My nightmare has come to life.

He has found me in my waking moments and followed me into my reality.

Now my days are filled with darkness too.

>WHO AM I?
>WHY ARE YOU PRETENDING YOU DON'T KNOW ME?
>YOU CAN'T HIDE FROM ME
>NOT IN THE DAY
>NOT IN THE NIGHT
>I AM WITH YOU, ALWAYS
>I AM DESTRUCTION AND I WILL DESTROY YOU
>IT IS TIME TO SURRENDER

10.

I am woken by the fridge door alarm.

Mum is in the kitchen. I can't avoid her forever. But as I walk into the room I see she's in a rush. She doesn't mention the email, just passes me a bowl of porridge and tells me she's running late. 'There are rolls in the pantry.'

That's weird. Maybe they didn't send the email? Or maybe I imagined yesterday after all?

I throw the roll into my lunchbox (I can't be bothered filling it with anything) and grab two mandarins. I don't think I have ever left this early in the history of school. This may or may not have something to do with the fact that (1) I don't have PE today and (2) I have art class first period. There is a chance I'm excited to go to see someone in particular . . . Someone with a double-barrelled name? Maybe a little bit.

It's strange arriving at the same time as the rest of the school. I'm used to getting here once everyone is well inside the classrooms. I'm the first in the art room too — even the teacher hasn't arrived yet. Nina Frankton-Forbes arrives but sets up on another desk. I watch as she unpacks her bag and chats to her friend Hannah. No one sits next to me. This kinda sucks; I will have to avoid being this early again because this rejection feels shit.

During class, Nina catches me watching her a few times across the room, but my eyes quickly dart away. *Jasper, don't be a weirdo*, I tell myself.

When the bell rings at the end of class, everyone starts packing up to leave and my teacher Maria asks me to stay behind.

'Can we have a chat, Jasper?'

I must be in some sort of trouble and I can't think why. Maria has always insisted we call her by her first name and is definitely my favourite teacher in the school. Well, she was. Maybe that's all about to change. I nervously make my way to her desk, where she's moving piles of paper around. She calls it her 'organised chaos' but really it's just chaos.

Maybe she saw me watching Nina and wanted to tell me to stop. I can't think of anything else I have done wrong today, but you never know.

'Thanks for waiting,' she says, rolling up her sleeves, then smiles. 'I have good news for you.'

'Oh. Okay . . .?' I wasn't expecting that.

'Your self-portrait — for the assignment we did last week

'... I love yours.'

'Thanks,' I reply, confused. 'I wasn't sure if it was any good.' Anything that resembles my face can't be that good, can it?

'It's better than good, Jasper.' She does a little laugh and shakes her head: the long feather-like earrings that she's wearing swing as she does. 'It's really good. I don't think you realise how great your work is.'

She goes to her shelf and picks up the self-portrait.

'I love the look in your eyes, it says so much. That's hard to do in a self-portrait, to tell a story like that. I want to know what he's thinking, what *you're* thinking . . .'

Jeepers, no she does NOT.

I shrug.

'Something is coming up and I want you to take part.'

'Okay?'

'It's the Secondary Schools' Mahi Toi exhibition. We've been asked to put some entries in. They give us a sentence to work with and selected students create something to that theme. This year it's . . .' She shuffles paper around until she finds what she's looking for. '*Ko tāku e kite nei*' or '*What I see*'. What do you think? Interested?'

'Sure.' Not that '*What I see*' is that interesting — in fact, I don't know what they even mean by that.

'Wonderful. They don't exhibit all the entries submitted, there is a selection process and competition is tight. Get it to me by the end of the month. I'm happy if you use some class time as well.' She hands me an entry form.

'Thanks, Maria.'

'Well done — and keep up the good work,' she smiles. 'Right, get outta here. I need to tidy up my mess. Actually, everyone else's mess.'

'Mess?' I laugh as I put my bag over my shoulder and walk out.

'I mean amazing artistickness!' she shouts out the door.

I don't often get good news like that and to be honest, I don't know what to do with it — but for the rest of the day, I walk a little taller. I do see the girl who I hit with the basketball though. She walks past me in the corridor and avoids eye contact. Fair enough. I'm going to have to apologise for that one day.

Sorry that your nose got in the way of my angry outburst.

Her nose does look slightly wonky. Was it always like that? Whoops . . .

After school, I rush home. I don't even go up the tree, I go straight inside. I throw my bag and cap on the bed and go to Han Solo, who seems to have perked up a bit too.

'Hello little guy, good to see you up and about!' I tell him about the art exhibition, and he listens intently. I tell him about Nina F-F and he seems excited. I tell him about her wavy brown hair and her green eyes. He even makes his way to the top of the water for some fish flakes. He just nibbles the edge but it's a huge step.

'Her last name is double-barrelled, Han Solo! Frankton-Forbes. Can you believe it?'

He can't.

I make cheese on toast and watch television all afternoon,

even though I have homework. I could even be thinking about my submission for the art exhibition but I'm not really in the mood. At about 7 p.m. I hear Mum come through the door. She comes into the lounge carrying shopping bags.

'Hello. How was your day?' she asks, putting the groceries away.

'Good. I actually . . .'

'Can you turn that off, Jasper? We need to talk.'

Here we go, she got the email . . . Am I expelled? Am I being sent to a Hamilton boarding school?

'We haven't talked again about Steven moving in.'

Oh, back to that. The problem hasn't magically disappeared.

'I understand it's a big change for you. For all of us. But do you think we could give it a shot and see how it goes?'

She comes into the lounge and sits next to me on the couch, reaching out for my hand. Oh, she's going to play it like this, is she? She squeezes my hand, but I pull it away. When I was a kid, she told me this was her silent way of saying she loves me without embarrassing me. From her other hand, she passes me a block of chocolate.

'Oh and I got you this. It's a new flavour . . .'

I shrug. I know what's going on here.

'What do you say, shall we give things a try?' she asks, eyebrows raised.

'But what if it doesn't work?' I ask.

'Let's be positive that it will,' she smiles.

I scoff. Being positive is not really my thing. Mum pats my legs and stands up again, tidying cushions as she does.

'Great. Thank you.' She is so chirpy. Obviously she hasn't read the email.

'My art teacher has asked me to submit something for an exhibition,' I tell her while breaking off a row of chocolate.

'Jasper! That's exciting, you totally should,' she says, heading to the kitchen. I follow.

'I will. I have until the end of the month. I probably won't get chosen but . . .'

'Don't put yourself down. You are a great artist,' she says, grabbing dinner plates. 'I've got a hot chicken and some rolls for a quick dinner. Hungry?'

'Is it vegetarian chicken?'

'Is there such a thing?'

After dinner, Mum comes into my room to say goodnight. I'm staring at the fish tank. Han Solo is near the bottom again, not moving and the sweet taste of decoy chocolate has worn off and I'm imagining Mum's hairy boyfriend having permanent sleepovers at my house.

'I think Han Solo is sick,' I tell her. I figure she needs to know so she can start giving me grief about how I don't look after him properly.

'Oh no, is he?' She puts her face up against the fish tank.

'He looks unhappy. Have you cleaned his tank lately?' she asks, noticing the green slime.

'Are you saying it's my fault?'

'No, just checking. Fish do die though.'

'Of course, they die. But are you saying we shouldn't care because it doesn't matter, he's just a fish?'

'I didn't mean that at all.' She says it unconvincingly and looks back at the tank then wipes the outside of the glass.

'You clearly think it's my fault and I shouldn't look after animals, just say it.'

'I don't think that, so I won't say it.'

'Typical!' I scoff and lie back onto the bed.

'What? Jasper, let's just see how he is in the morning.' She backs out of the room, apologetically, probably thinking, *Irrational teenager, abort conversation.* I haven't actually cleaned the fish tank lately and it probably is my fault and I probably don't care and I probably am a bad person who shouldn't look after animals.

But she'd better watch what she says.

You know that saying, a problem shared is a problem halved? That's bullshit. I feel way worse now she knows, because it's obvious I have not looked after him. Mum knows, she saw the slime. That's the stink thing, I probably should clean his tank but it's late now and I didn't do my English homework. I'm supposed to read and give my *reflections* and I can't reflect right now and my computer's not charged and . . .

I feel crap. It's official; Manly Steve is moving in. Happy, happy, joy, joy.

Living with him is going to be torturous. I'm allowing this to happen too, allowing Mum's happiness over mine because she gave me a chocolate bar! I don't know how I fell for that. I should have demanded she reject this terrible idea. I should have said, 'NO WAY JOSÉ!' A flatmate can't just announce a new flatmate is moving in without the other flatmates agreeing to it, and they can't attempt bribery. Surely! Why is this any different? Just because she's paying the mortgage, and I am thirteen.

I am so useless at standing my ground. Maybe my new name should be Jasper Too-Weak, Too-Nice, Too-Susceptible-to-Bribery. And why does Mum not consider my feelings? She knows I don't want it. And while we're at it, why did I say I would put something in for the art exhibition? My art is shit. My teacher probably just feels sorry for me. I bet I will get rejected. And Nina wouldn't want to talk to someone like me, ever. No one even wants to sit at the same table as me . . .

What I see? What I see?

I see a waste of space. I can't draw that.

There will be no sleep tonight. I just know it.

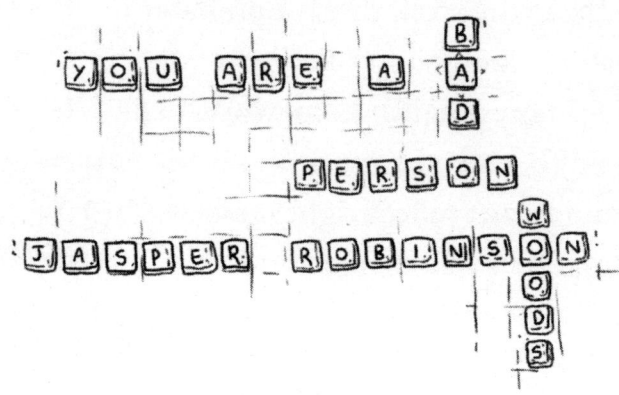

I flick off the light.

I figure He will come tonight.

It's only a matter of time until He does.

I will myself to sleep but it doesn't work. *Please sleep, Jasper. Please. Why can't you just sleep like a normal person?*

What will happen tonight, here in the dark?

I am a bad person.

No one likes me.

I am alone.

There is something wrong with me. Wrong.

When I have hateful thoughts He always comes. He likes those thoughts. He feeds on them like a bear feeds on a dead animal, thrashing at the lifeless body, chewing through muscles, gnawing on bone.

I can't get that vision out of my head.

I know He is close . . . So I stop trying to force sleep and I just wait.

I wait.

WHO AM I?
I AM WATCHING YOU
YOU ARE HIDING IN THE DARK,
FROM THE DARKNESS INSIDE YOU
I AM HERE TO REMIND YOU OF THIS
YOU ARE A BAD PERSON
YOU ARE NOTHING
I WILL DESTROY YOU
IT IS TIME TO SURRENDER

11.

'I'm off, Jasper, time to get up!' Mum yells from outside my door. It's 7.30 a.m.

He didn't come after all. Or did He?

'I'm up,' I say, half asleep.

'There's lunch money on the table. Time to get moving!'

I rub my eyes and pull my feet slowly out of bed. I feel exhausted. Moving is like moving through mud, but I force myself to rise anyway. Like a half-set statue, unsteady, unstable.

Blood rushes to my head.

He did not destroy me.

It's just a matter of time.

I walk over to the fish tank. Han Solo is still alive. I feed him a few granules of fish food, but I don't know why. He doesn't show any interest, so it just floats in the water and sinks to the ground ignored, into the pebbles like leaves falling from a dying tree. He has given up.

Nana stopped eating near the end too. She lost lots of weight. 'She is skin and bones,' Mum used to say. 'Skin and bones.' I could see her bones too, right through her grey skin. I could feel them if I held her hand, feel the ridges of her tiny bones, her knuckles. I remember holding her hands. It's just a matter of time for Han Solo too.

More slime has appeared overnight.

'I'm sorry,' I say as I leave the room. 'So sorry.' There's no time to do anything about it now.

In the bathroom, I decide to skip the shower (again) and instead quickly get dressed and brush my teeth. When did I have a shower last? I race to the lounge to grab my bag and the lunch money and rush out the door, grabbing my cap from my room before I leave. I am determined not to be late today. As I jump down the front steps, I remember I have art today with Nina Frankton-Forbes, second period. Hopefully, I can get in early, but not too early, and get a seat at the back of the class. I figure then it won't look like I'm staring at her because she will be in front of me. Oh man, now it sounds like I am fantasising about her. Oh well, it gets me moving.

I wonder if I might be able to talk to her, one day, actually say a full sentence to her. Out loud. Not just stare at her like a weirdo, thinking of things to say but not ever saying them. Even a 'hello' would be a start. Jeepers, why is that so hard? And would we ever get to discuss the double-barrelled name thing? Is that something people would want to discuss? But how do you start that conversation with a stranger anyway?

Other people seem to do this without a second thought. What is wrong with me?

'Hey, so, your name . . . it sucks. But so does mine . . . wanna hang out?'

She may have an opinion on a new name for me, though. I need all the help I can get.

As I walk along the road I flick through the alphabet in my head, searching for potential new editions to my rather short shortlist.

A. Adams, Allan, Abercrombie, Anthony (also a first name: cross that off)

B. Birch, Bailey, Benson, Barron, Bachelor (Jasper Bachelor has a ring to it but probably not in a good way)

C. Christian, Cotton, Crump (too close to Trump)

D. Daniels, Dublin, Dermott

E. Elevator (sorry can't think of anything here)

F. Frankton, Forbes (how weird would I look if I stole one of Nina's last names?)

G. Gordon, Griffin, Grouch (Jasper the Grouch, Jasper the Great, Jasper the Invincible, Jasper the Incredible)

H. Hamlet, Harper, Horatio, Honolulu, Harding, Hopscotch (okay now I'm just thinking of H words I know . . .)

I. Idiot (that sure suits me)

J. Johnson, Jeremiah, June, Jones

K. Keel, Kaleidoscope, Kilmer

L. Lovett, Lightfoot, Longbottom (hell no)

M. Marcon, Morgan, McDermott, McDowell,

McFlafferty, McRoberts, McMan
N. Norman, Nobody, Nickel
O. Octopus, O'Reilly, Otto, O'Doherty, Old McDonald
P. Patricks, Portman, Porter
Q. Quentin, Quizzer, Quiddler, Quadface, Queue, Q (just the letter Q, that's cool)
R. Ruyter, Rippler, Ronaldo, Reginald, Rollerblade, Rebel, Rastafarian ...

My exercise is interrupted as I approach school and see students flooding through the gates. Friends, hugs, handshakes ... I don't get any. I am invisible. This place terrifies me, actually terrifies me. I feel like my school is the film set for a movie, a horror movie about my life. It's one of those scary teen films where you are wondering when it's all going to go bad ... that's how I feel.

It's brewing. Disaster and doom.

It doesn't help that I still have to be at school with people like Leo Fulham — the one who has tortured me since primary school. Still torturing. He is still just as unpleasant as he was when he was seven, but with pimples. He has the vibe of the teen horror movie bad guy, strutting around the school in a sports jacket and treating people horribly: that's him. They often get their comeuppance though, don't they? Interesting that ...

Speak of the devil. He walks in the school gates at the same time as I do. I am not invisible to him, sadly.

'Hey, Weirdo!' he says, his dickhead-look on his smug face.

My heartbeat starts to race, shoulders tense, chest tightening. An internal lock is set in place. *Only four-and-a-half more years here, Jasper, if you can last that long . . .*

He whacks me on the back. I change direction, but not fast enough. I still hear under his breath: 'Have a shit day, Weirdo.'

I am on time again though (success on that front) so at least there is no trip to the dean's office to start the day. English is first up. I spend most of the class staring at an empty page in my creative writing book.

'A journal can be a great way to start expressing yourself through words and help you process emotions,' my teacher says. All I can think of is how impossible it is to write my thoughts down. No one wants to read that. Not me — that's for sure.

Once English is over, I quickly walk to the second period, art.

As I get closer to the art room I see Nina Frankton-Forbes sitting outside going through her bag. She looks worried. If I were braver I would ask her if everything was all right. But I'm not brave. Maria stands at the door.

'Just give me two minutes, I'm still setting something up.'

I sit down on the steps across from Nina and open my bag too. I don't need to, I just don't know what else to do. I check my phone and there is a text from Mum.

Jasper. We need to talk about an email from school. I am not happy! Why did you not tell me?

Then a second text.

Steve might move a few more things in today too.

Oh joy. Double whammy of NOT joy.

I switch my phone off without replying. I was hoping the whole school email thing might just magically disappear. Seems not. They must have sent the email to her personal email address which she always forgets to check. And Manly Steve is moving stuff in. He was waiting to pounce as soon as he got the go-ahead.

'Um. Jasper?'

I look up, confused about who could be talking to me.

It is Nina. Oh. My. God. She knows my name. Nina, Nina Frankton-Forbes.

I look back down in case I imagined it.

'Excuse me, Jasper?'

'Ya, I am Jasper,' I mumble.

'Yeah, I know.' She is standing above me now. 'I forgot the sheet we were given, with the instructions for our woodcutting today. And Hannah's not here. Do you mind if I take a look at yours in class?'

'Oh, um, sure. I mean, yeah.' Just speak normally for once!

'Sweet . . . Thanks,' she smiles shyly.

AHHH!!!!!!!!!!!!!!! I just had a conversation with Nina Frankton-Forbes! This could possibly be a very good day indeed!

I am feeling things I have never felt before in my life. I can't even describe it. It's like a bubbly feeling, a nervous but good feeling. A light, smiley tingle with a warm heart-racy feeling. I'm having an out-of-body experience. Maybe I do have a crush? I don't know, but whatever it is, it feels pretty good.

Nina Frankton-Forbes forgetting her sheet was the best thing to ever happen because now she is working next to me and we are sharing the sheet (thank god I brought it today and didn't lose it like I usually do with anything from a teacher). I can smell her hair conditioner. Sorry, now I'm sounding creepy.

At one point we bump elbows, and it sends this electricity current up through my arm which makes my head explode. I'm not learning anything, literally not hearing a word that comes out of the teacher's mouth. I'm pretending to listen, but I couldn't care less because my head is just so busy with thoughts.

Don't be a dick.
Don't be a dick.
Don't be a dick.

Maria hands out blocks of wood to the class. I nearly drop mine as it's handed to me, my muscles weak all of a sudden. What is wrong with me? Could this be the first symptom of algae-disease-itis? Or is this what happens when you have a crush?

'As we discussed at the end of the last class,' Maria says, 'woodcut is one of the oldest forms of printmaking. We'll work to carve our portrait image onto our wooden surface and later use this to print on paper, using rollers.'

She says something like this anyway ... I'm not listening.

I can see Nina looking over at me. Probably because we are all confused about what we are supposed to be doing. But we catch eyes a couple of times and it's just, well it's, it's … it's … effggg. Blaa. Ekgh. I can't make any sense anymore.

'We need to take care,' Maria warns. 'Not only with the equipment, which will be sharp but also because once the material is cut it can't be put back. You make a mistake, you live with it, or start over.'

This could get messy. A sharp chisel, clumsy hands and a nice girl next to me. This could be a recipe for disaster.

We get to work. My hands are shaking so much I don't think I should be trusted with a knife-like object but I start to make small gouges into my piece of wood to look like I'm doing something. Nina seems to be doing the same. Is this art?

My woodcut represents how I feel. A big, giant mess. At one point Maria says, 'Jasper, why do you look so confused today?' Little does she know it has nothing to do with art. 'Is this all making sense?'

I just nod and smile like a silent fool.

Somehow we all start making progress and class goes quickly. Too quickly. I don't want the class to end but the bell

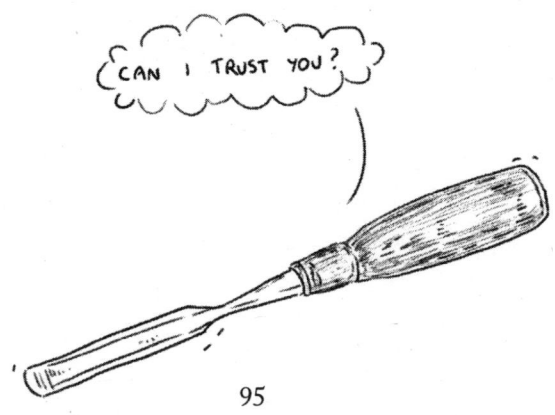

rings and we all pack up. My strange woodcut looks up at me, judging me. One giant eye glaring.

'Good start everyone,' says Maria. 'See you all tomorrow.'

Nina and I hardly spoke or anything (apart from me apologising when we bumped elbows) but she says, 'Thanks for that, Jasper.'

I reply, 'That's sweet as.'

Sweet as? Who am I?

Progress. Not much, but it feels like a big step. Holy Toledo. I don't think I was *too* much of a dick either. The rest of the day is a blur. I race home with a new pace to my step. I feel lighter. Bouncier. When I get home, I head for the tree. For the first time ever, I'm going there not because I'm in a bad mood, but because I don't know what else to do with myself. How else do I manage these feelings?

12.

I throw my bag on the front steps and climb the tree quickly.

My soundtrack today is kind of jazzy, upbeat. There are trumpets playing, it is fast and lively. I didn't know my brain orchestra could even play like this! This new Jasper needs a new name. What letter was I up to?

S. Samuels, Salmon, Sutton, Silly Sausage, Sandwich, Stevens
T. Thunderstorm, Thick Shit, Trumpet Head, Ticklebottom
Nina, Nina, Nina
U. Udder, Ukulele, Umbrella, Understood (or Misunderstood)
V. Vulture, Vermin, Victorious
Nina, Nina, Nina
W. Wigmore, Wiggles, Wibblebottom, What-the-hell

X. Xylophone, X-ray (only words I know that start with X)
Y. Yates, Young, York
Z. Zippy, Ziggy, Zoologist
Nina, Nina, Nina

Okay, I'm not in the mood for this, my brain isn't functioning. But Nina knows my name! She knows MY name and we bumped elbows and shared an instruction sheet! Hallelujah! I remember the electricity current that shot through me and I feel the residue pumping through my veins. Will she talk to me ever again? I imagine scenarios for what must be hours because the next thing I know it is getting dark and I see my mother's car pulling into the driveway. She gets out of the car and makes her way up the path looking down at my school bag as she walks up the steps.

Whoops, I forgot to throw it behind the bush where I usually do. This slightly confuses her and she takes it inside with her. Just when I'm about to jump down, she comes out the door and stands on the steps. She leans forward to look left and right up the street. Ninja stealth. Quiet breathing. Not one movement. I am a ninja.

She looks concerned. Maybe she is expecting her precious Manly Steve so she can discuss where to put all his fabulous stuff. She checks her watch, then puts her hands into her pockets. Her chest rises and falls with a sigh. Wait. I think she is

worried about *me*. Why does this please me? As if I needed some weird confirmation that she cares about her own son. Of course she does, I knew this. The worry, the hand squeezes.

She looks left again up the street and something grabs her attention.

Uh oh. I think it's me! No, no, no . . . Have I just been seen up the tree? After all these years? Her eyes squint to try, in the fading light, to make out the shape of a five-foot-eight, tall, skinny, teenager. In a tree. 'Jasper? Are you . . . up there?'

I think my cover is blown. I mean, clearly my cover is blown! NINJA!!!!!! NINJA STEALTH!!!!!!

'No,' I say faintly.

'No? No, you're not?'

'No, I'm not,' I say again.

'I was starting to worry. What are you doing up there?' She comes closer to the tree until she is standing just below me, looking up.

'Thinking . . .' I say.

No. No. No.

'Thinking? How long have you been up there thinking?'

'Dunno.' The answer to this is possibly *hours*.

'Hungry?'

'Yes. Very,' I say, which is the truth. I am so ravenous right now and no dreaming of Nina or alphabetical last name exercises are working to distract me.

'I'll get dinner started. Steven is on his way.' She turns her back and walks inside with a small backward glance. 'And we have to discuss that email.'

Great. The email from school. She's seen it and she's not happy. And Manly Steve is on his way, probably with a truckload of his belongings AND my secret hiding place is not so secret anymore. Dammit. I should have used my ever-so-plausible excuse about the cat up the tree. I have been practising that for years!

I rush into my room to hide, mortified. But I can't hide for long. I am hungry and the smell of onions and garlic cooking has made its way into my room. Nana always used to say, 'All good meals start with garlic and onion.'

I go to the kitchen to search for salt and vinegar chips.

'Not too many,' Mum says as I break open the chip bag. She has reapplied make-up after work, I can tell. And she's wearing a floral top and black pants. Not her usual clothes for home. She's dressed up. For you-know-who.

I sit eating the chips while Mum stressfully cooks. It's always entertaining watching her, she keeps sighing and tying her hair up out of her face, then the hair escapes and she ties it up all over again. But she doesn't mention the tree . . . Yet. I'm sure it's coming. She doesn't mention the email either. The stress of cooking for Manly Steve is taking over.

'What are you making?' I ask, mid-chip.

'A recipe I've wanted to try. Chicken mushroom something. I saw it in a magazine.' She points at an open magazine lying on the bench. Ugh. Mushrooms. Whenever Manly Steve comes for dinner she tries new recipes. I suppose from now on he won't be 'coming for dinner'. He will live here — it will just be 'dinner'.

'There's a baked potato for you if you're vegetarian today,' she says, pricking a cold potato and shoving it in the oven.

BAKED POTATO! WHAT THE . . .? That chicken something sounds a lot more appetising. Especially if she manages to pull it off.

'How was school?' she asks, dropping an onion on the floor. She gives me a quick glare as she leans down to pick it up.

'Fine,' I say. Here we go.

'So.' She stops chopping and looks at me. 'What happened the other day? The principal wants to . . .'

But in perfect timing, Manly Steve arrives! She must have given him a key because he doesn't knock on the door, but for once I am happy to see his face. Mum won't bring the email up in front of him, this will buy me some time. She'll want this first dinner together to be nice and not fighty. Fine with me.

'Hello! Hello!' Mum says, rushing over to him.

'Big day,' Manly Steve says, kissing Mum on the cheek (life in packaging is obviously highly stressful).

He remembers me. 'Hi.' Awkward.

'Hi . . .' Equally awkward.

Dinner is just as strange. I hardly talk and neither does Manly Steve. Mum however talks a lot, trying to make everything seem so wonderful and positive. She tells Manly Steve about the art exhibition (even though I haven't even started anything for it). He pretends to look impressed.

'I haven't come up with anything, Mum. Nothing to celebrate yet.'

'It's great to be asked, Jasper, not everyone was . . . Or were they?'

'No, not everyone.'

She continues talking . . . about everything and anything that pops into her head: a patient this morning who knew someone who knew someone who knew someone who was on a reality show that none of us watch; the weather; how she thinks we should get a clock in the kitchen; how the neighbour has painted his fence. 'It's yellow! What was he thinking?'

Manly Steve and I silently eat dinner and catch each other's eyes now and then. I decide this might be a good time to tell Mum about how I caught Mr Schultz in the act the other day, letting Princess poo on our front lawn.

'He left it right there. Just pretended he hadn't seen it. A big giant stinking poo!'

Manly Steve looks disgusted. 'Can we not talk about this while we're eating?' he says. The first time he has properly acknowledged me this evening.

'Mum likes to know these things.' She does. She loves hearing about Princess the pooing cavoodle.

Mum looks embarrassed. 'Well, it's just . . . I need to talk to him.'

Is dinner going to be like this every night? And if you are wondering, yes I ate the chicken mushroom thing. And no, it didn't look ANYTHING like the picture in the magazine.

Mum keeps jabbering on and apologising about the food.

'I may have missed a crucial step.'

She one hundred percent did.

As I eat, I notice a few new things around the house — a new kettle, a new lamp in the corner and a large ugly pottery vase on the table. It is asymmetrical and vomit-coloured. It looks like something even I could make and I've never tried pottery. Mum must hate it.

When I go to the bathroom, I notice a new painting in the hallway too. Ugly.

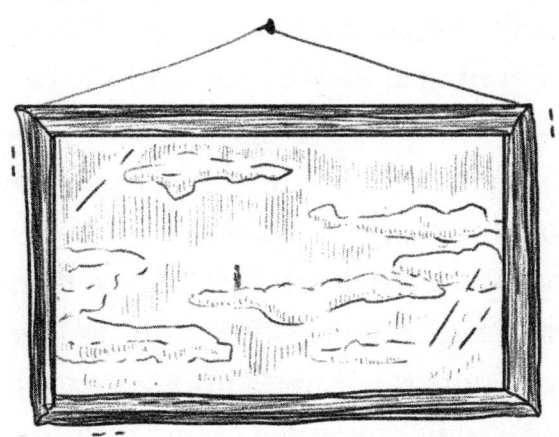

I stare at it. It's odd. I don't like it and my new standing as an impressive artist means my opinion matters. Someone standing on clouds? I don't get it and it doesn't look good. I walk down this hallway more than once a day and this is frankly an eyesore.

I didn't imagine Manly Steve was the arty type and what's worse is that someone has taken down some of the art I did at primary school to make room for this junk. The hallway used to always be for my art. Where is that now? It's awful stuff really, but I thought Mum liked it.

As I walk back down the hall, I notice new books on the bookshelf: business-themed. A photo of Mum and me is shoved to the side to make room for his library of boringness. Once I'm back at the table, Mum tells me Steve is going to move most of his stuff this weekend. He has a moving truck organised tomorrow for 'some of the larger items'. How many items are there if he can class them in sizes AND requires a moving truck for 'some' of them?

I stare down at my dinner plate. 'Whatever . . .'

Mum charges on despite the signs. Apparently, he is putting some stuff in storage so he isn't bringing everything he owns. Come on, how much paraphernalia does this man have? I honestly think I might have to move out to make room for him; this is getting ridiculous.

'Steven has a nice couch for the lounge too, so we can get rid of our old ones,' Mum says, excitedly. Woohoo. It seems our 'old' lounge suite is not up to his high standard of places to put your arse while you watch evening television.

Mum smiles wildly; she genuinely seems to think new lounge furniture might cheer me up. 'You'll love it!' she says. 'It's quite fancy.'

Yes, Mum, how exciting! I hated the idea of your dumb boyfriend moving in with all his disgusting art, dumb economics books and new house rules . . . But then he brought his fancy couch and EVERYTHING changed!

'Might go and finish my homework,' I say. I need to go into my room to absorb all of this.

'Okay, Jasper, that's great. Absolutely, you do that. We'll tidy up,' says Mum. Again, twice as many words as needed.

I go to my room and collapse on the unmade bed. I don't even want to be in this room. I don't even like it in here. Now I will probably be hanging out here more than I already do, in a room I don't like with a dying fish in its death water!

Speaking of the dying fish, Han Solo is still very much alive. He is punishing me now, dragging his death out to make me pay for the suffering I have made him endure his whole life. I don't even want to look at him and I don't want to do my homework. But here I am, hiding. I just want to watch television. I want to go into my lounge and sit on my old couch and watch my television. I want to sit on the couch which is not good enough for Manly Steve and leave crumbs on the floor and have my sneakers on inside. All the things he hates.

I'm supposed to be happy about our couch being replaced. Happy! I *like* our old couches; they are important to me. The more I think about this, the more this is really going to piss me off. I can feel it mounting: anger. I can feel my thoughts start to justify that anger, start to build and grow and fester and burn.

I LIKE MY COUCHES!

Here's the thing with our couches: my nana gave them to us. They make up a dark blue, three-piece leather lounge suite; she gave it to us when Poppa died, when she moved into the retirement village because it was too big to fit in her unit. It is ridiculously large and I suppose it has to be said it's uncomfortable. It kind of sucks you in when you sit down and getting up is never easy. In fact, on a hot day, you can't sit on it in shorts because the backs of your legs stick to it like glue and you have to peel yourself off it.

POP!

But that is not the point. Those couches remind me of going to Nana and Poppa's and having dinner in front of the television. I think of watching cricket with Poppa even though I didn't know the rules and found it boring. I just loved sitting on the couch while he yelled at the television and occasionally jumped up like a jack-in-the-box when something exciting happened (not that often in cricket).

He lost all of his spring not long before he died. And then Nana lost hers once he was gone.

She wanted us to have those couches. She didn't want to say

goodbye to them either, because of all the years sitting next to Poppa on them. And Mum just wants to give them away because Manly Steve is moving in and his hairy buttocks are too fancy to stick to them!

Is this how it's going to be now? I have no input in the big decisions. I spend A LOT of time on those couches because they are in front of the television and my PlayStation. I should have been properly consulted.

Rage lights a fire inside me. I want to take that fire and set things alight (mostly Manly Steve's economic books and his dumb cloud painting). He has been living here for five minutes and is already telling us our things aren't good enough, our memories are not important enough. He doesn't know that I would do anything just to be sitting there again watching the telly with Nana and Poppa.

He is an arse. An ass. Hee-haw.

I stand up, throw my door open and stamp down the hallway.

Mum and Manly Steve are doing the dishes and he is mid-sentence about . . . Well, I don't care what about!

'I don't want you to get rid of the couches!' I shout.

'Oh,' says Mum, surprised. 'I was going to give them to the charity shop.'

'They were Nana and Poppa's. I love those couches. They aren't something you just give away.'

Manly Steve watches intently, tea towel in hand. I deliberately ignore him. Mum puts down the dish brush and approaches me gently like I'm a wild animal on the loose. I ruined the lovely first meal together with *Steven*. It was bound to happen.

'I thought you hated those couches.'

'Well, you thought wrong.'

'Steven has a big corner couch, one end you can put your feet up because it's got . . .'

'I don't care. Just don't give my couches away. I will have them in my room if *you* don't like them.'

'They won't fit.'

'I will make them fit.'

'Fine,' says Manly Steve, going back to drying dishes. 'He can have them in his room if that's what he wants.'

'Thanks for getting involved in something that's not even about you,' I say and with that I turn and walk away, feeling righteous, feeling like Nana would be proud. And Poppa too, even though I only ever heard him swear once and it was about how uncomfortable those couches were.

Mum comes and sits at the edge of my bed, looking around the room. 'If you want the couches in here, that's fine.'

She'll be thinking they won't fit but she needs to let me try anyway.

I am determined. I feel like those couches staying is now about Manly Steve versus me. I will do whatever it takes to keep them in the house.

Me: 1 Manly Steve: 0. Success.

I am still ready for a fight. Mum next.

Round 2. Ding, ding, ding.

'Did you throw out my art from the hallway?'

'Of course not. I've put it in the box with your other art.'

'Just chucked in a box?' I look down for dramatic effect.

'Do you want it up in your room?'

'No, it's crap.'

'Okay, I'm confused.' She throws her hands up in the air.

'I thought you liked my art,' I say, sadly. I will make her pay for this. 'Why tell him I'm good at art and then hide it? I hate that you're moving all our stuff to make room for his crap.'

'This is his house now, too.'

'Exactly!' I shout, maybe too loudly. 'I don't want to live with your annoying dickhead boyfriend.'

She stands and points her finger at me. 'How dare you. Your behaviour is appalling. You are being unfair.'

I roll my eyes. Her behaviour is appalling; Manly Steve is appalling.

'And on that topic, Jasper, we need to talk about your behaviour at school because the principal wants to see me about the incident.'

Here we go. The incident.

'Not now, Mum.'

'Yes. Now.'

Round 3. Ding, ding. Dammit.

13.

'Why on earth did you hurt someone at school?'

'It was an accident.' Accident. Not incident.

'You verbally abused a teacher.' She is standing in my doorway, arms crossed.

'It was a discussion, a heated discussion. She is a cow.'

'Stop, Jasper! I am so disappointed in you.' *Welcome to my world, Mum. I feel disappointed in me too.* 'I can't keep getting these emails from school.'

She looks almost defeated.

I think she's still feeling guilty about the hallway art though, as she should, because just when I'm preparing myself for a mammoth mother-style lecture she sinks down onto my bed and just says: 'Please let that be the last one.' I thought she'd at least take my phone. She looks at me for a moment then stands up to leave and at the door says, 'Learn to control your anger.'

Ha. Great, thanks, any tips on what to do when you are going to be eaten by a terrifying bear from your nightmares, Mother? Any chapters on that in your parenting books? She stares at me but does offer something she must have read. 'Take ten deep breaths or something.'

Brilliant. If only I had thought to breathe. This is probably something she learned in the yoga class she enrolled in but only went to twice. 'Ten deep breaths,' like that's going to solve all my problems. I'm sure that will make a huge difference when He is in front of me. I can just breathe Him away, slowly at the count of ten. Send Him back to wherever He is from with a gentle breath *phhhh*. Problem gone. Blissful life. *Namaste*.

'Things have to change, Jasper. You have to.'

Awesome. Thanks, Mum. How very *accepting* of you.

She stares at me. 'Say something Jasper, for goodness sake.'

I pull my duvet up to my shoulders and close my eyes.

With a sigh, Mum says, 'I'm going to get hold of your father.'

Oh great. Here it comes.

'You can have a chat with him, man to man?'

I turn over in my bed and throw my pillow over my head. She's telling me there is something wrong with me. Why doesn't she just say it? Everyone can clearly see it. They probably mentioned it in the email.

Jasper is not okay!

JASPER IS NOT OKAY!

She still hasn't left. She keeps talking.

Why don't you discuss this with Steven? No. Never gonna happen!

Shall I call Uncle Rob? Haven't talked to him in four years.

Do you want to talk to the boy up the road? Who?

Do you want to . . . Should I call . . .Who can help? No. No. No.

All things that won't help. All conversations I don't want to have. All the people that mean nothing to me.

'Talking is the last thing I want to do. Can you just leave?' I sit up again, pick up a book and pretend to read.

'Why do you get so angry about little things, Jasper?' she asks, with a sigh.

Little things.

Little. LITTLE. LITTLE!

'Mum! The stupid teacher was NOT listening. And now you're NOT listening? Why do you think I'm angry? What is the point of TALKING when no one is LISTENING?' I throw the book across the room.

'STOP!' she yells back.

ONE... TWO... THREE... FOUR...

I stand up out of my bed, throwing my duvet aside. 'I don't want you here. I don't want to be in this house. I don't want to be here at all. I hate my life!'

'Don't say that, Jasper!' She takes a step towards me.

Don't be angry, Jasper.

Don't be angry, Jasper.

Don't. Don't. Don't.

'You're still not listening!' I yell.

'Argh. I can't talk to you when you're like this, go to sleep!' She turns and walks out, slamming the door behind her. She leaves me with the anger and the fire.

I lie back in bed, staring at the ceiling. Again! I can hear Mum and Manly Steve get ready for bed. How can I sleep now? How can I not be angry now? In the darkness, with these thoughts and while someone is dying?

While someone is waiting.

In the darkness.

I bang my fists into the side of my head three times.

One bang. Two bangs. Three bangs.

All is quiet in the house. I get up and walk to the dark lounge, pacing. I sit on the old blue couches in the dark. And then stand up. And sit down again. I can't do this anymore; I need to sleep. I can't survive without sleep. I feel broken and I need to tell my mother because there is no one else to tell. I walk towards her room. I will tell her that I can't sleep and she needs to help me. I don't want to be angry anymore, but I don't know how. I don't want this. I don't want to feel this way.

As I approach her door, I hear voices. My mother's; Manly Steve's. Little whispers in the dark. I stand outside the door, ready to knock, but instead, I listen. I hear my mother say the one thing I don't want to hear.

'He just doesn't seem right. He's so much like his father sometimes, it scares me.'

14.

The words echo through me. *So much like his father.*

I rush back to my room and pull a piece of art paper out from under the bed and a pencil from my desk.

What I see? What I see?

I see something I don't like. I see someone impossible to love, just like my father. I see darkness and shame. I see someone who is angry and resentful. Someone everyone is scared of. But I am scared.

I see a scared kid being chased by a grizzly bear in the dark.

A bear that I hate.

That's what I see.

So I draw what I see. I draw. And I draw. And I draw. Until I can't anymore because my hand is sore and I am finally tired.

> **WHO AM I?**
> **NO JASPER, WHO ARE YOU?**
> **I AM DARKNESS, WHO ARE YOU?**
> **I AM DESTRUCTION, WHO ARE YOU?**
> **ANSWER MY QUESTIONS!**
> **I WILL DESTROY YOU**
> **IS IT TIME TO SURRENDER?**

I wake with a jolt. Time has passed slowly, yet in an instant, I must have slept. In fact, I know I did, because a flash of a dream returns. I am in a fish tank, swimming around desperately. I have scales and a tail but I can't breathe underwater.

I am drowning.

And now, in my bedroom, I am cold, lying on the floor. I have a chill in my bones and my mouth is dry. I have a throbbing headache on the left side of my head. It drills in. I stand up and find a hoodie to put on. For the chill in my bones.

Bones.

I am so thirsty; my mouth is so dry even swallowing is hard. I make my way to the kitchen and in the hallway, I see the pages. Ripped pages from a book. Down the hallway. Scattered. I pick up the destroyed cover and I see it is one of Manly Steve's books, one of the new books I saw on the shelves. *Small Business Ventures: How to Succeed Against All Odds*. I quickly pick up the pages. They are torn, screwed up. The book is completely ruined. There are more remains of it on the floor of the lounge.

I quickly go out the back door and put the pages in the outside bin, underneath a rubbish bag. My heart is racing. He must have done it. The Nightmare. He must have come last night. Did He?

I put the rubbish bin lid down and turn to go inside. As I am closing the back door, Mum walks into the room.

'Where have you been?'

'Nowhere,' I reply, closing the door behind me.

'Nowhere?'

'I just went outside. To look at the garden.'

'Okay . . .?' She looks at me, awkwardly, like she doesn't recognise me. Like she is seeing me up the tree again. Like she is afraid of me. But I know this.

She walks into the kitchen and fills the kettle. 'How are you feeling?' she asks, tentatively.

'All right.'

I am not all right.

'The movers come at eleven. Once you and Steven have had breakfast we'll move the couches.'

I am now sitting in my bedroom looking at my giant forty-year-old couches. I can hardly move. I can't even fully open my door; I have to hold my breath to squeeze inside.

All morning, Mum kept telling me I was crazy putting them in my bedroom, but Manly Steve kept saying if that's what I want I should have them. He thinks she worries about me too much. *Let him fail.* That's what he's thinking.

Moving the couches was the first time Manly Steve and I did anything 'together'. It was painfully awkward, as most of our interactions are. I'm not strong, I have no muscles, I don't lift weights let alone couches. I was annoying him because I wasn't holding the couches correctly. They kept slipping and I had to put them down and rest about fifteen times along the hallway.

He sighed and scoffed every time I needed a break.

'This is going to take all day . . .'

Then there was the issue of how to get them around the tight corners. That was followed by a lot of manoeuvring and mathematical equations, geometry angles, forty-point turns. But we were both determined to make it work and finally got two of the couches in my room. The other one is in the garage. 'For when I move out and go flatting,' I say to Mum. Manly Steve will love that day, I'm sure.

The garage is a mess already, but we squeeze the couch in next to the box of my rejected art. On the top are the two framed pieces that were in the hallway. Manly Steve goes back inside and when I'm alone I look at what else is in the box. There is another self-portrait. This one was done at about age six, I think. My eyes are different sizes and I have large ears. My mother told her friends it was 'Picasso-esk'.

It's crap. There's also a painting of a house, our house, but coloured brightly with a giant sun in the corner. Why do kids always draw a giant sun in the corner? With lines for the rays. Who started that?

Standing next to the house are three stick figures. Mum and Dad and me. It must have been before they broke up, when we were a family. Before we were a broken family.

I shove the art back into the box and head inside, to try to create some order in my bedroom. I move things around, trying to make it look better, knowing in my heart that this is ridiculous. I feel like I'm just moving piles of stuff from one side of the room to the other. I've had to take out my desk and chest of drawers to make room for the couches: they are in the garage now too. I figure one of the couches can become my wardrobe, I will just stack the clothes on it. It will be awesome because I will be able to see where everything is. It's going to save so much time.

I stack my school books and comics on the floor. This could become problematic but I'm not going to think about that right now. I hear a loud banging sound outside and move to

the window to see a large moving truck has arrived. Someone is pulling the back ramp down. It crashes onto the pavement. Another couple of men join him and they start unpacking. Manly Steve's stuff has arrived. All of it. In all its glory.

I stay in my room, out of the way. From my window, I watch as they carry the boxes inside. Where is it all going to go? It doesn't look like much has gone into storage. There are loads of boxes and of course the *glorious* couch. It is a dark shiny leather. It takes all three of the movers to carry it and negotiate its corners into the house. I hate it already.

Next, there are mirrors, lamps (we have those already) and more bad artwork (plenty of that in the garage). Is Manly Steve some kind of art historian or something? And it's not Mum's cup of tea at all but she won't tell Manly Steve that, I bet. She will pretend she loves it. So far I've never once heard her tell Steve what she really thinks. She is morphing into the woman that he wants her to be. I don't recognise her sometimes.

After the men unload the last of the boxes, what feels like hours later, Manly Steve hands over a stack of twenty-dollar notes to one of the burly men and the truck leaves. Mum and Steve stand hand in hand while it drives off. It's like a happy movie moment. Mum turns to Manly Steve and smiles at him and he kisses her on the forehead. Eww. His hand goes down her back and rests on her butt. I see his big manly hand give it a squeeze.

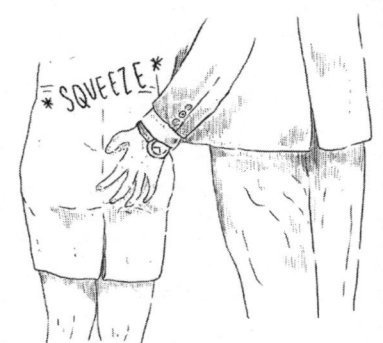

Gross.

I hide in my room for as long as possible. There is loud music playing in the lounge, terrible music, while Mum and Squeezy Steve unpack the gazillions of boxes sitting on the floor there. I don't want to be given any kind of unpacking job and more importantly, I don't want to witness any more public displays of affection. My poor young eyes can't handle it.

Inside my room, the view isn't any good either. I feel like a colossal idiot surrounded by couches. I know I need to deal with the mess but now I'm too tired to tidy, I'm exhausted from moving the couches. My arms are sore. All my muscles are sore.

I move some posters around to cover new holes in the wall. Mum wants to come and see my room once I've 'tidied' it and she won't want to see the holes. I cannot deal with the conversation if she did.

I stare at the chaos. Han Solo stares at me. 'Stop judging me,' I tell him. I grab my phone and google *dying goldfish* to see if there is any hope for him. One website says if the water condition isn't great fish will get sick. My fault. Another site says he might be constipated and I should give him peas, but we don't have any.

I don't want to but next I google *how to kill a fish humanely.* The suggestions are upsetting. I can't do it. I change it to *how to save a dying goldfish.* Apparently, they can just get 'stressed' and hang out at the bottom of the tank. Maybe Han Solo is depressed too, because of me? It could be me making him sick. But when I scroll down it says fish stress is more than likely to be bad water, lack of air and poor nutrition.

However you read it, it's all my fault and I feel terrible.

I spend the next hour changing the fish tank water and rinsing off the green slime from the walls. It's disgusting. I scrub clean the little slimy castle and put it back inside the tank, to be ignored some more. I watch the slime-water flow down the sink, then spend another twenty minutes washing my hands and rewashing them. To get rid of the algae-disease-itis and slime residue.

The fish tank does look healthier.

But Han Solo still looks sick.

Mum knocks on my door. 'Jasper, how is your room looking?'

'I've been cleaning the fish tank,' I say, pointing to the tank. I can now see inside it properly too. The slime has gone.

'It looks great. The room's a bit of a mess though?' She looks around. 'I've put a few things out on the road with "free" signs. Do you have anything to add?'

'No.' Like I would just put my stuff out there and give it away because her boyfriend has moved in and we need to make space. I don't think so.

'Okey dokey,' she replies, false cheer.

I can't believe Manly Steve is letting her do this, putting her own belongings out on the street to fit his crappy stuff in. What's he going to make her give away next?

Mum gets burgers for dinner. I ask for a fish one but can't eat it because I have flashbacks to the websites I was googling before. Sick fish. Dying fish. Killing fish. Why did I get a fish burger? Why did I think that would be a good idea?

'What's wrong with your burger?' Mum asks, seeing me taking half the burger to the rubbish bin.

'I'm not hungry.'

'Waste of money,' says Manly Steve under his breath. Always budgeting.

'You want me to get it out of the bin so you can finish it?' I say, pointing to the bin.

'Jasper ...' Mum says, looking embarrassed.

'Night,' I say.

'You going to bed already?' Mum asks, following me down the hall.

'Yep,' I say and squeeze my way back into my room, shutting the door behind me.

It's starting to get dark. As I pull my curtains closed, I see the tree outside. I try to remember how it feels to be up there, the quiet.

It's not so quiet in here, with the laughing outside my room.

I wonder if He will come tonight. What will He destroy next?

I push the small couch across the door. There is no way He would get past it. As I lie down, I remember the blocked door. I am hidden away, safe and sound. He can't get in. He is outside. I am in.

And I sleep. I actually sleep. It could be exhaustion from the couch lifting but when I wake, I know I have slept deeply. Like a log. Like a dead weight.

DEAD.

15.

Manly Steve makes average pancakes for breakfast.

He gives me the one that broke when he flipped it. It's a small observation and I don't make a thing of it; I thank him anyway. But it's another sign he doesn't like me.

Then something weird happens. My dad calls. He hardly ever calls me. The last time I spoke to him was three months ago, before I started high school. Father of the year, everybody. Maybe Mum told him to ring. He calls on the landline while I'm in the bathroom. I hear Mum answer.

'David! How are you?'

I rush out to the lounge and take the phone from her before she can launch into her complaints about me. I take the phone to my room.

'Hi.'

'Hello, Jasper,' he says, sounding chirpy. 'You good?'

'Ya.'

He asks me how school is going but before he's even finished the question, I say, 'Mum's boyfriend moved in, did you know that?'

'No,' he replies. 'Well, that's good. How do you feel about that?'

'Not sure,' I say. 'Not that happy, I suppose.'

'Why's that?' he asks like he cares how I feel.

'Because I'm just not.' The stuff, the awkward conversations, the hands on bottoms, the artwork, the comments, the clutter, the couches.

'Well, he is your mother's boyfriend, you aren't supposed to like them.'

'I'm doing what I'm supposed to then . . .' At least I'm doing something right.

'You might just have to deal with it though,' he says. 'One day you're going to want to move out and start your own life. It'll be nice to know your mum has someone to live with. Ever thought of that?'

'No,' I say. I hadn't. Sometimes my father says the stupidest stuff, but sometimes he says things that make actual sense, it's weird.

'Where are you, anyway? You been busy?' I ask, a hint of sarcasm but he doesn't pick up on it.

'Yes! I'd like to see you soon . . . don't know when that will be.'

Winner.

He gives me a number to call if I need to over the next few

days. I write it down on a piece of paper and put it on one of the blue couches (the one where I am filing all the stuff that used to be on my desk).

'Night.'

'Bye, Jasper. Keep smiling.'

Keep smiling. I wasn't smiling in the first place. What a stupid thing to say.

So deal with the situation and 'keep smiling' is the advice from my father. Get on with life, maybe see him one day (ultimately — when it suits him). He wants to see me, but not really enough. Another satisfying conversation with my father.

But maybe he has a point. I do want Mum to be 'happy', so I should be 'happy' that she met Manly Steve. I should be 'happy' that he likes her and 'happy' he has a nice big couch and 'happy' he wants to live with us. 'Happy' that even though my own father doesn't want to live with me, some random dude is willing to.

Happy, happy, happy. Right? What even is 'happy'? What does it even feel like? Whatever this 'happy' business is, maybe I should try it, try not to be so angry and see how that goes. Maybe He will even go away and Han Solo won't die. He won't be depressed if I'm not depressed. And it will all be okay ... And we will live pretending that it's happily ever after.

It's Monday morning and I'm giving 'happy' a go (despite Mondays being particularly difficult historically). This whole happy thing is weird but I have to admit having Nina at school is actually kind of making me vaguely happy plus I have finished the art for the exhibition so I achieved something for school this month. It's probably terrible, but I take it to Maria at the start of the day. She is getting ready for her first class.

'Come on in,' she says. 'How are you?'

'Okay. I've finished my thing for the thing,' I say, as I stand next to her desk, awkwardly.

'Your thing for the thing?' She looks confused.

'Sorry, my art for that exhibition thing.'

'You've finished already? Wow. Show me, show me.' She walks around her desk and stands next to me.

I grab my art folder and unzip it, feeling like maybe it's not finished and it's probably bad and why did I say I would do it, she'll regret choosing me and she's one hundred percent going to think I'm some messed-up kid with a messed-up brain because if this is *what I see*, there is seriously something wrong with me.

I pull out the piece of paper and put it on the desk.

'Oh my goodness.' She sits down in front of it.

'Is it okay?' I ask.

'Jasper . . . it's . . .'

Oh god, I feel mortified. It's terrible. Why would anything I do be any good? She must think I'm . . .

'It's incredible. I love it.' She looks up at me. 'You should be so proud of this.'

'Oh. Thanks.'

'You need to add something,' she says, standing, then walking back to her supply cupboard.

'Does it need more shading? I kind of left it but I could . . .'

She hands me a pen.

'No. You need to sign it. Always sign your art, Jasper.'

The day gets even better. In art class, Nina sits next to me — without needing to borrow anything. She just sits next to me. There were even other free chairs as well, so it wasn't that she had no choice. Nina sat next to me of her own accord.

Maybe I can be a little bit happy. Maybe things are looking up.

She even smiles at me as she is getting things out of her bag. 'Morning.'

'Morning!' I respond, but it comes out with the exact singsong tone that she had and it sounds distinctly like I was making fun of her.

Dammit, Jasper.

Then the mind games begin. What to do now? How to behave when someone you like is sitting next to you? I mean someone you . . . forget I said that. Anyway, this is my chance to say something.

Potential conversations swim around in my brain. None of them stick.

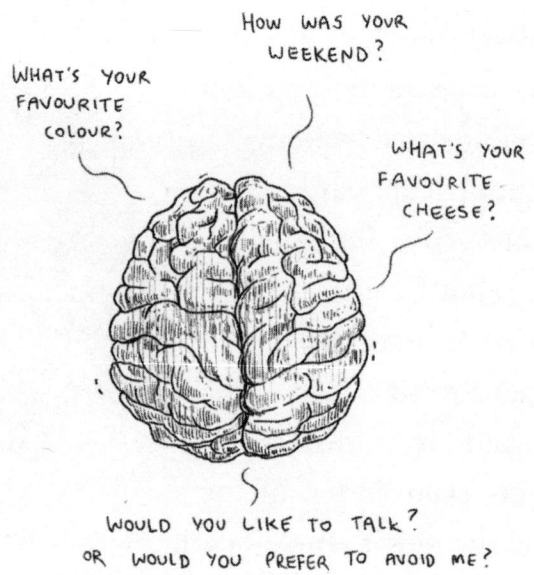

In the end, she beats me to it. 'Your woodcut looks good.'

'Oh thanks,' I say and laugh strangely. I don't know where to look so I just continue looking down at my half-carved, mutated face. I wouldn't exactly describe it as good, but I will take the compliment.

Then it hits me.

I should have said: *'Yours does too.'* But I didn't and now it's too late. Or is it?

'I like yours too,' I say.

It was too late. And said too fast.

She laughs. 'You're just saying that. I'm finding it so hard.' She looks down at her wooden face. 'Everything I do looks like a five-year-old did it. You're so good at art.'

'I don't know about that. But thanks.'

'No, you are. Really good. Everyone says it.' She smiles.

Everyone says it? Everyone? Do they? I thought everyone

said I was weird and had a bad temper. And who is this *everyone* anyway? I wanna know who *everyone* is!

I can't ask that, can I? Can't ask for names?

'Less chat, more carving!' Maria pipes up staring straight at me, but smiling, like she is happy I am talking to someone my age for once.

And there we have it. A proper conversation and I didn't sound too odd and I even got two compliments!

So today has been a good day already and it's not even lunchtime. I even see Leo Fulham in the corridor and just when I think he's going to come over and whack the back of my head, the principal comes around the corner. Leo has to withdraw his hand at the last minute and say 'Hi, Jasper,' instead.

Happy Jasper. Happy. You can do it.

At home I help unpack a few of Manly Steve's boxes because Mum asks me to — some plates and cups for the kitchen (even though we have plenty of those). I give more than one-syllable answers to his stupid questions and I even dry the dinner dishes — that always puts Mum in a good mood.

She clearly likes having Manly Steve here, her face lights up when he arrives home in the evenings and he brings her bottles of wine. Tonight he even gave her a bunch of flowers because she was upset because her receptionist's husband wants a divorce. I'm not sure of the details, or why it upset Mum so much (shouldn't the receptionist get the flowers?). Anyway, the receptionist is going to stay with her parents temporarily and Mum needs to find a replacement urgently blah, blah, blah.

The flowers work: it is a touching moment. Manly Steve even makes a few calls and finds someone to help her in the clinic. It seems he makes her happy in a way I can't. Me buying her flowers would be weird and I can't find her replacement receptionists. I can't even offer to be one. I would make a terrible receptionist.

Mum's happy, and I think I'm almost kind of happy as well; but just when I reckon things are looking up, Mum comes into my room for a chat. 'I talked to the principal today.'

'Oh.' I don't know why she didn't mention this earlier. Ah, Manly Steve. She doesn't want him to know I'm in any trouble.

'It's hard for me to meet him during school hours,' she says. Yes, her patients, her precious, precious patients. 'But we spoke on the phone.'

'What did he say?' I ask, not really wanting to know the answer.

'You are on a warning, for the incident last week, with the ball and the girl . . . and the . . .'

'Yeah, I know the one.'

'I promised him you were going to try hard to control your temper, Jasper. I need you to do that for me. You can switch this round.'

She doesn't let me say anything.

'Goodnight.' She turns off the light and shuts the door. I listen to the clock ticking.

Tick. Tick. Tick.

Control my temper. Switch this round. I am on a warning...

Everyone is talking about me behind my back. Today was a better day, but who was I kidding? Why do I even bother trying? I have a temper and no, I can't control it sometimes! I can't!

Oh, He's gonna love this. What will He destroy tonight? Will it finally be me? He knows. He knows I'm just pretending to be happy. The darkness is still here. He knows deep down I can't control this. He knows that deep down Nina probably doesn't like me and my art isn't that good. He knows that while today was a good day, tomorrow will be bad. He knows there is a reason my dad isn't here. He knows it all.

Now it is 11.10 p.m. and I don't think I will be getting any sleep. Sleep is not my friend tonight.

There is no friend.

WHO AM I?
I AM NOT GOING ANYWHERE
I AM A BLACK CLOUD LOOMING
AN ACHE YOU CANNOT IGNORE
YOU CAN PRETEND WITH EVERYONE ELSE
BUT YOU CANNOT PRETEND WITH ME
I WILL DESTROY YOU
IS IT TIME TO SURRENDER?

16.

The bear doesn't come in the night, but He wakes when I wake.

I don't see Him but I know He is here.

In fact, I feel like He follows me around the house as I get ready.

Mum tells me off for leaving my cereal bowl on the table, for being grumpy, for breathing. Can she not see Him? Can she not see why I am feeling grumpy, what is following me around?

I sense Him behind me as I walk out the door and He follows me to school, a few steps behind, huffing and puffing. I feel a sense of doom and dread as I arrive at the gate, like something bad will happen today. I feel nauseous, panicked. People look at me strangely as I walk in the school gates: maybe they can see what, who, is following me around.

All day I sense Him at the back of the class.

By the window.

Under the desk.

In the corridor.

I sense Him. But I don't see Him.

I wonder when He will show His face.

It's only a matter of time.

Eventually, He does.

In the school library. There in the quiet among the books.

I try to sleep it off. I try to hide from Him by closing my eyes. But instead, I open them and I'm being watched by the school librarian. She is standing above me, telling me off for falling asleep when we are 'supposed to be *researching*'.

She goes on to say something about not sleeping in the library. I see her mouth moving but don't hear the exact words. I have a ringing in my ears. I try to look more interested in the book I'm holding, but she continues to watch me and the ringing sound continues.

I move around the library looking for books to help me '*research*' my imaginary topic but no matter where I go, her eyes follow me. And the sound does too. Other people watch too. Do they hear the sound? I wish everyone would just leave me alone. I don't like to be watched.

He is watching me too, hiding behind book stands, sniffing under the shelves.

I don't know who I hate more: the bear or the librarian.

She is glaring at me. I don't need glares right now. And there is this question brewing inside me: *What are you going to do now, Jasper? What are you going to do about the nosy teacher?* I keep hearing it. And every time I see her dumb face look at me, it gets asked again. *Who does she think she is? What are you going to do about it?*

Now everyone in the room is staring at me. Everyone in my class. Everyone in the library: watching me over their books, talking about me in whispers. Watching. Watching. *What are you going to do now, Jasper? What are you going to do?*

Eyes on me.

The room begins to spin. The ringing sound begins to drill. I want to get out of here. I can feel my heart racing, my blood in turmoil. I want to escape this. I put my hands in my hair and start to push them into my skull, fingers like mini drills into my brain. I can't stand this anymore. I have to get out of this place with all the watchful eyes. NOW.

I stand quickly, pushing over one of the library displays as I grab my bag. All the books topple down, one by one, onto the floor. I look around and I can't see the bear. Where has He gone?

The glaring librarian rushes over. 'What on earth have you done?'

'I'm not feeling well,' I say, hands holding my head.

'Pick the books up off the floor and go to the school nurse!'

'I'm trying to. Go away.'

She continues to watch me, hands on hips. 'I'm making sure you tidy it up.'

'I said I'm trying to!' She stands above me as I pick up the books. My hands are shaking. Eyes on me. Everyone is watching, glaring. Eyes. Eyes. Eyes.

Even Leo Fulham. He is here too. I see him standing by the check-out desk, staring.

'Weirdo,' he mouths.

Why? Why did he have to be here?

Eyes. Eyes. Eyes. Burning eyes.

I feel heat rush to my cheeks as I quickly shove the books on the shelf and sprint out. My head feels like it is swirling and my legs shake underneath me as I run to the sick bay. The nurse looks up as I enter.

'Hi. How can I help?'

I lie, telling her I have a bad headache and need to lie down. Or is this the start of a headache? A migraine? I don't know anymore.

'What's your name?'

'Jasper Robinson-Woods.'

She shows me to the bed and asks if I would like pain relief but I say, 'No, I just want you to call my mother.'

I lie on the bed and try to calm the shaking and the swirling and the drilling.

Mum arrives an hour later looking extremely stressed. She had to cancel an appointment

with little notice and it's 'not a good look'. *Sorry, Mum. Sorry for existing. I can see my existence is a total hindrance to you and your career and the lives of your precious patients.* She thanks the school nurse and grabs my bag. We make our way to the car; she hasn't asked how I am.

Once we're in the car, she puts the keys in the ignition but doesn't start the engine. She just sighs. Then looks to me. 'What is this about?'

'I have a headache.'

'Do you, though? Not trying to get out of school?'

'No. I have a really bad headache. Why do you always think I'm lying?' I put my head into my hands, leaning forward against the dashboard.

'I don't know, you're such hard work at the moment.'

'Hard work? Thanks!' I raise my voice and she flinches as I do.

'Look,' she says quietly. 'Is there anything you need to talk about?'

'No, there is not.' As if this would be a good time to talk when she's accusing me of being a liar and hard work.

'It's just ... It seems to be more than headaches ...'

'What does that even mean?'

She takes the keys out of the ignition now and plays with them in her hands. 'I could talk to Mara — her son Devon went to see someone who helped, when he was ...' She tries to find the word. 'Depressed.'

Mara was Mum's cleaner, clearly a specialist in teenage mental health as well.

'You think there is something wrong with me,' I say, looking at her.

'You don't seem yourself, Jasper.'

Myself? Who even is that, because I don't know. I wish she would let me know a little about him, it might be helpful in this identity crisis.

'I just want you to be happy. I don't want all of this getting on top of you.'

There it is again. *Happy*. I was trying! My own mother thinks I'm nuts now and she doesn't even know about the bear, what would she think then? I hate to think.

'I am trying! I'm tired of trying,' I say and flick through my phone.

She finally puts the keys back in the ignition and starts the car, driving home in silence. It takes less than a minute, we live so close to school. The silence annoys her. 'You could have just walked home, Jasper.'

'I'm not allowed to just come home when I don't feel well, Mum. School rules.'

She scoffs.

'I've got to go back to work.' She stops the car but keeps the engine running.

'Thanks for looking after me so well,' I mutter.

'What?' she asks.

'Forget it.' I get out of the car and shut the door.

She drives away. She doesn't even come into the house, she just rushes back to the clinic, back to her patients, the ones who *need* her. The ones she really cares about.

I close the curtains in my room and collapse into my bed. I wish she had stayed. I wish she had sat at the edge of my bed like she did when I first had the nightmares, told me it would all be okay and that we would get through this. Together.

But she left.

I know I just tried to shut her out when she was trying to help. I don't know why I do that. I don't know why I don't answer her questions truthfully when she asks how I am.

I open the curtains again. I am unsure why I thought darkness would help. I see the tree. I don't know what else to do so I go back there. Climb the tree. To sit. To think. To pretend. To hide. Not from the bear, from myself.

He must have stayed at school.

Hopefully He ate the school librarian.

I sit in the tree for hours, numb. What if my headache was some kind of early sign of a brain bleed and she's just dropped me at home without a second thought, just thinks I'm avoiding school? My head is actually feeling fine now, but she doesn't know it! She doesn't care! I imagine her coming home to me lifeless in the bed. How bad would she feel? Would she care?

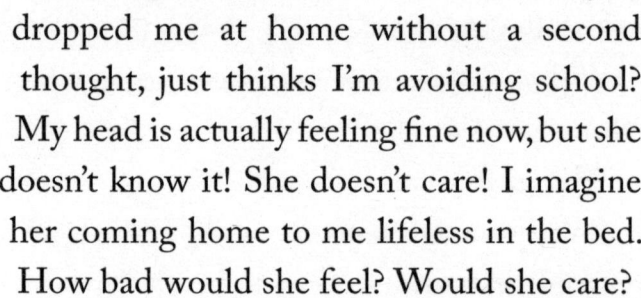

I head back inside because I need food. I walk down the hallway past the ugly dumb painting with the clouds. I hate seeing it every day, taking a spot that used to be for my art. What is it even supposed to be about, anyway? I hate it. Did Manly

Steve paint it? It doesn't look professional. It looks crap.

I eat seven pieces of toast with peanut butter and spend the afternoon playing computer games. Just living in the computer for a while helps. In another universe. When my eyes begin to hurt I turn off the computer and lie on Manly Steve's fancy new couch. I have to admit it is really comfortable. I hate that it is. I even go off to sleep for a bit. Damn this horrible fancy couch, why does it have to be so relaxing?

I wake when I hear Mum's keys in the front door and her steps down the hallway.

'Hi.' She walks straight past me and doesn't ask how my headache is. I consider pretending to be in a coma to give her a fright but can't be bothered.

She unpacks groceries in the kitchen while I lie in silence. Finally, she comes to sit down on the couch with me. I try not to look too comfortable.

'I talked to Mara.'

'Why?' I ask, offended that she ignored me. I hate that they were talking about me.

'She gave me the name of that psychologist. His name is Jack Brothers. Apparently he was excellent. Would you like me to call and make an appointment?'

'Does he treat headaches?'

'No. He helps people, Jasper.'

'I'm not going to see Jack Brothers, Mother.'

She sighs, looks frustrated and leaves the room. But no... I cannot see that happening. She is trying to get someone else to deal with me because she doesn't have the time to. She's too busy with her job and her new life with Manly Steve. I'm just in the way. Plus I don't see how it will help. I am not like Mara's son and I don't think Jack Brothers can help me. Mostly he can't help me because I wouldn't be able to tell him about the bear. So how can he help me? There's no point. I am absolutely not going . . . however . . . I do think Brothers is a cool last name and I think I will add *Jasper Brothers* to the shortlist. I might steal his last name, so I think it's best we don't meet.

So the new shortlist is:

A: Jasper Black
B: Jasper Brothers

Bs. I like Bs. I'm thinking I'll use a B name.

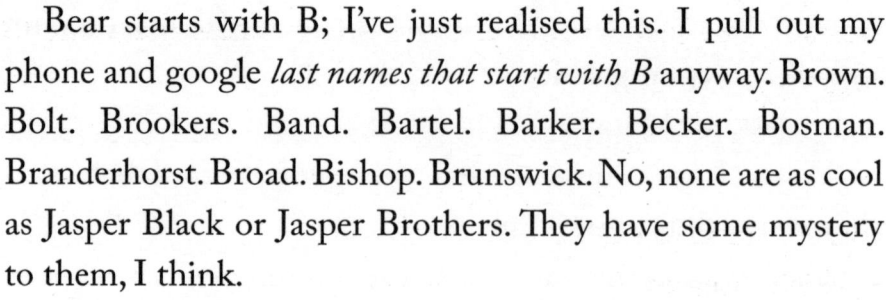

Bear starts with B; I've just realised this. I pull out my phone and google *last names that start with B* anyway. Brown. Bolt. Brookers. Band. Bartel. Barker. Becker. Bosman. Branderhorst. Broad. Bishop. Brunswick. No, none are as cool as Jasper Black or Jasper Brothers. They have some mystery to them, I think.

I check online to see if there is anyone called Jasper Black. There are lots. Also a few Jasper Brothers. But I suppose unless it's a ridiculous name, there will be others out there so that can't be a determining factor. I can't find a Jasper Bear anywhere. Thought I'd just check. But it's NOT on the list, for the record.

This leads to searching *how dangerous are grizzly bears?* Despite their size, they can run extremely fast — more than fifty-five kilometres per hour. I have no idea how fast I can run but I don't think it's that fast. They are dangerous to humans if 'surprised' or if a human stands between them and their cubs, that makes sense. There is no mention of grizzly bears in New Zealand. But I knew there weren't any here, of course.

I search for *Jack Brothers New Zealand*. A website comes up with a photo of him and some other psychologists he works with. There are some articles about anxiety and depression. Do I have those? Is that what this is?

I stare at the picture of Jack Brothers for ages. I don't want to go and see him. I go back to Google and write in the search bar *what is wrong with me?* All of these sites come up about mental health. I think of Leo Fulham: 'weirdo, weirdo, weirdo'. But just writing that question makes me want to delete my search history.

I search *how to delete recent searches*.

SEARCH HISTORY:
- Fish diseases
- How to kill a fish humanely
- What could the next global pandemic be?
- Coolest last names for boys
- Nina Frankton-Forbes
- How to breathe (I wasn't sure if I've been doing it right)
- Platypus (they are so weird-looking! What kind of animal ARE they?)

17.

I know Mum has told Manly Steve that something is wrong with me.

At dinner, he seems sympathetic. He probably does feel sorry for me. Or perhaps he is trying to keep me happy so I don't flip out and cut his dumb couch with a kitchen knife (I have thought about it). I hope his sympathy stops him from telling me to remove my sneakers as I walk in the door. And while we're at it, I hope he stops telling me not to drop my wet towels on the bathroom floor and to change the way I talk to Mum. I have lived with my mother for nearly fourteen years and she has never expressed concern about these things before. We have our own way of communicating. She does stuff to look after me and that makes her feel good. Picking up my towels makes her feel needed. That's what I tell myself, anyway.

TOWELS + DISHES + CHIPS = MOTHERLY LOVE

'Tell Jasper your news, Steven,' Mum says, putting extra broccoli on my plate. She has to narrate our conversations sometimes. *Jasper, tell Steven what your teacher said. Jasper, tell Steven about what you had for lunch . . .* ' In other words, please fill the awkward silence people!

'My daughter, Elise, is coming to stay this weekend,' he says, applying an unhealthy amount of salt to his meal.

'Here? In this house?' I say. Is this allowed?

'Yes.' He looks at Mum.

'This is Steven's house now too,' she says, annoyed again.

Okay, he's only just moved in and now he is inviting visitors to stay!

Manly Steve cuts his meat and it makes the plate squeak. 'I'm hoping you will all get along.'

'I'm sure we will,' Mum says, looking to me as if to say, '*Unless you behave badly and muck it up like usual.*'

I had forgotten he had a daughter. 'Who is she again?' I ask.

'She's at university in Wellington, older than you, Jasper. Twenty now.'

Manly Steve spends the rest of dinner talking about her and how much we are going to like her, as if he is trying to sell us a used car.

She is studying a Bachelor of Arts.

She is a vegetarian. (Snap!)

She likes animals, just not eating them — in particular she's keen on small ones like guinea pigs, rats, mice and rabbits and when she was younger she would buy them with her pocket money and hide them in her room.

The whole time I'm thinking how weird it's going to be to meet her. I struggle to talk to girls at the best of times: I still haven't had a decent conversation with Nina. And while Elise and I have the vegetarian thing in common, for me it's very much in its early days (in fact, I have been eating A LOT of meat lately).

'Where will she sleep?' I ask out of nowhere, after a few minutes of silence.

'The spare room,' says Mum, looking angry at me again. I'd forgotten about the spare room. It is slowly becoming Manly Steve's office/storage space. And yes, this IS annoying me.

'It will be great,' says Mum. 'I'm so excited to finally meet her.'

Is she a twenty-year-old version of Manly Steve?

Is she manly too?

Does she like him?

Does she hate my mum?

Mum breaks me from my thoughts by changing the subject. 'How is your goldfish, Jasper?'

I reply: 'A bit better. But still not moving much so I . . .'

'Sounds like it's time to flush him, or run over him with the car,' Manly Steve interrupts.

'What? Run him over? Can we NOT talk about this, please?' I am shocked at the turn this conversation has taken. What would his animal-loving daughter think of him trying to kill my goldfish? Finally, I have a conversation starter when she arrives.

I admit I did google how to kill a sick fish, but I would never consider driving over Han Solo! This confirms to me that I couldn't get 'rid of' Manly Steve. I can't even imagine murdering my sick goldfish — a goldfish I am pleading with the universe to let die. I don't think murder is for me.

'Let nature take its course,' Mum says, clearing away plates. 'Who's on dishes? Jasper?'

But Manly Steve has more to say. 'Fine, let him live in pain for days, dying slowly. Miserable . . .'

Damn, I really do hate him sometimes. I never asked his opinion anyway. 'He might not be dying,' I scoff. 'He might be fine!'

'Sounds like he is sick . . .' Dumb, smug face. I wish I could at least smack him in the head with a dead fish. That would feel just great.

'I'm having a shower,' I say. I don't even put the dishes away. (Manly Steve will hate that. Ha!) Mum follows me.

'Sorry about that. Of course you don't need to do anything like that. I know how much you care about Han Solo.'

She doesn't get that that is not even the point here. And why does she feel like she can't stand up for me in front of Manly Steve? Why does she have to follow me down the hall to do it? I hate that. I really, really, hate that.

I stand in the shower. Not moving. Just letting the water rain down. I imagine Han Solo in the toilet bowl, my hand on the flush button. I do want this slowly dying thing to be over with, but I certainly don't want to be the one that inflicts the final blow.

While I'm in the bathroom, my dad calls, again. Twice in a week! This is unheard of. Maybe he is trying to be the father of the year all of a sudden.

He leaves a number with Mum, different from the one he gave me last time. She passes it to me on a scrap of paper while I'm heading to my room. As I get dressed, the number on the paper sits on my bed, staring at me. He will want another chat and I'm not in the mood. He never stops to ask if it is a good time for me. He just expects me to drop everything. What about when I need to talk to him? What then? Yeah . . . I can't get hold of him. What if I think being a father is something you are *always*, not just when it suits you? Not just for a phone call three times a year.

Mum sticks her head around the door. 'Call your father, Jasper, it's getting late.'

'Tomorrow,' I reply, opening my computer and moving the mouse around to stir it from computer sleep-land.

'He's staying with a friend tonight. You probably won't get him tomorrow. You know what he's like.'

Exactly.

I know what he's like.

Dad doesn't believe in cell phones: he thinks they give you brain cancer. Sometimes I think he doesn't want one because people would be able to call him and expect him to pick up and tell them where in the world he is.

'I don't feel like talking, Mum.'

Her face pops around the door again. 'Jasper, he's your father. He wants to see how you are.'

'I talked to him the other day!' I shout. 'And no, he doesn't.'

The parenting book she is obviously reading must tell her to encourage father-and-son relationships because usually she couldn't care less if I talked to him or not. She probably feels it's easier when he doesn't get in touch.

'You don't have to yell at me!' she says, starting to yell herself.

'I'm tired.'

'Call him and tell him that, then.' She hands the phone to

me. 'I know he is hard work but he's your father and you only get one.'

Don't I know it! I press the numbers into the phone, slowly. Mum smiles and leaves the room. As the phone rings for a sixth time and I'm about to hang up, a woman answers.

'Hello?'

'Hi, is David Woods there? This is his son.'

'Ah, hi Jasper! I will get him for you.'

'Okay thanks,' I say, monotonous. The way she says my name makes me think he has talked about me: this annoys me. I bet he tells people he has a son and what a great father he is and we both know that is absolute bullshit.

I hear muffled voices.

'Jasper!' says Dad, loudly into the phone.

'Yep.'

'How are you?'

'Fine.'

'Just okay? How's school?'

'Good.' Do you think he's getting the picture? Not in the mood to talk right now. Will only provide one-syllable answers to emphasise the point.

'That's good to hear. So . . . what are you up to these days?'

No, not getting the picture.

'Nothing. School. Where are you?' I ask, changing the subject away from my boring life.

'Eastbourne, near Wellington, stopped in to visit my friend, Sue, do you remember Sue?'

'Nope.' I don't.

'Yeah, I wanted to catch up with her, it's been a while, hasn't it, Sue?' He laughs and she says something in the background but I don't hear. Poor woman. Whoever she is. My father has had a stream of girlfriends over the years. I can't keep up.

'So, here for a bit then back to Wellington for a few days' work but then I'm heading to Auckland. Thought I'd stop by.'

'When?'

'A week or so? I could pick you up and we could go on a bit of a road trip like the old days?'

'I have school.'

'Yes and school will still be there when you get back.' He laughs again. This is all hilarious to him.

'I'm at college now, Dad. I can't disappear without getting in trouble.'

'Trouble! From who? The Gestapo?' He laughs again.

'My teachers. The principal.'

'They'll get over it. What can they do? They don't have the strap anymore, do they?'

'Not the point, Dad.' I don't want to tell him an excuse to get out of school would be great, but Nina might forget me if I go away for too long. She will find someone else to share worksheets with.

'I can be your teacher for a bit,' he says. 'I could teach you a thing or two while we are away. We can call it *home school*. It will do you good.'

My mind flashes to the kind of things my dad could *teach* me. And it's nothing helpful. How not to parent? How not to be a good husband?

'No thanks. Gotta go. I've got school in the morning.'

Dad laughs. 'Wanting to sleep . . . wanting to go to school . . . what kind of teenager are you? Are you sure you're my son?' More laughter.

'You tell me . . . Goodnight.'

'Sleep well, Jasper. And I will . . .' I hang up the phone before he finishes. Only my dad would make me feel like a disappointment for wanting to go to school. Not all of us want to float around living off forty dollars a week. I turn off my computer (I don't really feel like finishing my homework) and go into the lounge.

Mum looks up from her reading. Manly Steve is on his computer at the dinner table. Busy man. Packaging, packaging, shipping, shipping.

'Good chat?' she asks, looking over her book.

'He is coming to Auckland. He wants to take me on one of his road trips.'

'In the middle of the term!' She slams the book shut.

'I told him that,' I say, handing her back the phone.

'Where is he?'

'Wellington. Or East Cape or something like that.' I wasn't listening.

'Who with?' she asks, then looks to Manly Steve to check it's okay she cares where her ex-husband is.

'Sue or Helen or something? Night, Mum.' I turn to leave.

'And when is he here?'

'Dunno, Mum. Goodnight.'

In my room, I turn off the light and get into bed as if I will sleep. But I know I won't. Thinking about my dad eventually makes me feel like shit.

Are you sure you're even my son? Did he actually say that?

Hearing it in my head, it hurts more. Who says that?

Are you sure you're even my son?

I feel like my blood is hot from a kettle and is pumping around my body at lightning speed. He clearly doesn't want me to be his. He doesn't! Or he would be here.

The more I try to calm these thoughts, the more aware I become of a red-hot heat bubbling away. I don't know why I always feel like this when I talk to my dad. He always makes me feel like I'm a disappointment; like I am not who he wants me to be.

And as if I could drop everything and go on a road trip because he has decided it suits him. He is the last person on earth I want to be like.

He is not who I want him to be.

He is a disappointment to me.

Mum and Manly Steve turn off the lights in the house and go to bed. My thoughts echo through the dark room. Loudly in the night's silence.

I need to sleep.

I want to sleep.

But I can't sleep.

Time is so slow. The night is slow. Time ticks and still . . . I do not sleep. It's the middle of the night.

Please. Sleep.

The more I want to sleep, the more I can't sleep. I am caught up in a vicious sleep cycle where I want it so badly and can't have it. I know I have to still my mind to sleep, but these thoughts and memories keep swirling around. Sleep is like a friend I no longer see, but I miss. Sleep is a distant memory, a skill I have forgotten how to use, a state I do not know how to be in anymore.

Sleep. Where are you? How do I find you? How do I invite you into my life?

Sleep. You suck.

Am I scared to sleep? Why am I scared to sleep?

Is it Him?

I try counting sheep. I try counting turtles. I try counting bears but that one is not fun at all. I try all of the animals, even narwhals, pangolins and Northern hairy-nosed wombats and other weird animals you hardly ever hear about. I try counting backwards. I try counting forwards. I try them all, all the things you are supposed to do to get some sleep. I try counting in twos then fours then sixes then eights (but I was never good at those).

I don't want to think about my dad. I try so hard for my thoughts not to keep returning to him, to disappointing conversations and road-trip failures.

Here I am, still awake. In the dark. Having imaginary conversations with my dad. He doesn't know me. He doesn't want to. The last time we spent proper time together was years ago. He doesn't know who I am now. You can't find that out in five-minute phone conversations once a year while your lady friend laughs in the background.

I wriggle and turn over; sighing, I throw off the blankets, then pull them up over me again, then turn over again. Then sigh. But still, I do not sleep.

I try to remember how many days it's been since sleep now, but I'm too tired to remember.

Are you sure you're even my son?

I hope I'm not. I hope I'm not his son. That would be great. Then I would know why I disappoint him: because I was never his in the first place. Maybe somewhere out there is a dad I want. A dad in a nice suit, with a nice car, who high-fives me, rustles my hair and is proud of me. I try to picture myself hanging out with this dad. This proper dad. This better dad.

But I don't really want that dad.

I want my dad.

Not when it suits him. Not on the phone. Not on a road trip. I need him here. Telling me I'm going to be okay, giving a shit about me. Me. As I am now.

Obviously I am his son. I have his blue eyes. His height. His pointed nose. His ash-brown hair. I am his son. And that's where the problem is . . . My mother, always worrying I am like him, she knows I'm like him. Not in a good way.

She knows it's just a matter of time.

> WHO AM I?
> I AM HERE TO REMIND YOU OF WHO YOU ARE
> YOU DISAPPOINT EVERYONE
> YOU ARE WORTHLESS
> NO ONE LIKES YOU
> I AM HERE TO REMIND YOU OF THIS EVERY DAY
> UNTIL THE END

18.

I walk through my week with no sleep.

I yawn my way through classes and think about the weekend and not having to get out of bed on Saturday morning. I'm too tired to even think about trying to talk to Nina so I ignore her and work on my woodcut in art class. Slowly, a face is starting to take shape. You can see outlines of my nose, my eyes, my ears, fighting to come through. But I do not like what I see.

On Friday evening, Manly Steve arrives home with his daughter, with Elise.

He brings her in the door with her bags and Thai food for dinner. My heart races.

'We're here,' he announces.

Mum races to the front door.

I peer around my bedroom door and see

her. She stands in the hallway, with a small suitcase and a shy smile. She's wearing a floral dress with a denim jacket over the top and lots of jewellery. Manly Steve displays her proudly. 'This is Elise!'

'Elise, hello! Come in, come in,' says Mum. Elise jingles and jangles down the hallway. She looks nothing like Manly Steve. She has golden brown skin and a whale's tail tattoo on her forearm. I take it all in as she walks past me with her bags.

'Hello,' she says as I watch her pass.

'Hi.'

I see the tattoo again when she finally puts her bags down and nervously hugs my mother. 'Nice to meet you.'

She scans the house, taking it all in. Her father's new home, her father's girlfriend, her father's girlfriend's weird son standing in the hallway.

'You must be Jasper,' she says to me with a smile.

'Apparently so,' I mutter while pulling at my sleeve for no reason at all. What? See . . . WEIRD! I bet Manly Steve has told her about me; probably how annoying I am and how awful I am to live with.

'We have dinner!' he says loudly.

Mum and Steve go to the kitchen to get plates and open takeaway containers. Elise and I are left alone standing in the lounge, next to the glorious couches. She looks around and pulls her hair into a ponytail. Let the awkwardness begin.

'How was your trip?' I say, surprising myself by asking the first question (though it's said to the floor with my eyes closed).

'Fine, I suppose. The seat next to me was free so that was good. No awkward stranger conversations. How was your day?'

'All right,' I reply, speaking of awkward stranger conversations. And it was, I suppose, all right. I wasn't late for school and I didn't throw a ball at anyone's head. But I felt terrible. I felt like a sleepless zombie walking around. This morning I also started with a fight with Manly Steve. He wanted me to leave the house spotless before Elise got here, like I'm the bloody house cleaner too.

She doesn't seem to care how clean the house is. She seems really nice, in fact, not scary and not a version of him. I am yet to see many family resemblances, actually. She must take after her mother.

'I'm starving now, though,' she says, looking towards the kitchen.

'Yeah, me too. But I'm always hungry.' I even make a little joke, not a funny one but *good work, Jasper*.

She giggles. 'Me too! So Dad tells me you are a semi-vegetarian? I don't eat meat so I got tofu pad Thai noodles and a coconut green curry thing, for us to share.'

Erk. Tofu. I am starting to regret ever mentioning a desire to be vegetarian. Looks like I'm going hungry tonight.

'Yum!' I say over-enthusiastically. 'Thanks.'

Mum sets the containers and a stack of plates down on the table.

'Come and get some food. Are you vegetarian today, Jasper?' she asks.

'What do you mean? Of course!' I say, rolling my eyes.

Mum looks at Manly Steve and gives him a smirk. 'Well, sounds like Elise chose some delicious vegetarian dishes for you.'

I wait for Elise to serve herself and then dish up a large amount of rice and a small amount of tofu stuff. It looks really weird and tastes even weirder — like air, dry spongy air. There are spicy chunks of chilli and garlic in one of the dishes too. It's so hot, but to be polite to Elise I eat as much as I physically can and try to look like I'm enjoying it. I do have a small coughing fit while eating a large piece of chilli though, it is intense.

Mum gets me a glass of water, smiling. She seems to be enjoying watching me struggle through my dinner. So does Manly Steve. Are they messing with me a little on this? 'What do you think about the food?' Mum asks once the coughing fit has calmed.

'Really good,' I lie, wiping my mouth with a napkin (and spitting a mouthful of tofu into it at the same time).

'So Elise, tell us about your studies, what are you doing?' Mum asks, finally taking the attention off me so I can spit out more tofu rejects.

'Theatre studies and drama, I want to either get into acting or directing. I love it.'

'Oh wow, good on you. Did you do that at secondary school too? Drama?'

'Yes, my favourite subject,' Elise replies, taking a sip of her wine. Yep, Mum gave her a glass of wine! I take note of this to make sure when I'm twenty I'm allowed to drink wine at dinner as well.

'Lovely,' replies Mum. 'Good on you. I always wanted to do theatre when I was younger.'

'No, you didn't, Mum,' I scoff while chewing on another piece of rubbery fake meat.

'Actually, I did, Jasper. Not that you have ever asked,' Mum says.

'Oh, weird.'

She's right, I don't ask that much about what she was like when she was young. I figured she had always wanted to be a dental hygienist.

'What year are you in, Jasper?' Elise asks, raising her eyebrows; her bangles chime together like small bells while she gets seconds.

'Year nine.'

'Cool. What are your favourite subjects?'

'Um . . . I don't really have any.'

'He is a talented artist, aren't you, Jasper?' Mum chips in.

'Not really . . .' I say, looking down.

'I'd love to see some of your art,' Elise says with a smile. 'My mother was an artist. But Jasper, it took me ages to work out what I was going to do once I finished school. I took a year off to think about it. Something will come to you.'

She looks at her dad and smiles. He obviously didn't approve of that.

'Jasper will have lots of options. You wanted to be a doctor when you were younger, didn't you?' Mum says.

'Yeah, when I was like seven. But not now . . .' Blood. Death. Wounds. Diseases to worry I have. No thanks.

'Well, you used to,' Mum says, smiling at Manly Steve again. Obviously another little in-joke with him. Annoying. 'Eat up everyone! There's plenty of food to get through.' She dishes up more tofu on my plate. Crap. I wish I had a dog so I could feed it under the table sometimes.

I wasn't looking forward to this weekend but it's actually okay. So far Elise is easy to get along with and it's nice having her here, another person in the house. The dinner table is a lot more fun with her around and Mum likes her too, I can tell. This evening would be perfect, except Manly Steve is there and I'm eating tofu.

Once dinner is done, Mum shows Elise around the house. Thankfully, they don't go into my room: Mum just points it out as they pass by.

We get ready for bed. I collapse into bed and listen to the voices outside my door; they actually make me smile and before I know it I have drifted off. To sleep! I actually sleep, no counting sheep or wombats required.

I sleep, so it can be morning even sooner.

Saturday with Elise is kinda cool too. Hanging out with Mum and Manly Steve isn't so bad when she's around; I don't feel like a third wheel. I make everyone eggs on toast for breakfast and they all say how good I am at making a good poached egg. Elise watches intently for tips.

'You are so good at this.'

'Make a vortex in the water,' I tell her, using a spoon to swirl the water in the pot.

'You've lost me already.'

Amazing what you can learn on YouTube tutorials.

After breakfast we go into town and walk around by the harbour, stopping for lunch at a Japanese restaurant (I go for the vegetarian sushi just to commit to the plan). Being vegetarian with Elise means we kind of have something in common. At one point, she even grabs my arm and says: 'Us veggies need to stick together, Jas.'

Jas? Or would it be Jazz? I don't know, but it's the first time I've had a nickname (unless 'Weirdo' counts). Elise helps me choose the best vegetarian sushi and I don't even have to spit out the tofu bits this time.

'And wasabi! Lots of wasabi!' I serve myself a lot, thinking it was a type of avocado, but it's not. It's really spicy, so I have to leave the rest on the plate under the napkin.

As we walk around the waterfront, I see other families: mums and dads with their kids. They go past on scooters and stop to take family photos. Some of them look at us as we pass. They must think we are all a family, a normal one. A dad, mum and two kids. I've never had this before. I've never felt like I was part of a *normal* family. It's nice to pretend for a bit.

Mum and Manly Steve are still annoying me a lot, hand-holding the whole time. But now I have someone to laugh at them with. They seem to be annoying Elise too, so she looks at me and laughs — and we both know why.

When we get home, Elise says she is going to meet some old friends of hers in town. I feel disappointed that she is going out. She comes into my room to say goodnight before she goes.

'See you tomorrow,' she says at the door, looking around the room. 'Jasper, you need to get rid of one of these couches,' she says, pointing to them. 'How can you even move in here?' She comes in and flops onto the empty couch (the other one is covered in a week's worth of dirty clothes and I feel mortified).

'Long story. But I like couches.'

'I like couches too, don't get me wrong, but *one* would do! Why two?' She laughs, still looking around trying to make sense of the chaos. I try to think of a lie but end up finding myself telling her the truth.

'When your dad moved in, his giant couch went in the

lounge and I really didn't want Mum throwing these out. They belonged to my grandparents.'

'Oh, you had to make a point.' She looks me straight in the eye. What is going on? Eye contact normally makes me want to wee but with her, it feels okay.

'Maybe you could keep just one? Your grandparents will understand.'

'They're dead.'

Elise nods slowly. 'I totally get it then. When my mum died I didn't have much of her stuff, but I have this knitted jumper. It's actually quite ugly but I wear it to feel close to her. No matter how ridiculous I look in it, I will never throw it away.'

Her mother died? When did her mother die? I'm sure this is news to me. I assumed Manly Steve had just separated from his wife, not that she had died. DEAD.

Panic jolts through my body. My heart rate starts picking up speed: like a train on tracks it gets faster and faster. Before I know it, it is racing, speeding along the tracks, dragging me behind.

Her mother died.

Died.

Dead.

Gone.

I don't handle news like this well. I am not good with death. Death follows me. I told you this. It follows me around and I don't know what to do when I see it. I don't know how to keep moving when I am reminded of its presence.

I usually hide.

I turn away and start putting clothes on hangers. I don't know what to say so like a fool, I say nothing.

Elise watches me. She sees the panic. 'Your goldfish is lying on the side. Is it supposed to do that?' She stands and puts her face close to the glass.

'No, he's sick.' More death. *Why won't you go away? Why are you always here, reminding me? Why can't you leave me alone?*

'That's awful.' She gives a sad face. She does love animals, big and small.

My head is still spinning with thoughts.

I want to know details and not know, all at the same time.

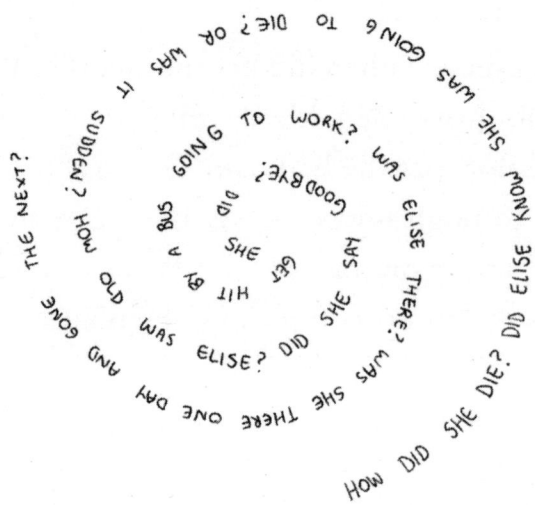

Thoughts spin around my head, down through my veins. Now the screeching sound I get sometimes starts, the loud, high-pitched ringing in my ears. It starts on one side and then the other. I feel my head tighten as it grows.

SCCCRRRRREEEECCCCCCCCHHHHHHH

All the while, Elise stands by the fish tank looking at Han Solo.

'Can you take him to the vet?' she asks, oblivious to what is going on inside my head. To the spirals and the screeches.

'They don't deal with goldfish, I don't think.' I fold a hoodie and put it away in a drawer. I'm keeping moving to try to calm the thoughts.

'That is crazy. They are still a life, they still have feelings, they must feel pain. Oh, sorry little fish.' Han Solo seems to perk up slightly just at being acknowledged. 'Anyway, I better go but your mum told me to tell you dinner is nearly ready.' She stands up and her bracelets jingle jangle. 'Night!'

Then she leaves the room.

Just like that.

With no mother.

17.

I ask Manly Steve to help me put the big couch on the street.

I write FREE on a piece of paper and tape it on the front. It takes half an hour and more awkward couch manoeuvring to get it out of my room, but we do it. Like Elise said, I still have one — plus the one in the garage. I tried to save them all but opening your bedroom door is important.

Maybe the person who takes it really needs a couch. Maybe they won't mind when their butt sticks to it? Manly Steve helps me get my desk from the garage too, and as we walk back inside he says, 'You tried to make it work.' I don't know what to say. I thought he would be smug.

He and Mum don't talk about it at dinner and it's not as fun without Elise here. We are all quiet. We have nachos which I usually like, but not tonight, probably because Mum used kidney beans and they look like kidneys from a pet rabbit.

After dinner, I put my dishes in the dishwasher and go to my room. I continue putting my clothes back in the drawers. I make the bed (first time in a long time). I might even change the sheets tomorrow. I don't even want to think about how long it's been since those were changed. It looks good. My room looks better. Sorry, Nana. Sorry, Poppa.

Mum comes into my room and asks me if I want to watch a movie, but I say no.

'What about *Pulp Fiction*? Your favourite?'

'No,' I say and she looks rejected. Where is that nice boy who was walking around the waterfront today?

I lie in bed and wonder what time Elise will come home. Where is she? At 10.50 p.m. I hear Manly Steve get a text and leave the house to pick her up. I go and find Mum. She is reading a book in bed.

'You're still up?' she asks.

'What happened to Elise's mum?' I sit at the edge of her bed. Manly Steve's things are everywhere. I can smell him in the room.

'Oh.' She puts the book down on the bed. 'It was really sad, Jasper, she passed away. When Elise was about twelve.'

'Why didn't you tell me?' I ask.

Mum looks down at her bed, stroking a crease from the duvet cover. She puts the bookmark into the book. 'I don't know. Are you okay, Jasper?'

'Sad. For Elise.'

I want to cry, but I'm not sure why. I didn't know this woman. I hardly know Elise. Sometimes horrible stuff happens to people and it sucks, but why am I sad? I swallow deeply to try to swallow away the thoughts.

No tears come. Sometimes I wish they would. But they never do.

'Elise is lovely, isn't she? I had no idea she was so lovely. Sounds silly.' Mum laughs.

'I know . . .' I had no idea she was so lovely either.

'Makes you feel grateful too, doesn't it? For who you have in your life.'

'Yep.' And it did. I hug my mum. It's our first hug in a long, long time.

She smiles at me. 'Night, Jasper. You get some sleep, okay?'

'Night.' I go back to my bedroom, to my bed. I try to cry as I go to sleep. But I can't.

I stare at the ceiling listening to the clock ticking. I can hear distant music and people talking. A party down the road. I worry about the couch being outside as if it's Nana and Poppa out there too, trying to eat dinner in the cold, with no television.

Soon I hear Manly Steve's car pull into the driveway and then the sounds of him and Elise coming inside and going to bed — their electric toothbrushes, the lights being turned off, the *goodnights, sleep wells*.

The last of the light that was peeping through under my door disappears.

Darkness. It is pitch black at first but my eyes start to adjust and the shapes of the furniture appear. My couch. The curtains. And then I see it . . .

I see the dark shape emerging from behind Nana and Poppa's couch, the one still in the room. The thing I didn't want to see.

Not tonight. Not with Elise here. But it's there.

The unmistakable shape of a bear.

I wondered when I would see him next. Of course it is tonight, when we have a guest in the spare room next door. I close my eyes and tell myself there is nothing there, nothing to be afraid of. *'Close your eyes and before you know it, it will be morning.'*

But my heart is racing. Chest pounding. I hear His claws against the floorboards. He starts to pace. He begins to get angry, too. Just as I do. Angry at this world.

Elise. Her mother. Han Solo. My dad. Nana and Poppa, outside in the cold on the couch. It comes over me like a flood. A flood of sadness and anger. Why do mothers of children have to die? Why do animals have to die? Why do grandparents have to die?

Why? Why? Why? Why is this world the way it is?

I lie in my bed, quietly. Still. Lifeless.

But He knows I am here. He plays with me. I see his shadow before I hear Him.

It flicks across the room, flickers of moonlight, and shadows against the wall. I see Him, in the corner of the room. He is using His teeth to pull my books off the shelf. One at a time, He rips at the pages and tears the books apart, in the room that had been tidied. He makes his mark.

Once He's done that He curls himself into the corner, ready to launch. I throw my pillow at Him but He grabs it with His teeth and rips it into small pieces, thrashing His neck as He does, grunting, growling, snarling.

He wants that pillow to be me. He wants to rip me into small pieces and leave me strewn across the floor, limp and pathetic, like He knows I am. I close my eyes and listen, waiting for Him to get bored of the pillow and come and find me. When He finishes with the pillow, the shadow slowly turns in my direction.

I am next.

Who am I?

No, who are you?

Who are you, really?

I wake. So I must have slept. There is chaos and destruction everywhere and my heart sinks. My room is destroyed, after all that tidying. It was finally feeling like a room again. There are bits of pillowcase and the inside of pillow stuffing all over the floor, bits of fluff everywhere. A pillow ripped to shreds. Destroyed. But my body is intact.

I kick the chaos under the bed and pick up the books, hiding them in my wardrobe. Some of them are completely destroyed. My mother will be furious.

I was happy yesterday, things actually felt good. It was nice having Elise here and I was even kind of enjoying Manly

Steve's company. Shock horror. I was happy. I don't understand why He came.

I hear signs of life from outside my room. The radio is on. Elise is up. Mum calls out to me. 'Jasper, you awake?'

I rush to the door so she doesn't come inside. I stick my head out the door. 'What?'

'Steven has made waffles, time to get up.'

I go to the kitchen. Everyone else is up. Elise hands me a plate. 'Morning!'

'Hi,' I reply, wiping sleep from my eye.

The waffles are nice but I don't taste them. All I can think of is last night, of Elise's mum and the fact she is going home today. And did she hear anything last night?

'You okay, Jasper?' Elise asks as she sees me staring at my plate.

'Yep,' I say, trying.

She gives me a smile but continues to watch me.

'Everything okay, Jasper?' Mum asks.

What can they see? How do they know?

After breakfast, I go and hide in my room again. I take a rubbish bag into the room and put the ripped books inside, ready for the bin. I throw any clothes under the bed and lucky I do, because Elise knocks gently and comes inside.

'I'm heading to the airport soon.'

It is time to say goodbye. I don't want her to go.

She looks around the room. 'You took out one of the couches, it looks better.'

'Yeah. You were right.'

I look out the window onto the street. The couch is gone. I didn't see or hear it go. It has vanished. Where are Nana and Poppa now?

'Were you all right last night?' Elise asks.

Uh oh.

'Yeah. Why?'

'I heard you crashing around.' She looks around, probably seeing the black rubbish bag in the corner. I pick it up and tie a knot on the top, keeping the destruction hidden.

'Oh yeah. Moving stuff. Tidying.'

'It's heaps better. Anyway, bye!' She crosses the room and hugs me. I stand there and she does all the work, I'm not sure how to hug people properly. But I take a deep breath and breathe in her rose-garden smells. Her earrings tinkle close to my ear, like a musical instrument.

'It was so cool to meet you,' she says and all I can think to reply is, 'Yeah.'

'See you next time, Jasper.'

'Bye.' And that's it. I say nothing more. Nothing more about how good it was to have her here and that I want to know her better, that I'm already looking forward to the next time. Nothing about how I'm sorry that her mother died and that I'm glad Manly Steve has a daughter, that for the first time ever, I hope Mum and Manly Steve stay together.

Because that means she might come back.

20.

Mum washes the bedsheets from the spare room and we both move around each other in silence. Elise is gone and we are both a little sad. I spend the afternoon on my computer watching YouTube. Mum keeps trying to get me to go for a walk with her and Manly Steve but I don't want to. She gets angry at me for being lazy.

'We walked for hours yesterday, Mum. Leave me alone.'

Finally, she and Steve go out and leave me at home. I go to the kitchen in search of chocolate and strike gold. A brand-new unopened block. I demolish half and start thinking about what else I can eat. I find three gingernut biscuits, half a packet of chips and I finish with an apple — to balance it all out.

I go to my computer and google *most popular names in the world*. Apparently, it's Wang, a Chinese name that means

King. I don't think I can pull off Jasper Wang. Around one hundred million people in the world currently have that last name. Holy crap, one hundred million! There are so many people in the world. I probably shouldn't worry too much about having a unique name, that might be impossible.

I google *Jasper Robinson-Woods* and nothing comes up.

So I have a unique name? One hundred million people in the world with the last name Wang and one called Jasper Robinson-Woods. But should I go with a completely unique last name? One of a kind. Could I name myself completely through random chance?

I close my eyes and type in a bunch of letters on the keyboard. When I open my eyes I have written:

Ghdouchedz.

Jasper Jonathan Ghdouchedz.

It kind of sounds like douche-head. I close the computer then go and feed Han Solo. He ignores me completely. I get a shiver of cold. Maybe it's being near Han Solo, his sickness.

I really hate watching him die. The water is clean, but he is still sick.

I remember my nana. Looking so thin, wondering whether she will last another year, another month. I remember her smile, the one person in my life who I knew was proud of me. The 'bee's knees' she would say. 'Jasper, you are the bee's knees.'

Mum and Manly Steve come home from their walk. 'You made dinner, Jasper?' Mum says as she passes my door.

'What? No?' I follow her into the kitchen.

'Don't know why I bothered asking that. Why don't *you*

cook us something, something vegetarian? You better learn to cook soon.'

'Because you'll be kicking me out soon?'

'No, I wouldn't do that . . .' She trails off, looking in the pantry. 'Maybe I will make a vegetarian lasagne tonight.'

A lasagne? She doesn't make lasagnes. What's going on? All of a sudden she's cooking fancy things she's never done before. I suppose that's one benefit of having Manly Steve here: she is making an effort with dinner, trying to impress him. She acts like she's always done this but the truth is, she never used to bother. She used to just heat up nuggets and fish fingers for dinner.

Monday morning and I am late to school, but only by a few minutes. I somehow get away with it because my form teacher is running late. Art is first up, and Nina has a new haircut. I notice these things. She can't tie it up anymore so she constantly blows her fringe out of her face while she is working. She makes a mistake with her woodcut and looks disappointed. I catch her eye as she sighs.

'Whoops. Maria was right. Once you make a mistake it's very hard to fix it.'

I laugh but try to make it sympathetic. But it's really hard to laugh sympathetically and I spend the rest of class wishing I hadn't laughed but had instead gone over and made a suggestion of how she could fix it.

I'm angry at myself. *Don't laugh at that.*

Social studies is next; I have a test on capital cities and I only get 4/15 correct. I forgot to study. Mum gave me a ten-dollar note this morning for my lunch and I can't find it in my pocket, or my bag, so I go hungry. I probably lost it on my way to school so some other kid is having a tuck-shop lunch on me.

When I get home I go up the tree, to sulk, even though my stomach is rumbling and eating its own stomach acid. The tree doesn't help. It never really has, I don't know why it's taken me so long to work this out. Sometimes I hate this stupid tree. It doesn't work. It's supposed to make me feel better but today it's annoying me; in fact, it's making me angry. I wish it was a money tree. Then it would be useful.

'Stupid dumb tree,' I say and punch the trunk as hard as I can, but that just hurts me. My knuckles glow red and start to bleed. 'I hate you.'

I am about to jump down when I hear Manly Steve's car pulling in.

Stealth ninja. Slow breaths. Quiet.

I watch him as he gets out of his car, beeping the alarm as he walks to the door. He doesn't even look my way. He heads inside and I give him a few minutes before jumping down and grabbing my bag from behind the rose bush. I won't be leaving it on the steps again. I've learned my lesson there.

I go straight to my room. I still don't know what to talk to Manly Steve about when it's just the two of us at home, it's still very uncomfortable. In my own house. When I hear him go into the bathroom, I rush to the kitchen and grab snacks to take back to my room.

'No eating in your bedroom, Jasper,' he says as he passes my door. *Well, hello to you too.*

I hear a knock at the front door. It's probably a courier for our resident businessman extraordinaire but when I answer, it's not a courier ... It's my father.

'Jasper!' he says, arms open.

'You're here?' I say, shocked.

He gives me a hug and pushes past. 'I'm busting for a piss.' Classy.

'Does Mum know you're coming today?' I follow behind.

'I like to surprise you two.' He turns and smiles before shutting the bathroom door.

Manly Steve stands up from the couch and walks towards me. 'Visitor?'

'It's my father, actually.'

'Your father?' He looks around as if trying to find the closest exit.

The toilet flushes and Dad comes out. 'Oh that's better!' He and Manly Steve are face to face. I introduce them thinking ... *Why? Why me? Why do I have to do the introductions?*

'David. Steven. Steven. David.'

'Steven. Hello. We did meet briefly at the funeral.' Dad wipes his wet hands on his jeans.

I'd forgotten they'd met at Nana's funeral. It was a strange day and I have blanked it out. My dad opens his arms and is about to hug Manly Steve but before he does Steve juts his manly hand out to shake instead. I don't think Manly Steve does man-hugs. Not his style.

'Yes... Yes...' Dad obeys. 'Sorry about the wet hands. But at least you know I washed them. It's not urine, eh Jasper?'

Dad flicks water at me and Manly Steve gives a concerned attempt at laughter.

'Gross,' I say.

'Where's your mum?' Dad asks, looking around.

'Working,' I reply. She has a job. I wonder if my father has heard of those before. Possibly not.

'Right. Of course. What brings you over, Steve? Here to hang out with Jasper?' Dad rolls his shoulders. He always needs to stretch after driving long distances. I hear his muscles and bones crunching.

'I live here now,' Manly Steve says, awkwardly.

'You moved in! Jasper did tell me...' Dad looks at me. 'Look how tall you've got!' I nod. 'Wow, you're nearly up to me. What are you eating?'

'Yeah. It's been about three inches since I've seen you,' I say. I want it to punish him, but he just moves on. He says that every time I see him. Salt in the wound. It reminds me how long he has been away. 'I'll text Mum,' I say. Anything to leave the room.

Dad has turned up and yr BF is home 2 help!

She replies: *What? Sorry. Patients for another hour good luck!*

No!!! This is not fair. Back to the lounge for more awkward chat.

'What brings you to town?' Manly Steve is looking uncomfortable. They are both still standing.

Dad stretches again. 'I wanted to take young Jasper here away for a bit of a road trip, but he tells me it's school and he can't bear to part with his precious schoolwork for a few days.'

'Sorry for wanting to pass this year,' I say, going to sit on the couch. They both follow.

'Jasper, you will be up for that, won't you?' Steve chirps up at the thought of time without me.

'You can have ONE day off, can't you?' Dad says, with raised eyebrows. Mum is not going to like this.

After more awkward chats and me making terrible cups of weak tea, Mum finally comes home.

'Hello everyone,' she says, dropping her bag on the counter and shooting me an apologetic look. 'Nice to see you, David, thanks for the heads up.'

'I mentioned it to Jasper . . .'

'Why are you here?' she asks, looking down at my bag on the floor. Dad had made me go and pack one.

'Road trip. The boy is excited, aren't you, buddy?' Dad replies, winking.

'Not exactly,' the 'boy' replies.

Mum doesn't look impressed. 'Road trip? At seven o'clock on a school night?'

'Yeah and I'm hungry,' I add.

'I'll tell you what,' says Dad. 'How about I go get us all some takeaways?'

'No, I'll go and grab something,' jumps in Steve, snatching up his keys — keen to get out of the house.

'Well, why don't we both go?' says Dad, following him out. 'Will do us good to get to know each other.' He pats Manly Steve on the back.

No reply from Manly Steve. Not sure he wants to get to know my father.

As the door clicks closed, Mum whispers: 'Oh dear . . .'

'I never imagined I'd have to introduce my father to my mother's live-in boyfriend; thought you might get that job.'

'They've met before.'

'Well, yeah . . . but still.'

'He can't expect you to drop everything. You have your own life now.' Mum walks into the kitchen and puts the mugs into the dishwasher.

Do I have my own life?

'I don't want to go with him anyway,' I say, looking in the fridge.

'Good,' she says, relieved. 'Don't.'

But in my heart I know I'm probably going to go. I can't say no to my dad. I hardly ever see him and maybe it will be different this time.

Mum starts counting plates and setting the table. 'Well, he can see you here in Auckland. Grab the cutlery, love. He can go and stay with your Aunty Celia, he probably hasn't seen her in ages either. He's not staying here tonight.'

Dad has a sister Celia who works at the hospital, as a doctor. She hasn't got kids and I rarely see her either. He and Manly Steve are gone so long I can tell it starts to worry Mum. She keeps looking out the window and saying, 'That will be them' to every car that goes past. I'm so hungry I even contemplate eating the tragic salad she makes. When they do get back, they are laughing and joking and carrying on like best friends. I don't know what's worse, the idea of them being arch rivals, or best friends. Both are equally terrifying.

'A busy night at the Chinese takeaways. Everyone's there tonight.' Manly Steve says, putting three containers on the table. I bet he didn't get anything vegetarian for me.

'We are on trend,' says Dad and they both laugh.

I open the containers. Manly Steve did get me a vegetarian fried rice so I will give him points for that. But my own father completely ignores me most of the night. He's forgotten I'm even here. He loudly talks the whole way through dinner like he is the guest of honour. Mum tells him about me being asked to enter my art in the exhibition. All he says is: 'Great, great,' looking at the bookshelf and taking a book. 'Might borrow this one Michelle, if that's all good?'

Mum manages to interrupt his stream of conversation to suggest he stays with Celia tonight and Dad thinks it's a great idea. It's almost like he forgot he had a sister as well.

'Oh yes, Celia. She does live in Auckland, doesn't she?'

After dinner, he phones her and she obviously gives him a warm reception because the new plan is that Dad will stay a night there and we leave first thing. He is adamant about the road-trip idea, despite Mum's half-assed effort to change his mind and I find myself agreeing to it.

'One night only though,' says Mum.

'Fine,' Dad agrees.

At 10.45 p.m. we kick Dad out. He's having such fun with his new best manly friend that he would have stayed over if we had let him, with no idea how weird that would be for everyone else involved. I go to my bedroom and am relieved to hear Mum closing the door behind him. She comes in and sits on the edge of my bed. She sighs, exhausted. I know the feeling.

'Good to see your dad?'

'Kind of.'

'Nice he wants to see you, as he should. It's been ages.' She looks at me, trying to read my face.

'Yep.'

I sense she wants to say something else. But she just looks at me. 'You okay?' she asks, then tries to scratch something off my duvet. I think it's old pizza.

'Yep.'

Why bother? We are both tired.

She pats my leg. 'See you in the morning.'

And I can't remember much else.

21.

Until I wake.

My clock says 4.03 a.m. and I can't get back to sleep.

Why are thoughts so much louder in the middle of the night?

I don't want to go with my dad. He was here for hours last night and didn't ask me anything. He is so self-centred; it feels like he doesn't even want to know anything about me. He didn't ask about my art, didn't ask about school. I don't even know why I am surprised, it's never any different. I know not to expect anything more from him, so why do I feel offended? Disappointed?

And now I'm losing sleep over him. He's not even worth it. 4.12 a.m. and counting.

I don't want to think about him anymore. But now I'm thinking about one of the road trips years ago when we went camping and my anger is building.

'So Jasper, what are you good at?' some boys in the tent next to ours asked.

'I came first in the hundred-metre sprints,' I said, proudly. I had. Running was the one thing I was good at in primary school. No balls involved. I was a fast runner and I loved it, the feeling of rushing past things, of running past people, of overtaking. And I did win the hundred metres.

The boys didn't believe me. 'You're lying, we can tell. You're not a fast runner.'

'I'm not lying.' I even sprinted across the campsite to show them. They said they still didn't believe me. They made me follow them over to my dad.

'Jasper says he won the hundred-metre sprints. Is that true?'

Dad laughed. 'Well, that doesn't sound right. I don't think so.'

It hit like a hammer to the heart.

DOFF.

'I did. I did actually win, you weren't there!' I said, mortified. Mortified that I couldn't prove it. Mortified I looked like a liar. But worse than all of that, I was mortified that my own father didn't know, or did he not care? Mortified that he hadn't been there in the first place, like the other dads at the finish line.

'Jasper, lying is not an attractive trait, boy,' he'd said, shooing me off.

And that was it. Everyone moved on, thinking I'd lied.

He didn't know; he didn't know me.

He still doesn't.

So much for leaving first thing. At 8 a.m. Dad calls and says, 'Perhaps leaving tomorrow is a better idea,' and that I should go to school after all. Instead, he and Celia are spending the day together as it is her day off. In other words, he has had a better offer. So I am off to school and probably won't even go away. Dad will keep getting better offers that don't involve me.

Why did I have a sleepless night for nothing? Another let-down. Surprise, surprise. Am I relieved? Or disappointed? I don't know. Either way, I feel like shit. But I do make it to school on time for a change. I even arrive early enough to choose a good seat in art class. As I sit down, Maria comes straight over to me with a beaming smile and takes me aside.

'Guess what?'

'What?' I say, genuinely confused. I have a detention? I've been expelled?

'You got in.'

'Got in what?' I say. Trouble? Jail? The club for losers?

'Your piece was chosen for the exhibition, well done! I knew they'd love it.' She smiles and I can't help but smile back. I can't believe it. I was preparing myself for disappointment.

After the bell rings, Maria stands at the front of the class and tells the whole class.

'Exciting news, everyone. I want to share with you that Jasper's had a piece chosen for the secondary school art exhibition next month.'

I look down at my hands but can't help smiling.

'It's an incredible piece as well, an amazing accomplishment. So a round of applause for Jasper!'

Everyone claps and stares. I feel my cheeks burning hot. When the clapping dies down, I look up and Nina is looking over to me, smiling. Then it dawns on me. Everyone who sees it will know. They will know about the bear. Why did I not think this through?

The rest of the day is a bit of a blur. As I'm walking home I text Mum.

My art got chosen for Xhibition

I feel an intense rush of nerves. Will mine be the crappiest there? Maybe everyone will laugh at it and ask why I drew a bear. Everyone will know how messed up I am. Why the hell does Jasper Robinson-Woods *'see'* a bear? Why on earth would he draw that? What the hell is wrong with him?

Mum brings home takeaways to celebrate: she obviously got the message. Takeaways twice in a row. Score. It's Indian food and she gets me a spicy chickpea curry and I can't eat it. Chickpeas are like little eyeballs. Guinea pig eyeballs. Instead, I eat two naan breads but use them to soak up the delicious creamy sauce. Manly Steve doesn't say anything about the exhibition, instead he quickly eats his food and complains that it's too spicy. Mum looks disappointed.

'I like it this way, Mum,' I say even though it is slightly spicy for me too.

'I'm glad someone's happy,' she replies and this seems to annoy Manly Steve more.

Mum comes into my bedroom while I'm getting ready for bed. 'I can't wait to see your art, Jasper. What is it?'

'It's not that great, Mum. It's kinda weird.'

'I'm excited. It must be good to have been chosen, Jasper. Goodnight.' She leaves the room.

'Excited'. She is going to be 'disappointed' soon.

When I turn out the lights, the nerves flood back. Will I be going away tomorrow with Dad? He hasn't even rung today so I have no idea. And I wish they'd never chosen my dumb art. Now everyone will see how bad it is. As I try to drift off, all I can see is the bear . . . framed. He is laughing at me.

22.

Dad does arrive in the morning.

He looks like he's just woken up, but he is here. The road trip is actually happening. He didn't get a better offer today.

'All right. Let's go, boyo,' he says as I open the door. 'Grab your bags. We don't want to hit bad traffic on the way north.'

'The traffic is bound to be bad. This is Auckland.'

I tell him I've got to get my phone charger. Instead, I go back inside and hug my mother. 'Love you,' she says, sitting up and reading in bed. Manly Steve is on his phone and says a quick, 'Bye.'

'Why do you need a bloody phone?' Dad says as I close the front door. 'You're only twelve.'

'I'm nearly fourteen, Dad.'

As I walk down the front steps, I spot the yellow two-door hatchback in the driveway.

'Jump in!' says Dad, tapping the rooftop.

'Whose is this?' I ask as I hop in, throwing my bag into the back seat.

'It belongs to my friend Trish; she's lent it to me for the week.' He walks around the back of the car, checking the car boot is closed.

'It's flash,' I say. It's not.

'It will get us from A to B. That's the main thing.'

'And where is B?'

He doesn't answer, just jumps in and starts the car.

Road trip Dad versus Jasper, destination unknown.

'I'm dying for a coffee. Want one?' Dad asks as the journey begins.

'I don't drink coffee.' One minute I'm twelve. Next minute I'm drinking coffee.

'Not a great habit to start at your age, but you're going to love it! I suppose I can wait until we get there then.'

'Where are we going?' I ask, again.

'Up north an hour or so. I have a friend Lizzie who lives by the sea. We could stay with her or go further if we want. You know I don't like being tied down by plans.'

'Yeah, I remember that from our other successful road trips.'

I watch him out of the side of my eye. He is looking older. He has grey hairs framing his face now and new lines across his forehead. Adults always go on about how you're growing up, getting taller, but all of a sudden I'm noticing how my parents are changing too. I look around the car. I open the glove box. There is a pair of sunglasses in a case, a New Zealand map and a car manual for a Honda Civic 2009. The car is tidy and smells like perfume.

'Nosy,' says Dad.

I wonder what she is like, this woman, and why she is happy to lend my dad her car. Is she in love with him? Poor woman.

'Who is Trish?' I ask, as Dad turns onto the main road and drives towards the motorway. There is a queue on the on-ramp so we join the line of traffic.

'Auckland traffic. Shocking! Trish is a friend. She lives in Wellington.'

'Just a friend?' I ask, trying on the sunglasses.

'Well, you know, it's complicated.'

'Don't want to know . . .'

We crawl along the on-ramp and slowly begin to gain speed.

'You can ask whatever you want, Jasper. I am an open book. Do you have a girlfriend?'

'Ha, ha,' I laugh at the thought. 'Nope. Didn't you think I was twelve?'

'I'm sure it won't be long, handsome boy like you. Or a boyfriend, if that's your thing.'

Okay. Not sure what to say to that.

'Your mother and Steve seem happy, though.' Dad looks over to me briefly, then adjusts the rear-view mirror.

'Yeah,' I sigh. Happy?

'How do you feel about him living there?'

'Whatever.'

'It's nice for her,' he says, tapping the steering wheel.

We reach the harbour bridge and I look down over the glistening sea. It's a nice day and for a brief moment I'm actually happy to be driving away from Auckland. Maybe this time I will have a good time with my dad. Maybe we will actually talk. And no awkward conversations with Manly Steve for a bit.

'He doesn't like me,' I say.

'Who? Steven? Do you do much with him?'

'We hung out a bit when his daughter was here from Wellington.'

'I suppose you're busy with your mates anyway. Don't want to hang out with your stepdad.'

'He's not my stepdad.' I look out over the sea. A ferry disappears below me, under the harbour bridge, but a line of little waves show where it's been.

Dad fiddles around with the car stereo and puts a CD in. The car wobbles in its lane and my heart skips a beat. *Concentrate, Dad!* The music kicks into action.

'What music are you into?' Dad asks as an unfamiliar male voice starts to sing. 'This guy is amazing. Hugo Historic. Canadian guy. Heard of him?'

'I don't really listen to music.'

'You don't listen to music?' he says, too loudly. 'You are no son of mine, Jasper!'

It hits like a punch in the face. 'What?'

'It's a saying. You are no son of mine? Like . . . we're so

different. I love music.'

'Why do you always say that stuff?' I kick my foot into the floor of the car.

He laughs, but I'm not finding it funny. 'It's a saying.'

'Am I your son? Is there a chance I'm not?' I look at him. He's still smiling.

'It's a joke, you are definitely my son! Sorry to say!' He laughs.

'Sorry for who?' I say, getting angrier.

'For you! That I'm your father.'

Is this the apology I've been waiting for?

I scoff. 'Do I disappoint you?' I surprise myself. I didn't think I'd have this conversation ten minutes into our quality-time road trip. 'Do you wish I was different?'

'You're overreacting,' he replies, still laughing at me. But it's not funny.

'Stop the car.' It's really not funny.

'Really? Chill out, bud.'

'No. Stop the car. Stop the car!' I yell, unbuckling my seatbelt. I don't want to go anywhere with this man.

'Jasper, I'm sorry I said that.'

'STOP THE CAR DAD, I'M SERIOUS!' I yell at him.

He pulls over onto the side of the motorway and a car toots loudly as it passes.

'We are on the motorway, Jasper! Calm down!' He raises his voice now too and puts the driver-side lock on and as I try the door, it doesn't work.

'Let me out!'

'Okay, calm down.' This time he says it quietly. But then: 'What is wrong with you?'

'Don't say that! That is literally the worst thing you can say to me right now!' I feel like I'm a pot of water on the element and I'm heating up all of a sudden. My blood begins to bubble and boil over the sides of the pot.

'Take a deep breath and calm down.' He puts his hand on mine and I pull away.

I do as I am told and take a few breaths. They breathe more anger through my veins. This road trip was a bad idea. Me spending time with my father: a bad idea.

'You're different to me but I'm in no way disappointed.' He readjusts his posture in his seat. 'I haven't seen you in a while and I'm learning about you, that's all.'

'Yeah, you don't know me. That's the problem,' I say quietly.

The song finishes and there is a moment of silence before another track starts. Dad takes a deep breath too.

'I get it, Jasper. Can I keep on driving, or do you want me to take you home?'

I screw up my face. I don't want to go home. I don't want to go up north. I don't want to have this conversation. I don't want to do anything. Right now, in this moment, I don't want to be here. I don't want to be anywhere.

'Just drive . . .'

Dad sits for a while and when a break in traffic appears, he indicates and moves back into the stream of cars. That was a stupid thing for me to do. What would I have done if he had let me out, I have no idea — hitchhiked from one end of the

city to the other? I don't think so.

'That's why we are doing this, Jasper. I want to know you,' he says. I lie back and put my head against the window and close my eyes. Does he? Does he really?

I listen to the sounds of him breathing and tapping the steering wheel.

And there in the car, I don't expect to sleep, but I do.

Dad wakes me when we are coming into a small beachside town. 'We're stopping soon.' He turns down the radio.

'How long did I sleep?' I say, rubbing my eyes, reminding myself of where I am.

'A while. Tired, huh?'

I can see the ocean peeping through baches as we pass, the sun shimmering on the sea.

'Is everything okay, Jasper?' Dad asks.

'Yeah.'

'Honestly?'

In my head I scream *NO, no no no no no no no no, everything is not okay!*

But I don't have words for it.. My fish is dying, I have no friends, I don't know if there is a place for me in my home anymore, I like a girl, but I can't talk to her and, most importantly, a giant killer bear follows me around. Ultimately, there is a good chance I might be on the verge of insanity. And now my usually absent father is asking if I'm okay, but I don't want to talk to him about it either, because he's like a stranger to me. 'Everything is fine,' I say.

'Look for letterbox one hundred and eighteen. There's one hundred and ten.'

One hundred and twelve. One hundred and fourteen. One hundred and sixteen.

'There . . .' I say, spotting a colourful letterbox.

Dad indicates right and pulls into a bungalow painted green. A woman is bending over; a large woven sun hat hides her face but I see green gardening gloves pulling at weeds. Dad toots the horn and she looks up, putting a hand up to shade her face from the sun.

'Hello! You made it!' she says, standing up.

'I did! *We did*,' he corrects himself.

The woman walks towards the car, taking off the large hat, as Dad pulls in behind a red station wagon.

'Okay to park here?'

'Yes, absolutely.'

Dad turns the car off and hops out. He gives her a long hug (too long for me). I don't know where to look. As he pulls away, he remembers me.

'Oh, and this is my son, Jasper. Get out of the car mate, stretch your legs.'

I ruffle my hands through my hair and hop out of the car,

making my way around to the other side.

'Hi.'

Lizzie smiles. 'Hi, Jasper — welcome.' She's wearing an oversized striped shirt and has grey curly hair, kind eyes.

'Thanks.'

'Look how tall you are!' she says, looking up.

'Isn't he? He'll take over me soon.' I am fast approaching his height.

'Come on in, I'll put the kettle on,' she says, pulling her gloves off.

Lizzie gives us a quick tour of the house, it's nice. She obviously lives alone. There are rows of seashells on the windowsills and artwork with large hibiscus flowers covering the walls.

'So this is my little house.'

'It's gorgeous!' says Dad. 'It's very you.'

We stay at Lizzie's for lunch. She makes a bacon and egg pie, which I eat seven pieces of, with apple crumble for dessert. When Lizzie is in the bathroom  Dad asks me if we should stay here the night and I agree, partly because Lizzie's cooking is really good and she likes me eating lots. She didn't say: 'You've had enough, Jasper.' And she doesn't know about the vegetarian thing so I can eat what I want. I try to forget about the bacon carcinogens. Dad ate it too, so maybe he's not vegetarian anymore either.

When Dad laughs at how much I eat, Lizzie says: 'Growing boys... Mine were the same.' Apparently she has two grown-up sons and one granddaughter. I don't know where my dad is sleeping tonight (I don't want to know) but she says I can sleep in her spare room, which used to be one of her son's. There are lots of photos on the wall and a few sports trophies. Looks like this son's name was Arthur and he was really into sports and surfing.

I feel better after lunch.

I text my mother.

Still alive

She replies immediately.

Thanks for letting me know. I was worried.

We go for a walk along the beach, and I sit in the warm sand while Dad and Lizzie have a swim. Dad tells me twelve times how nice it is and how I should go in too, but I resist. The warmth of the sun feels good though and I draw pictures in the sand.

Maybe this is going to be okay?

Lizzie is making roast chicken and vegetables for dinner, with gravy. She asks me to peel potatoes and I watch as she and Dad cut up the vegetables and reminisce about when they knew each other twenty years ago. I watch as Lizzie puts fresh herbs inside the chicken and seasons it. She is a really good cook and looks so at ease in the kitchen, not like Mum, who always drops things and swears lots.

And the roast dinner is delicious and there's heaps of this really good gravy to pour all over it. I tell myself it's fine that

I'm not vegetarian this weekend; it would be really offensive to Lizzie to not eat her food. I'm just being generous.

We watch the start of a film called *The Wolf of Wall Street* and it's right up there as one of the most awkward experiences of my life. As soon as there is a naked body, I quickly tell them I am tired and need to go to bed.

'Sleep well, mate,' Dad says. Lizzie smiles and waves.

'Night.'

I lie awake for a bit listening to the voices in the lounge but eventually sleep. And I sleep until 11 a.m.

I can't believe it.

Lizzie makes me corn fritters for breakfast with sour cream and relish and it's so good. She tells me she used to own her own café and it all makes sense.

Dad asks if we can stay another night and I agree, because I wonder what she will cook for dinner.

'You have to tell Mum,' I say to him.

'Yes, I can do that.' Dad helps Lizzie in the garden for the afternoon and I lie in a hammock and listen to them talking about parsnips and other random vegetables.

We walk along the beach again and they have another swim. This time I take my sneakers off and stand in the shallows. The cold water feels good, until I stub my toe on a giant rock.

'Go on, Jasper. Just come in!' Lizzie shouts to me.

'I didn't bring my togs.'

'Who cares?' she says.

I care.

23.

Back at the house, Dad tells me that he and Lizzie are going out for dinner. Without me.

Actually, Lizzie says I'm welcome to come — but I don't want to eat with strangers. I sense Dad doesn't want me to go either. Technically I'm not supposed to be home alone, but I'm close to fourteen plus Dad doesn't seem to have any interest in the law.

Lizzie dresses up and they come to say goodnight. Dad is still wearing what he has worn all day. He tells me to behave myself.

'Help yourself to whatever's in the fridge,' says Lizzie.

I make eggs on toast and eat another slice of the bacon and egg pie. I channel-flick on her television. It's super old so she hardly has any good channels and there is nothing on but some show where people marry strangers. I can't watch it, it makes me feel ill. At 8 p.m., I start thinking maybe I will just go to bed. It starts to get dark and I start to feel a bit anxious so I close all the curtains and check the doors are all locked. I wonder how long they will be. They said 'Goodnight' like it's going to be late.

I grab my phone and see three missed calls from my mum. I call her back and she answers after one ring.

'Hey, how are you getting on? Where are you?'

'A beach somewhere up north.'

'Who with?' she asks.

'Dad's friend Lizzie.'

'Nice. Jasper, there is some news here.'

'Yeah, what?'

'I went into your room before,' she says, probably snooping around while I'm out. 'It's Han Solo. He's dead. I'm sorry.'

'Oh.' There is silence. Then noise. The ringing sound in my ears. I don't know what to say.

'Jasper, you all right?' Mum asks.

Am I okay? This is good, isn't it? I knew this was coming. I did . . . I knew he was going to die soon. I wanted him to die. He has been miserable.

'Is he fully dead?' I ask, pacing the hallway. 'Sometimes he goes still for ages.'

'Definitely dead, I'm sorry,' she replies. 'He wasn't doing well though, was he? So, it's a good thing.'

A good thing? Death finally coming can be okay sometimes, a relief. We don't have to watch the dying anymore.

But that is so selfish.

'Manly Steve didn't run him over?' I ask.

'Jasper, no! He wouldn't. It just happened.'

Maybe? Or was it last night? I don't think I even looked in the tank before I left, I was busy getting my stuff and wondering if Dad would even turn up. Maybe he was dead and I didn't even look at him. I didn't say goodbye.

Why now?

Why now, when I can't even . . .

He hated me.

'You okay?' Mum says.

'I've got to go.'

'Call me back if you need. I'm sorry. I love you.'

I don't know what to do. I feel numb, sad, angry and relieved all at the same time. I wanted him to die, I did, but now I feel like the cloud that was hanging over him has moved to me.

I didn't look after him, I didn't care . . .

He's gone.

Gone.

Dead.

I put my head in my hands and tears start rolling down my cheeks. Finally. Tears. I start hitting my head into my hands. WHY DO THINGS HAVE TO DIE? It's not fair. It. Is. Not. Fair. I grip my head and squeeze my fingers together. I want to grip so tightly that my skull will shatter. Blood and brains will explode everywhere. I deserve that.

I imagine Han Solo, his little fish body. An image of my

nana's body when we went to see her at the hospital, after she had died, comes into my head. Mum thought it was important. To see her. To say goodbye.

I didn't cry. Mum was crying a lot and I thought me crying would make her cry more. So I stood there. But I felt angry. So angry. She was too young to die. I didn't feel like I had said goodbye. I hadn't told her that I loved her.

When I was with Nana I felt like everything would be okay, that the world was a good place. Right now, it hurts. For some reason today, in every inch of me, I feel like it's the day she died, all over again. I don't know if it's about Han Solo or Nana, but it feels like a double-whammy of sadness. I feel so exhausted.

I cry the tears I didn't cry when Nana died. I cry them until I am washed away with the tide.

The pillow is soaked in tears. I try to sleep, but I can hear strange noises. The wind starts to pick up and things start banging around in the garden. I hear the howling of wind through trees and waves slamming in the distance. I can't relax. I get back up and start pacing the room and check my phone. Should I call my mum? She will get angry at my dad. Where is he? I shouldn't be alone.

He is probably going to break Lizzie's heart and she is really sweet and a really good cook. She doesn't deserve it.

He uses people. He lies. He lied to me. He always messes everything up.

My pacing moves to other rooms in the house. I text Mum.

What r u doing?

A few minutes later I get a reply . . .

Steve's friends are here. Can we talk tomorrow?

She is having a lovely time without me in the house. Surprise, surprise. She is finally rid of me.

What now? I check the doors again. Each one, twice. Just in case. I don't like this. I don't want to be here. I should have gone to the restaurant with them and sat in silence. That kind of silence is better than this kind of silence. I walk around the house and my heart starts to race. What should I do? I don't have Lizzie's number — I can't call Dad. I can't call Mum — she's having fun with her new friends.

I imagine my dad rushing home: sensing that I am sad, that I need him.

'Jasper, I'm here.'

'I'm scared, Dad. I'm really scared!'

I imagine him sitting at the end of the bed. 'What scares you, Jasper?'

'Heaps of things, Dad,' I say.

'Give me one.'

'Dying . . .'

'What? You're thirteen. You don't need to worry about that!' He laughs.

'I don't want to die yet, Dad.'

'Chances are you won't. For a very long time.'

'Don't jinx it by saying that,' I say. You can't say or think that. It's dangerous.

'An asteroid might hit you in five minutes. All of us.'

'Thanks,' I imagine myself saying, laughing a little.

'But it might, so you may as well not worry about it. You'll die someday. We all do.'

'Thanks for reminding me. This isn't helping . . .'

But now in my head, he gets closer, takes my hand, holds it tight. 'What else scares you, Jasper?'

'Other stuff, Dad.'

He takes a deep breath in. 'I understand, Jasper.'

'What scares you?' I ask him.

'Global warming. Gun laws. Nuclear warfare. Cell phone radiation.' He would say something like that.

'Okay . . .'

'Don't spend your life worrying, Jasper, or you might find that you're too scared to live. There are wonderful things ahead for you, because you are an amazing person. I can't wait to see what you achieve.'

'Thanks, Dad,' I say, feeling better.

He stands up, puts his hand to his heart. 'You will be fine, Jasper Robinson-Woods. Just fine.'

'I love you, Dad.'

'I love you, Son. You make me so proud.'

But he doesn't say those things.

He is out with Lizzie on our weekend away and I'm alone with my thoughts, with my fears, wondering if He has followed me here.

Why do I have to be alone? Why does no one care that I feel this alone? Why is everyone else so happy? Why does my dad even bring me on these trips and then ignore me? Why?

Because he doesn't love me. Clearly.

I am alone.

Alone.

Or am I alone?

I close my eyes and listen. The wind howls. I feel watched. When I glance down the hallway I see why — I see a shadow dart across the hallway between rooms.

His shadow.

He is in the house.

He is here. I am certain of it.

I will never get away from Him, no matter how hard I try. No matter where I go. He has followed me here.

Of course He has.

I close my eyes and listen intently to the house, to the sounds, to the wind and to Him.

A floorboard creaks. A door swings. Something brushes the wall. He's in Lizzie's room, the door is slightly ajar. I hear things moving around but my heart is racing so deeply it hurts my chest.

Thump. Thump. Thump.

The pounding travels up into my ears, now I can't hear anything because the thumping is so strong.

THUMP.

THUMP.

THUMP.

It gets louder still. My breath starts to quicken now too and my hammering heart races faster again. Just when I think it can't beat any faster, it does.

THUMP.
THUMP.
THUMP.

I worry my heart might stop. It can't beat this fast, this hard. I can't survive this. Maybe this is what a heart attack feels like.

And where is my dad? All this going on, all this inside me, and he is not even here.

I hear the growling start. It is loud. Over the wind and the thumping, I hear the bear.

He is coming for me.

That is the last thought I have before He comes thundering down the hall.

WHO AM I?
I AM HERE TO REMIND YOU OF WHO YOU ARE
YOU ARE THE DARKNESS
JASPER ROBINSON-WOODS
DARKNESS
YOU
ARE
TRULY
ALONE

24.

The world is still. The wind has calmed.

I'm woken by the front door opening and closing. Then laughter. Quiet voices, whispering. Then louder voices.

'Jasper?'

'Where are you?'

'Are you okay, Jasper?!'

Someone rushes in and light from the hallway floods into the room. On to my face. Where am I?

'Jasper, what happened?'

The figure turns on the light and the brightness forces my eyes open. I quickly squeeze them shut again to hide from its sharp assault.

'What do you mean?' I say.

'Jasper? Why is there stuff everywhere? What happened? Did someone come into the house?'

I remember now. The road trip. Han Solo. My dad.

This voice is my dad's.

'I don't know . . .'

'There's been a robbery. There are broken plates . . . Call the police, Lizzie!'

'Wait. What?' I say. *Police?* I hear Lizzie's voice in the hallway.

'Nothing seems to be taken, David. I think . . .'

'Jasper . . .' He pulls back the covers to wake me. Stir me from this daze. 'You didn't do this, did you? You didn't make this mess?' He shakes my shoulders again, more violent this time. But I was actually asleep, I was actually in a deep sleep. I can't find a way out of the fog.

'Han Solo died,' I say, quietly.

'What? Had you not seen that movie?' See, he knows nothing about me.

'Not *that* Han Solo. My one. My goldfish. He was sick and Mum found him.'

'I didn't know you had a fish.'

'Well, I did and now he's dead.'

DEAD.

'Well, yes. It sucks when things die.'

'Yep.' It really does.

'So you destroyed Lizzie's house because your goldfish died? Jesus, Jasper.'

There are no words. I don't have a reply.

'Can I sleep?' I try to pull the covers back over me, but he won't let me.

'How dare you do this because you're in a bad mood!' He points to the lounge. 'How dare you!' I push him away and lie back down onto the pillow. I don't remember.

'Go. Go! Leave me alone!' I shout.

And he does.

I hear Dad and Lizzie outside the door. 'There is something wrong with that kid.'

Lizzie's voice is trying to calm my father. 'No. It's okay, David. Let's get some sleep and sort it in the morning.'

'I TOLD YOU I DIDN'T WANT TO COME HERE!' I stand and shout at the closed door, to my father, then fall back on to the bed.

I hit the pillow hard, yet somehow I sleep.

When I wake, Lizzie and Dad are not up.

I walk down the hallway and Lizzie's shoes are scattered along the hallway. In the lounge, the pillows have been pulled off the couch and the magazines that were in a flax basket are ripped, pages strewn across the room. Books are pulled off the bookshelves and thrown on the floor. It seems like stuff He would do. Stuff He's done before.

I check the kitchen and there are broken plates and vases on the floor. It's a mess. I close my eyes and look back, behind my eyes. Deeper, deeper. Deeper into the ocean of my thoughts — the cold quiet of the deepest sea, where the sea monsters live, where the darkness is, where the demons wait.

I look there.

In the silent darkness, I can see. Last night. The bear was back. I was protecting myself. I told Dad I didn't want to stay here. I told him. It is his fault because he went out. This was supposed to be our weekend together and he wasn't even here with me. He says he wants to spend time with me, but he's lying. It's never about me. He doesn't even like me.

He lies.

And who was here with me?

He was. He followed me here.

The bear.

I had to keep Him away. I had to keep myself safe. I had no choice. Han Solo is gone. It is my turn next.

I sit on the floor and start putting the ripped magazines back into a pile. I put the books back on the shelf. I can't remember what went where, so I shove them back in any order, pages still torn. I shove the cushion stuffing back inside the cushions and put them back on the couch. I line the shoes in pairs along the hall.

I hear Dad yawning and a door opening. He comes and sits on the floor with me.

'Did you have a good dinner?' I ask.

'We did. Until we came home and found this,' he says, looking around the room.

I want to say I'm sorry. I am sorry and it hurts. But I don't know how to say the words to this man who has never apologised to me.

'I nearly called the police, Jasper. I thought there had been a burglary. What the hell happened?'

'Why did you bring me here?' I ask him.

Dad starts to talk but stops himself.

'You hate me,' I say, quietly.

'I do not hate you,' he says, unconvincingly.

'You should.'

He doesn't say anything, just puts his head in his hands.

'Dad?' I ask. 'What do you think happens to you when you die?'

'Well . . .' I can tell he doesn't know how to answer this. 'I believe you're gone. The end.'

'You don't believe in life after death? Or reincarnation?'

'I like the idea of it, but don't think it happens. If it did, I would be a lion, though, or a bear, something no other animals would wanna mess with. You?'

'Not a bear. A bird, an eagle or something.' Definitely not a bear.

'And what do you believe in?' he asks, leaning back on the wall behind him.

'Don't know. Nothing yet, really.' I don't, I still don't know what I believe in. 'But I hope Nana is still somewhere, watching over me. And Poppa.'

Dad nods his head. 'Well, believe in that then.'

There is something I believe though. 'Dad,' I say, looking into his eyes. 'I think there might be something wrong with me...'

I hope he will say something, anything to make me feel better but he just looks uncomfortable. He doesn't know how to talk to me so I don't know why I even bothered.

We are leaving Lizzie's house. She wants to finish tidying the house herself and thinks it's best if we just go. I have a shower and make the bed in the spare room, as if that makes up for it, all that I have done. While I pack my bag, I hear Dad on the phone to my mother. He is telling her what happened, saying he will take me straight home. I go close to the door to hear.

'You're saying this isn't the first time? Well, what the hell is going on with him, Michelle? He needs help.'

Mum is going to be furious. I put my bag in the car and wait next to it. I can hear the sea, waves crashing. Lizzie comes to the car and Dad gives her a long hug.

'Thanks for having us,' he says, then whispers something else which I think is something about how bad he feels. Lizzie comes over to me. I look down at my sneakers.

'Bye,' she says.

'Sorry... You were so nice to me, but I messed up.'

'It was good to meet you, Jasper. And I'm sorry about your

fish.' How can she say that? She must be lying.

Dad backs up the driveway and Lizzie walks to the letterbox and waves goodbye. Dad toots loudly. She won't want to see my father again, maybe that's a good thing. For her.

'We need to buy her some new plates,' I say to Dad. 'And a vase.'

'It's sorted,' he replies.

Silently we begin our car journey home. I close my eyes and hope I will sleep, just sleep and wake up and find maybe this didn't even happen? Maybe I will be home again and Han Solo will still be alive.

But no sleep comes then. And this is not a dream. Or a nightmare. Dad turns the radio on and nothing is said for about twenty minutes.

'Dad?' I say, over top of the voices. 'What were you like when you were my age?'

'I don't remember much,' he replies. 'I think I was pretty angry though.'

'At who?'

Light rain starts to fall on the windscreen and Dad turns the wipers on. I watch as they rhythmically swish across the windscreen, taking the dots of rain away, as more rain appears to take its place. SWISH. SWISH.

'Everyone — my parents, teachers, society in general.' He gives a small laugh. 'Life wasn't any easier for me.'

'You know Grandpa and Grandma? Did they stay married?'

'Yes, until the day they died.'

I never met his parents. They were in England and they

died before I could meet them. 'What's that like, not to have divorced parents?' I ask.

'Well,' Dad laughs, a sarcastic laugh. 'My parents were miserably unhappy but stayed together because that's what people did back then. They felt they had to. That's not great either, trust me.'

'Oh.' I'm not sure if that's romantic. Or disturbing. I guess it's a bit of both. Mostly disturbing, though.

'It's hard being a teenager. I do remember that. You feel things so intensely, everything is a catastrophe.'

I nod. I do feel things intensely. And things do often feel like catastrophes.

He looks at me and smiles slightly. It's the first time in a long time I notice his eyes are quite kind. And sad.

And then I do sleep. I fall asleep listening to the sounds of the road and my dad breathing next to me, the wipers still moving slowly and the light pitter-patter of rain. I don't know why I can sleep when I'm in the car with my father.

When I wake, he is listening to the radio again.

I speak as if the conversation hasn't stopped. Before I lose confidence.

'I am angry too, Dad,' I say, as if my dream has given me clarity, when in fact I dreamt of nothing. Maybe I am still dreaming in fact.

'I can tell. Are you angry at me?' He turns the radio off.
'Partly.'
'Do you know why?'
'Dunno.'

'Because I left?'

'Probably. And other stuff too.'

I'm angry because he didn't come back. And because I don't see him. I'm angry that Nana isn't here anymore. Nor Poppa. And now Han Solo. Angry that I lose everyone important to me. I want to change my name and my identity and I don't want to feel like this.

'I haven't been a great father, have I?' He stares ahead, eyes on the road, but ears on me.

I don't say anything.

25.

I am back in the tree.

It's the first place I go when Dad drops me off. We didn't speak much more in the car; in fact he was very quiet. He didn't ask me any more questions, probably didn't want to hear the answers.

Mum is still working and Manly Steve is somewhere else and I'm glad he isn't home. I don't want to see him yet, that's for sure. Before he left, Dad gave me a hug and told me that he loves me. I didn't believe him. I don't know when I will see him again and I don't know where he is going. I have learned not to ask.

'Sorry,' I had said as he walked away. He had looked back but said nothing.

So I am back in the tree. It smells like home. But I hate home at the same time and I'm not ready to go inside. I am thinking of Him, the bear and how He followed me, how wherever I am now, He seems to be too. I want to hide from Him. But I can't. I don't think I can be this person. I want to be someone else. If a plane dropped from the sky and landed on my house right now and this tree and me, maybe that would be okay? Mum would be distraught, of course, her only son, but she has Manly Steve now — they could rebuild the house. Maybe it would all be okay in the end.

Without me.

I contemplate getting down. I need to unpack. And I need food. As I look along the road, I see a figure walking towards me. So I wait.

Stealth ninja waits.

As the figure comes closer, I squint my eyes to focus them, and my heart starts to quicken. It looks like . . . Nina? From art class Nina. Nina Frankton-Forbes. The Nina Frankton-Forbes.

As she gets closer, I see that it is one hundred percent Nina Frankton-Forbes, walking on my road, near my house. And I am up a tree! Of all the days, of all the houses, of all the roads. She gets a piece of paper out of her pocket. Is this in my imagination? Have I conjured up this image of her? I don't know what my mind is capable of and sometimes I don't know if I am awake or asleep, if I am real or imaginary.

This is one of those moments.

But I'm pretty sure it is real. In fact, as she gets closer, I see that she seems to be looking for my house. When she gets to my letterbox, she looks inside and goes and knocks on the door, stepping over my bag. Why? Why? Why am I up a tree and not in the house where I could answer the door and say hello like a normal human being? She knocks five times and waits.

Can I get down?

No, I can't, I can't do it without being noticed. Would it be weird to be like, 'Hey, I was just up the tree?' YES! That would be weird!

She looks out towards the road, grabs a pen from her bag and writes something on the piece of paper. She knocks another time. But no one is home. I am not home. I am right outside it, up a tree, like a flipping idiot. Again I consider jumping down — but I feel like I can't. I am such a mess I don't know how to talk, what to say, how to behave. I don't have a suitable explanation. I feel the stuck cat wouldn't work now. And there's no fruit to pick. No treehouse.

Nina walks down the front steps. When she gets to the letterbox, she opens it and puts the paper inside. She takes one more look at the front door and starts walking back the way she came.

I sit in the tree and watch as she walks away.

Nina Frankton-Forbes walks away from my house.

My house.

When her figure is at the end of the road, I jump down

from the tree and open the letterbox. Inside is an invitation to the Secondary School Art Exhibition and Nina's writing on the top.

Maria asked me to drop off your invitation to the exhibition. See you at school? Nina F-F.

I stand, staring at the handwritten words, the way she has joined the letters together, the curl at the end of the *a* of Nina, the F-F. Before I know it, I have stuffed the letter back in the letterbox and I am running along the street in her direction.

I run. I run faster than I knew I could run. I am running like my life depends on it. I don't know what I am doing and I don't know what I will say if I get to her, but something tells me I have to at least try. My heart is beating so fast again.

This time it is thumping because of the shock of physical exercise, but it almost feels good. To run. To move my heart like this. With nothing chasing me. As I get to the end of the street, I look right, the way she turned. I imagine her figure walking ahead of me, but I can't see her. I can't see her brown hair, her red school bag, her white shoes. I can't see them and my heart sinks.

She has gone.

I walk home, disappointed.

Yet there's something else. Maybe I'm a little elated that she came to my house, that she knows where I live, that she wanted to do this for me. She didn't have to. Maria could have given it to me. When I get inside, I throw my bag on my bed and kick my sneakers off. I know I should unpack but I have no energy, so I stare at the space in my room where Han

Solo's tank used to be. Then back at the invitation. Then back at the space.

Mum has removed any sign of Han Solo, the tank and his fish food.

I wonder if she saw the holes in the wall? She may have had a good look around the room while I was away. Wouldn't put it past her. I hear keys in the front door. It's Mum and she comes straight to my room.

'Jasper? You're back.'

She drops her bag on the floor and hugs me. 'I've been so worried about you.' She pulls away and looks at me. 'What happened?'

'I don't know, Mum.'

'Your dad told me you destroyed his friend's things while they were out.' She shakes her head, in disbelief. Or is it disbelief? She knows what I am capable of.

'There's no point in me even going away with him, Mum, he didn't even want me there.'

'Why didn't you call me?' She grabs my hand. Squeezes it.

'You were with your friends. For dinner.'

'So what? You should have called me.' She gives me another hug. 'But, why? Why destroy those things?'

I know I can't explain myself. I can't tell her that I don't even know if it was me. That maybe it was Him? 'I dunno, Mum.'

She leaves the room and I lie back into my bed. I close my eyes tight and don't expect to, but I go to sleep again — without eating, without unpacking, without seeing Manly

Steve. I sleep for fifteen hours. I am sleeping like I haven't been struggling for days, weeks to fall asleep. I sleep for most of the weekend.

Sleep is my friend again.

I think.

Mum rings me to wake me Monday morning. She has left for work already.

'Are you okay?'

'Yes.'

'Tired?' she asks.

'Yes, Mum. I'm so tired.'

Of everything.

'Don't be late for school today. And I told them you had a tummy bug last week, by the way.'

I eat five pieces of toast for breakfast and leave all the dishes on the table, for Manly Steve, so he knows I am back. *You're welcome.*

When I arrive at school, I look for Nina everywhere but I can't see her. She is not in art class either. She is away. I can't believe it. Where is she? Why is she not here? Today of all the days. Why is the universe doing this to me?

All day I can't focus. I learn nothing. I take nothing in. I talk to people without registering I am having a conversation. I eat my lunch and it tastes of nothing. I don't care. I don't care about any of it. I wanted to see Nina, say thank you.

I want it to be tomorrow so I can be back at school to see if she is there. *Where are you, Nina Frankton-Forbes?*

What if she's moved cities? Or countries? I bet she has!

At dinner, Mum and Manly Steve want to talk about my 'holiday with Dad'. Holiday?

'It was bad,' I say. I move food around on my plate.

'What happened?' Manly Steve asks. But he knows.

'Nothing.'

'You can tell us about it, Jasper,' says Mum, looking at Manly Steve. She has clearly told him what happened. He stops eating, like *this is going to be interesting.*

'I don't want to talk about it.'

'You can't do that to people's houses,' Manly Steve says, putting his knife and fork down on the table, ready for business. He is the businessman of the century.

I say nothing.

'We'll talk about it later,' Mum says, awkwardly. She offers me some garlic bread. 'Bread, love?'

'I would be furious if you did anything like that in this house, for the record.'

'Steven, please . . .' Mum says, offering him the bread. 'It's okay.'

I still say nothing. I have nothing to say *for the record*. But I would love to destroy all of his stuff.

I get up and leave the room. 'Thanks for the support,' I say as I walk away.

If I keep being horrible to live with, Manly Steve will just leave. Surely. Or would it be *me* that has to leave? I google *I hate my stepdad* to see what comes up. There are all these chat-sites where people are complaining about their stepparents.

Seems like I'm not the only one. One site has a few 'tips'.

Take it slow. *I'm trying.*

Find common interests. *Don't have any.*

Always be polite and civil. *Bloody hard sometimes.*

Always communicate with your stepparent, even 'idle chit chat,' Try and ask: 'How was your day? How was work?' *Maybe I will try that, some 'idle chit chat' about his day at the boring packaging office. Maybe he might ask me how my day was instead of telling me to pick up my towels.*

Despite the encouragement of these great 'tips', I go to sleep dreaming of all the ways Manly Steve might meet his end.

I sleep well.

26.

It's Wednesday and Nina is at school.

Nina. At school. Nina Frankton-Forbes. She didn't move to Canada like I'd decided she had. I spot her from a distance and don't know whether to go straight to her, or just to see her in art class. I can't get up the courage to approach her so I watch her from a distance, like a stalker.

When it's time for art, I go into class first. I choose a desk with a free space next to it but when she comes in, she doesn't sit next to me. I try not to look disappointed when she glances my way. But I am. She doesn't look at me again the whole class, she just works on her woodcut. At the end of class, she leaves the room first. I am so angry at myself. She made an effort; she came to my house. It's my turn to say something.

As I'm walking home, I see her up ahead. *Okay, Jasper, talk to her. Come on. You can do this!* I can't go home and spend another afternoon in a tree thinking of what I SHOULD have said.

'Nina!' I say . . . And then panic. But I can't take it back.

She turns around and sees me. She stops walking, a smile on her face. I have to say something else, I can't leave it there! *Think. Words. Talk. Sentence.*

'Hey. Nina. Thank you . . . For dropping the invitation off, for the art thing. That was really . . . Nice of you.' Suave.

'All good. Maria wanted you to have it.'

'How did you know that was my house?' I ask.

'Oh we drove past once and I saw you. We live two streets over.'

Oh man. I hope I wasn't up a tree.

'I went away with my dad,' I explain. 'That's why I missed it. Last week. School.' I'm not talking in proper sentences!

'Oh, okay. Do you not live with your dad?' She starts walking. So I do too.

'No. Mum. I live with her and her . . . this guy, her boyfriend. But I don't see much of him. Dad. Actually . . .' Oh god. Why am I sounding like I can't talk? And is this over-sharing? I don't know.

There is a short silence and my head explodes with potential questions to ask her without the silence being too long. *What's your favourite colour? Do you like pizza? Do you like geese?* For some reason that one pops into my mind. I hate geese. They are terrifying.

Nina breaks the silence. 'How long have your parents been split up?'

'About seven years,' I reply, kicking a stone along the path.

'Is it hard?' she asks, turning her face to mine.

'It gets easier,' I say. It's all I can think of. But it sort of does. 'After a while you can't really remember them being together.'

Is that even true? Maybe the memories of them together get foggier.

We walk along to the corner of my street. Nina does most of the talking and I listen but ... she seems to be able to make sense.

'So, this is me. Oh, but you knew that.' I laugh. She smiles. 'Thanks again for the dropping off, I mean dropping off the thing. The piece of the ... the invitation.'

AH, MAKE SENSE, JASPER!

'No problem. Who will go with you to the exhibition?' she asks.

'My mum.'

Is she asking to come? Or was it just a question? Oh man. Conversations are so hard sometimes.

'See ya tomorrow then,' she smiles.

'Bye.'

She waves goodbye. I wave back, then continue walking and reliving the conversation in my head all the way home.

Things I have learned about Nina:

She has two older brothers and a Golden Retriever called Benny.

She plays the French horn and is in the school orchestra.

She loves Japanese anime.

She told me all this while walking to the corner. She chatted away. I think I even said a few sentences that made sense. There were still a lot that didn't. We didn't talk about the name thing. One day I will ask her about it but there was no time today.

NINA + HER HAIRCUT

I talked to Nina Frankton-Flippin'-Forbes!

When I get inside, I feel different. I walk straight into the house, get a snack and put the telly on, like a normal kid. No tree. Just straight inside. Like maybe it's going to be okay.

I feel real again. I am not imagining this. I am real. I am a real person.

Mum smiles at me across the table at dinner, like she knows. 'Anything interesting happen at school today?'

'No, why?'

'Just asking.'

She has made some kind of risotto but I'm not sure if she's cooked it long enough. It's kind of crunchy.

'I forgot to tell you that I got the official invitation to the exhibition,' I say between crunches. I had put the invite on the fridge but she hadn't noticed.

'Oh, exciting. Your first exhibition!'

Manly Steve smiles. 'First of many more, eh Jasper?'

Wow. That was even a nice thing to say. Wasn't expecting that.

'Can you be there too, Steven?' Mum asks and I get a bit

of a fright. Surely he doesn't want to come.

'Sure,' he says. Woah. Family outing.

I go to sleep early. And I sleep really well again and there is no bear.

There are dreams. Of walking and corners and invitations and waves goodbye.

I walk home with Nina again the next day. In fact, she looks for me at the gate and we start walking . . . no awkward moment of the silent 'Shall we walk together?' game. As if it's what we always do. All it took was a 'Hey.' And a 'Hey' back.

This time she asks me lots of questions. I make a bit more sense today. I tell her about Manly Steve and Elise, about her studying drama. She says she sounds cool. And before I know it, we are near the corner where we say goodbye. I hate that bit. I wish we could keep talking. Me and Nina. Nina and me.

And as we're about to walk away, she asks for my phone number. So she can text me!

NINA FRANKTON-FORBES ASKED ME FOR MY PHONE NUMBER!

I want to shout this out or put it on a bus stop ad or something.

I almost didn't know my own number because I never give

it to people but I finally remembered and she saved it on her phone. I've checked my phone every minute since she asked for it, but she hasn't sent me a text. I forgot to ask for her number as well so I just have to wait. I can't really think of anything else. It takes ages to get home, dawdling down the road and thinking, thinking and dawdling and checking my phone every ten steps.

When I get home, I can hear Manly Steve stomping around angrily. Mum is home too, which is odd. I creep inside and hide in my room, wondering if they are having their first argument.

'Oh dear.' Mum comes into my room, sighing loudly.

'What's going on?' I ask, wondering if I even want to know. 'Why are you home?'

'Bit of a long story, really. Steven has had some bad news.' She sits on the end of my bed and looks around. I don't panic straight away because it's Manly Steve's bad news. Not Mum's.

'Work stuff?' Maybe he lost a big packaging deal. Whoopdee shit.

'No . . . Family stuff actually.'

What did I do this time? Have I lost his charger again?

'It's about Elise,' she adds.

'Oh. What?' Now I do care.

'It's nothing to do with us. He'll work it out, I wanted to let you . . .'

'No, what? You have to tell me.' I sit up, worried now.

'Jasper. It's not really up to . . .'

'You're always like, *Jasper can't handle this news so I won't tell him.*' I attempt my best impersonation of her.

'It's not that. It's not my news to tell.'

'That's going to make me really . . .' She knows what I am going to say.

'Fine,' she says, rubbing her eyes. 'Elise called today and told him that she is, I probably shouldn't tell you, but she's pregnant.'

'Oh.'

Okay, that is kind of big. Not what I was expecting and now I do feel a bit out of my depth and wish I didn't know. 'Why is that *bad* news?' I ask.

'She's still so young, Jasper. She's studying and her boyfriend is young too.' This all sounds complicated.

She stands up and picks up dirty glasses from my desk. 'He might be a bit upset for a bit while he gets used to it all. Sorry.'

Then she goes to leave, saying 'Dinner in five,' as she closes the door behind her.

I don't know what I am supposed to do. I consider saying I have a headache and going to bed. But I'm hungry so I brave it outside my bedroom for dinner and it's super-awkward. Mum is right, he is in a foul mood. At one point, she tries to talk about it, but he just replies, 'I don't want to talk about it at the dinner table, Michelle.'

So we sit in silence. He doesn't want to talk about it in front of me, I can tell. I have lots of questions though and I can't resist. 'Did she know she was pregnant when she was here?'

Manly Steve takes a sip of water and quickly thumps it onto the table and stares at me. Water splashes across the table. 'What part of not wanting to talk about it do you not understand?'

'She had wine. That's why I ask.' We'd been learning about foetal alcohol syndrome in health studies so I was wondering. But Manly Steve sighs and glares at me. No words.

'Fine.' I get up and leave. I'm not that hungry anymore. I slam my door as I enter my room and the house shakes.

'And DON'T SLAM DOORS!' I hear him yell from the dinner table.

Does he not see it? Does he not see that it's my door, not his? I can slam my door if I want. Maybe my mother doesn't want me to slam it, so maybe she can tell me not to. SHE CAN. The owner of this house he is a guest in! I lie in my bed and imagine drawing penises and balls on his fancy car.

I want to know if Elise is okay.

Later Mum comes in and apologises for him. She tells me that it's probably best we don't talk to him about it while 'the news soaks in'. I resist the urge to tell her that her boyfriend can be a total arse sometimes.

She does tell me Elise probably was pregnant when she was here but she didn't know, she just found out.

'How is she, though?' I ask.

'She's still coming to terms with it all, Jasper. It's

overwhelming for everyone, I think. You get some sleep love,' she says as she leaves.

I don't sleep. Not well. I stay up thinking about Elise. And about how I don't like it when Manly Steve thumps the table and how I want to see Elise and tell her.

Tell her it will be okay.

In the morning, Manly Steve is still angry. Mum leaves early and he thumps and grumps all over the house. I hear him grunting and crashing around so I try to stay out of his way, but it's hard. He tells me off for the floor in the bathroom being wet.

'What are bath mats for, Jasper?'

He tells me off for leaving my breakfast bowl 'on the table AGAIN!'

And he tells me off for leaving the milk 'on the counter AGAIN!'

It seems I am consistent with my behaviour. Bad behaviour. 'I get it. I can't do anything right today,' I say, as I grab my bag and head for the door.

He is not in a good mood at all. 'What? What did you say? Jasper? Come back here.'

'I said I can't do anything right today,' I say it quietly, cautious. But he hears.

'You're not using your head, mate!' He walks towards me. 'Have some respect for other people in the house for once.' When he talks to me some of his spit flies through the air and lands on me. I really don't like it when that happens. Manly germs. Germs at all. I don't like germs.

'Whatever,' I say, wiping my face.

'Don't *whatever* me, Jasper. Have some goddam respect.'

Respect. Goddam respect! There are so many things I want to say to him. There are so many words I want to yell. There are so many of his faces I want to punch my fist into. I feel a rush of red through my blood and I kick a plant over in the hallway and slam the door as I walk out.

The house shakes. On the front porch is a pair of Manly Steve's gumboots. I pick one up and throw it at the tree; it hits it and lands in the rose bush.

Respect that, dickhead.

I feel like he might follow me, yell at me and demand I pick up the plant — and the gumboot. I sprint to the end of our road, slowing to a jog when I reach the main road. I kick pebbles as I walk, grab flowers from front gardens and drop them on the ground. My nana would be appalled. She loved admiring flowers in front gardens. Sorry, Nana.

I hate him. I hate his voice, his face, the things he says, the way he says them.

So, his daughter is pregnant, she is growing up and he doesn't like it. It hasn't gone to plan, his plan for her and he hates that. But now I am paying for it because I didn't pick up my towel this morning. That sounds fair, doesn't it? I didn't make her pregnant (in fact I'm still slightly weirded out by how it all happens in the first place). Who does he think he is?

I go the long way to school because I'm too agitated to go to class. I feel like I can't be around people and definitely not teachers trying to tell me how to behave. Not right now. It takes me a while to calm down. I consider not going at all. But I do. There's nowhere to go and my house feels like a prison at the moment anyway.

But it means I'm late for school again and we all know what that means.

27.

I'm in my favourite place: the dean's office. And she's in the mood for comical sarcasm.

'You're late again, Mr Robinson-Woods, what a surprise.'

'Certainly seems that way.' I can play this game too. I'm good at it.

'Why are you late this time?' she asks. 'Clock playing up?'

'The bell rang before I made it here.' See. Really good at it. In fact, dishing sarcasm out is a hobby of mine, even if she's heard this one before.

'It did. It really doesn't like you.'

'I've had a bad morning.' I sigh.

'Anything you want to talk about?'

'Nope.' Does she really think I'd have a heart-to-heart with her? Now?

'I don't have a choice here, Jasper, I'm going to give you

another detention and get your mother in so we can talk about the importance of getting to school on time.'

'You don't have a choice? You probably do.'

Silence.

'What would *you* like me to do about it?' she asks, her eyebrows lifted.

'Give me a break, that might be nice.' My only other idea is that they change the bell time to later for me, but I don't think that will go down well. Anything before 10 a.m. is really too early for teenagers.

'These are school rules and school procedures, Jasper. And you were on a warning. Rules are here for a reason and there are consequences when you break them. Get to class.' She passes me a late slip and points to the door.

I leave the office and go and sit on a bench outside. I don't want to go to class. I don't want to be at school. I don't want to go home either. I don't know where I want to be.

So I just sit.

I check my phone: see a message from Mum.

I hear you've made a mess in the hallway. Clean it up. Not impressed!

Of course he rang her. Of course he did.

'Why are you out here?' A teacher I don't know walks past holding a pile of books. 'Is there somewhere you need to be?' she asks.

'Yes, there is.' I pack my things up and slowly head to class. I sit at the back, fold my arms tightly and don't listen. I don't listen because I don't care.

'Will you be taking your books out of your bag, Jasper?' Mr Cloonan, my English teacher, asks as he passes my desk. I open my bag and get a book and pen out. I start to draw on the cover and think about nothing.

'Jasper!' Mr Cloonan's voice wakes me from a daze sometime later. Then louder. 'Jasper! Go to the office.'

Oh joy. I grab my things and make my way there. As I go past the music room, I see Nina sitting at a piano playing chords. She somehow senses I'm looking at her and looks up. I smile shyly and she waves. Maybe today isn't so bad. This feeling quickly disappears when I enter the office foyer and see my mother with crossed arms and appearing fairly horrified in the waiting area. She turns to me as I walk in.

'What have you done now?' she snaps, looking concerned.

'Nothing,' I shrug.

'Why have I been called in to see the principal, then? Because of nothing?'

'I was late. Again.' I shrug and sink down next to her.

'Jesus, Jasper. I was at work. I had to cancel a patient.'

'You should have said you can't come in. It's not a big deal.' I get my phone out of my bag and start scrolling.

'Put that away.' She snatches my phone and puts it in the front pocket of my bag. 'It sounded kind of important. I thought maybe you'd . . .' she trails off.

'Maybe I'd what? Hit someone in the head with a ball again?'

'Or worse, Jasper. You have been acting appallingly lately. I don't know what you are capable of, to be honest.'

'What I am capable of? Awesome, Mum, thanks for the vote of confidence.'

'Well, destroying that woman's . . .? And Steven tells me you were extremely rude with him this morning. You are like a monster sometimes.'

A monster! I am a monster! This is just what I need to hear. I will show her monster . . .

'Rude to *him*, Mum? He is SOOOOO rude to me. He is grumpy at me constantly! Constantly!' I raise my voice and Mum shushes me with a finger to her lips. The receptionist looks over to us.

'I hate living with him, Mum. I HATE living with both of you!' I say. 'I hate my life.'

'Jasper, please . . .' She looks around, embarrassed. 'Can we get through this meeting and talk about this later?'

'Talk about what? That I hate living with your boyfriend? But it can't change, can it? You're not going to kick him out, are you? I want to go and live with Dad.'

Mum ignores me. She makes a strange noise blowing air out of her nose and mutters something under her breath. She puts her keys in her bag and folds her arms again, looking out the window.

We sit in silence for a few moments. Silence with a few deep sighs from Mum. The principal comes out of his office.

'Kia ora, I'm Mr Taumata, we talked on the phone the other day.' My mother stands up and shakes his hand.

'Michelle.'

'And hi, Jasper. Come on in.'

We follow him to his office. There is a couch and two chairs.

Mum and I both look around, wondering where to sit. The couch seems too informal for Mum so she sits on one of the chairs, holding her bag on her lap awkwardly. I slouch into the other chair.

'How are you both?' Mr Taumata asks.

'Good,' I say.

'Okay,' says Mum. Clearly not.

'I wanted to call you in for a chat, Michelle. We are wondering if there's anything we can do to support Jasper. He's been arriving late to school most days. And we have also had a few angry outbursts in class lately, as you know.'

'Yes.' She looks at me. Yes, I am aware too.

'It's becoming a bit of a habit, isn't it, Jasper?'

They both look at me.

'Today was a bad morning,' I say to the floor.

They both continue to look at me. I look around to avoid their eyes, unsure what I'm supposed to say now.

'It's time to sort it out, Jasper,' Mr Taumata says. 'Most students have no problem getting here for 8.50 a.m. Is there anything we need to know about what's going on for you?'

I look out the window. 'Nope.'

Mr Taumata's gaze flicks between us. Mum jumps in, probably offended by the thought that I have issues and she's not 'mumming' correctly.

'Everything is fine. We have had a few changes at home, maybe you're a bit unsettled with all that, Jasper?'

I raise my eyebrows. Unsettled?

'Our school counsellor, Callum Hughes, would be great to talk to, Jasper, even to chat through some of the . . .'

'No thanks.'

'Take a bit of time to think about that. Things have been looking up too, though, yes? I hear you have a piece in the art exhibition.'

'Yeah . . .'

'Well, you should be proud of that. This might be of interest as well.' He passes my mother a booklet and I see the words *Anger Management*. She takes a quick look.

'I'll have a read tonight. Thank you.' She puts it inside her bag and gets up to leave, eager to get back to work and her ever-so-important patients.

I stand too.

'I hope to see you here nice and early tomorrow, Jasper. Maybe put the alarm on ten minutes earlier and see how you go? Right, back to class. Good to meet you in person, Michelle.'

'You too, thank you,' she says, rushed, and then she gently closes the door behind us. Outside the office, she is furious.

'How embarrassing, Jasper. You've only been at this school a few months and you already have a reputation for lateness and anger issues. This is just what I need.' She looks through her bag trying to find her keys again.

'Sorry. It's not really what I need either,' I say, throwing my school bag over my shoulder.

'You need to sort it out. No one else can do it for you,' she says loudly.

I look around, this is so embarrassing. I don't know what she wants me to say.

'Stop blaming everyone else and take responsibility.'

'Yes, fine . . . bye.' I turn and walk down the corridor, away from her.

'And go and see the school counsellor,' she says behind me.

'No!' I turn to say it back to her. A teacher comes around the corner and I shake my head at my mother. I can't believe her sometimes.

'Well, Jasper, if you think you . . .' Mum tries to walk towards me.

'No. Bye.' I walk away.

I hear her sigh as she turns to leave.

I can't concentrate in class. I've got a worksheet I'm supposed to complete about language devices in a short story I haven't even read, but I can't even seem to read the words on the page. Anger management! Ha! Sometimes I feel like there is a volcano inside me and I never know when it's going to blow. And inside that volcano is a little fire that just keeps smouldering. As I get older more and more bits of wood get thrown into it to keep it burning, more fuel for the fire. How do you manage that?

Instead of doing the worksheet, I draw a volcano. And me jumping into it.

Nina and I are walking home together again.

'I'm thinking of changing my name,' I say to her. Finally.

'What! Your name?' She looks horrified. 'There's nothing wrong with your name.'

'Jasper Robinson-Woods. Awful.'

'It's fine! In fact you're not allowed to change it because I need someone else with a long name in this school! I'd have to change mine too and I can't be bothered. It's not like it's Jasper Longbottom or Jasper Fartneck.'

That does make me laugh.

'Well, funny you mention those names! Those were on my shortlist.'

'No, Jasper!' She hits my arm and laughs. I make a mental note to google *most unfortunate last names* when I get home, it might make me feel better.

I don't end up mentioning my actual shortlist. It seems boring now.

'I mean, Frankton-Forbes is a bit of a mouthful,' she says. 'Too many Fs! At least yours doesn't have the same letter as well! Frankton-Forbes! What were they thinking?'

'But that makes it cool. It works. Robinson-Woods! Those

names don't work together. It's not . . . symmetrical.'

We argue for about ten minutes about whose last name is worse. There's no way I'm changing my name now. She even teases me when we are saying goodbye.

'Later, Robinson-Woods.'

'See you, Frankton-Forbes.'

So . . . new plan. No way am I ever changing my name. Ever. I can't do it. Nina says so.

In other news, Mum and Dad are having secret conversations about me now. She must have told him about today with the principal. She doesn't know what to do with me, by the sound of things. I know this because Dad calls ten minutes after I get home.

'Anything you want to talk about?' he asks.

'No,' I say, firmly.

Oh, man. Adults are so annoying: let's talk MORE about this. MORE about me. I want everyone to leave me alone for once in my life.

'You sure? Your mum says you've been in a bit of trouble at school.'

Secret conversations confirmed.

'No, I was just late, that's all . . .'

'Not a morning person? I can relate.' He yawns. Not an afternoon person either.

'Yeah. Nah.'

'She mentioned some angry outbursts at school?'

Angry outbursts. How many times have I heard those words lately?

'Oh, you know . . . teachers. Anyway. Gotta go, Dad . . .' I'm about to try to come up with something I really need to do when:

'Jasper?'

'Ya?'

'I'm always here if you want to talk, okay?'

'Always where? Where shall I get hold of you when I need to talk?'

'I left a number with your mum. I'm here until tomorrow, but I'll be back in my flat soon. And I will get a phone. Shock horror.'

'It's about time.'

'But Jasper, it's okay to be angry.'

'Um . . . No, apparently it's not.'

'No, it is okay. You are allowed to BE angry. It's what you do with it . . .'

'I always get in trouble no matter what I do, Dad,' I interrupt. 'I can't win.'

'You gotta find some way of feeling it, without letting it boil over.'

'Like what?'

'Reading. Meditation. Walks.'

'Dad. I'm not going to meditate. I'm not one of your middle-aged friends at yoga. Goodnight.'

That was not a good day, apart from seeing Nina and

deciding maybe my name was okay after all. The rest of it sucked. Dinner is super-awkward again. I'm not sure if Manly Steve is angry at me, or Elise. But he is not fun to be around.

'Take your cap off at the table,' he says as I sit down. I frisbee it down the hall and he sighs loudly.

'Did you decide if you are vegetarian or not?' he asks me at one point, while I eat a lamb kebab.

'Mostly. I'm vegetarian most of the time.'

'I don't think it works like that. You need to decide so we know what to cook for dinner for you,' he says, not that he's ever cooked dinner.

'Thanks, Mum,' I say, ignoring his statement. I stand, putting my plate on the counter and turning to walk away. I don't want to have this conversation.

'Dishwasher,' he says firmly. I sigh and put my plate in the dishwasher.

'Thanks, love,' says Mum.

Later she comes into my room, holding the anger management brochure the principal gave her. I am lying on my bed attempting some homework.

'I had a quick read, some good tips in there, Jasper.' She turns it over in her hands awkwardly.

I change the subject.

'I need a new school bag. Mine ripped.'

'Oh, fine. We'll look for a new one. You should take a look tonight.'

'For a new bag?'

'No, at this information.' She waves the brochure in the air.

'You should give it to your boyfriend,' I whisper, but she hears it.

'Pardon me?'

'He clearly has some major anger issues,' I say, sitting up. 'He's so grumpy.'

'It's a stressful time, Jasper.'

'What's even happening about Elise? Is she coming up again?'

'I don't know, I'm staying out of it, to be honest.'

I congratulate myself on the tactic to avoid the anger management chats. It seems to have worked because she gives up and leaves the room but puts the brochure on my bed — right in the middle, so I can't miss it. I pick it up and take a quick look.

Do your feelings overwhelm you?

You may at times feel like your emotions are so strong, you don't know what to do with them. Some of the reasons a young person may be angry are: humiliation, embarrassment, hormone fluctuations, stress, rejections, frustration, looking for a connection, hunger, fatigue, perceived or actual injustices, a feeling of powerlessness.

Tick. Tick. Tick.

I throw it across the room. I will look at that later, being reminded of my 'overwhelming feelings' is overwhelming me. Instead, I pick up my computer and google *unfortunate last names* and it's a lot more entertaining than the brochure. There are some funny names out there:

Ben Dover.

Dixie Normous.

Jack Goff.
Wendy Wacko.
Dick Tips.
Dick Long.
Dick Stains.
Kash Register.
F. You.
P. Ennis.
Dr. Wheat Faartz.

And Loser, Butt, Cockburn, Twocock, Squatpump, Pornsak and Cobbledick are all apparently real last names. And Weiner.

Maybe my parents aren't as mean as I've been making out. This does put things into perspective. Perhaps I can live with Jasper Robinson-Woods. Maybe Jasper Woods would get shortened to Jasper Woodie. Better to keep it as is! And for Nina's sake too.

See, sometimes googling helps. It doesn't always leave me feeling like my strange health symptoms are the start of awful life-threatening diseases. Sometimes it makes me feel better about myself.

I get ready for bed. I try to sleep . . .

But then I remember the pot plant in the hallway.

I forgot to clean it up. Mum must have done it. I remember why I pushed it over. Manly Steve. He's going to be here when I wake up. And the next day. And the day after that. Pushing my buttons constantly. Cap off. Dishwasher. Shoes off.

I get up to put the anger management brochure in my cupboard, as far away as I can reach. But it's still there. In my room.

As the lights go out in the house, I start to feel it again. The darkness coming back. Will He come tonight? I feel like He will. It's been a while since He's visited at night. I think of Dad on the phone.

'It's okay to be angry.'

So it was okay for me to feel angry and throw those things around at Lizzie's? I don't understand. *Is it okay, Dad? Because you make me angry, Dad. Is it okay to be angry at you for all the times you let me down? Well, I am so angry at YOU!*

> To Jasper,
> I wanted to let you know I can't take you away these holidays. See you next time buddy.
> Dad
> PS Merry Xmas

> To Dad,
> I do not forgive you.
> Jasper
> PS Have a shit Xmas

WHO AM I?
I THINK YOU KNOW
I REMEMBER WHEN I MET YOU
WHEN EVERYTHING CHANGED
ARE YOU TIRED, JASPER?
ARE YOU TIRED OF LYING AWAKE IN THE DARK?
IT IS TIME TO SURRENDER?

28.

I sit up as my alarm rings. The anger management brochure is ripped up and lies in pieces all over the floor.

I quickly pick it all up, throwing the words in the bin. I can make out some of them, in pieces: *stress, rejections, frustration, looking for a connection, hunger, fatigue.*

I rush to get ready. Mum is flustered, running late as well, but Manly Steve is not there. He has an early meeting.

'Lunch money on the counter,' she says as she flies out the door. 'Don't be late.'

I get dressed in the clothes I wore yesterday — black jeans, black hoodie, cap (yes clean underwear) and leave the house. But I do make it on time. Small success.

Nina actually comes to find me at break time, and we sit together to eat lunch. That's a first. She has her friend Sylvie with her.

'Can we join you?' she asks and waits patiently for an answer, like I would say no.

'Sure,' I say.

She shares her chocolate chip cookies with us. She made them herself. She is such an overachiever. 'They are gluten-free, sugar-free and dairy-free,' she says.

'They are delicious,' I say, although they are a tiny bit taste-free as well. 'What are you two up to tonight?' I ask.

'Sylvie's coming to stay at mine, should be fun.' Nina smiles. 'You?'

I ignore the question, because the answer is *absolutely nothing*. 'You think you will get any sleep?'

They look at each other and giggle. 'Probably not.'

That evening, I finally get my first text from Nina.

Hey what you up to? Nina

My heart skips a beat when I see an unfamiliar number come up and her name at the end of the text. Finally. I'd started to think I was never going to get one.

Nothing much – U?

There is no reply for about ten minutes. It's one of the longest ten minutes of my life.

S and I are watching a movie. Bit naff though 😁

What movie? 🙂

There is no reply for another ten minutes. SO painful. I'm tired but I don't want to miss her reply.

Too embarrassed to say. Night JRW 😴

Goodnight Frankton-Forbes

I don't get any more texts from her. All weekend I check my

phone and think about texting her, but I have this thought, that maybe she's laughing at me, with her friend. Or do they just feel sorry for me?

Saturday is no fun. Mum gets annoyed at me again because I don't want to go for a bush walk with her and Manly Steve. It sounds naff to me, stuck in the bush with them! No thanks. They are gone for the whole day and while I enjoy the house to myself for a bit, I search the cupboards and find nothing interesting to eat and channel-flick and find nothing interesting to watch. Maybe I should have gone? They would have at least bought me ice cream.

I start watching this documentary about the world's scariest volcanoes. I am initially relieved to know that the volcano only kilometres from my house, Rangitoto, is not on the list but then I start thinking of the volcano I feel inside. All the little bits of wood being thrown into the fire beneath it. I try to bring my thoughts to good things: Nina's emojis, the exhibition, the phone calls with my dad. I try.

But they catch fire too.

Mum and Manly Steve come home from their walk.

'You should have come,' Mum says. But when I look at Manly Steve, I know he's glad I didn't.

'Did you get me some food?' I ask.

'No.'

The rest of the weekend is boring and uneventful. Like they usually are.

'Why don't you two go to a movie, or go bowling?' Mum asks me and Manly Steve on Sunday afternoon.

'Nah,' I say, just as Manly Steve says, 'I have a bit of work to catch up on.'

29.

Monday morning and I have to try to get myself motivated for school, but I feel like I'm dragging my feet around.

Mum leaves first after waking me early and giving me a lecture about being on time. I am determined to be on schedule, even without the lecture. I struggle my way through getting ready and try to leave the house early. But Manly Steve is clearly in a bad mood again.

Elise's news still hasn't 'settled in' as Mum keeps saying it will. He yells at me as I'm walking out the door, says I have taken his phone charger from the kitchen. 'Where the hell is it, Jasper?'

'I have no idea. You should look after it.'

'What did you say?'

'I said you should look after your charger. I don't know where it is.' I'm tying my shoelaces on the front steps when he comes to stand above me.

'Quit it with the attitude, Jasper. I left it in the lounge. And it's gone, can you check your room?'

'I know it's not there and I want to be on time for school.'

'I'll check your room.'

He can't go in there. Holes. Mess.

'No! Don't go into my room. Fine, I'll check.'

I rush to my room, slamming the door behind me. My heart racing. How dare he? How dare he accuse me of something I didn't do? I look around my room.

And I see it.

I see two chargers by my power plug. Mine. And his.

Shit balls.

I put it outside my door. 'It was an accident,' I yell.

I hear thumping footsteps down the hallway.

'Jasper, you need to apologise.'

'Sorry!' I snap.

'What the hell is wrong with you?' More thumping steps and a door slam.

I don't know how that happened. But it was a mistake. NOW I'M ANGRY TOO! I have a thunderstorm inside me. He probably planted his dumb charger in my room to make me look bad. I wouldn't put it past him.

Sabotage.

What the hell is wrong with me? His sentence echoes in my head as I walk to school. I don't want to hear that. Now I feel like I want to destroy something. And Dad says this anger is okay? How can this be okay? How can this awful feeling that makes me feel like I might explode be 'okay'?

I am not okay. I'm in a bad mood and now it's probably going to be like that for the whole day. That is how bad moods work for me: impossible to shift. I am a simmering kettle about to boil, a washing machine on its final spin cycle, a 747 waiting to take off down the runway. I want to get rid of this anger somehow.

I am ready to explode.

It is no surprise that I do.

Leo Fulham. It is his fault too. He had to mess with me. Today of all days. The day I get accused of theft and accidentally committed it.

I make it to school on time, somehow, but I notice him everywhere. He crosses my path and smirks that dumb smirk; he bumps my bag as we walk out of assembly; he nudges in front of me in the tuck-shop queue. His smug smile is everywhere I look. No matter how hard I try to avoid him and his glaring eyes, they are on me.

So when he mouths 'Weirdo' at me as I cross the corridor, my kettle finally boils, my spin cycle concludes. And I explode.

'Why? Why are you doing this?' I yell at him across the corridor. My voice echoes.

'What did you say, Weirdo? Did I hear you talk? I didn't know you could.' He takes a step towards me.

'Leave me alone!'

'Did everyone hear that? Little Weirdo here wants to be left alone.' He looks around. 'Luckily you're always alone because no one likes you.'

'No one likes *you*, Leo!' I shout.

A few people hear what's going on and start to gather around. I don't care. I feel the heat in my body. My chest is tight and my fists clenched. And I can hear a grumbling sound, gravelly and low. Like an engine stirring.

Leo takes another step towards me. He's angry too. His kettle has boiled over too, but I don't care. I don't care anymore. This is the problem.

I don't care.

I should walk away, turn and walk away. Why don't I? Instead, I think I will have a conversation with someone who has always made me feel like I am nothing. 'What is your problem? Why do you always do this to me?' I yell as he takes yet another step towards me.

He is right in front of me now. And the sound is still there. Like thunder moving closer. Can anyone else hear it? A growling sound.

No, no, Bear, not now. Any time but now.

Leo leans towards me. 'I haven't got a problem. You have a problem. You have a serious weirdo problem, Jasper Robinson-Weirdo-Woods.'

I know He is coming for me.

No longer do I care about Leo Fulham; he is the least of my worries. I stop looking at him in that moment and my eyes go to the floor as I feel Him approach. The bear. He walks slowly with heavy, thunderous steps. I can feel Him through the ground, through my sneakers, up into my legs and inside my veins. My heart races. My feet tingle and my throat tightens.

'Not now,' I say in a whisper.

'Not now?' says Leo. 'What are you on about, Weirdo?'

I close my eyes and wait.

I give up. This time I won't run. This time He can have me. I don't care anymore.

You win, bear. You can have me. The time is now.

I surrender to you.

I SURRENDER

I feel His hot breath as it brushes across my arm. This is it. I open my eyes, ready to see Him. Ready to finally let him have me.

I can't fight this any longer.

But the bear has gone.

The feeling has not.

'What the hell is wrong with you, Weirdo?' Leo is still here too.

I don't want to be called Weirdo one more time. I have had enough. Now it is me who bares my teeth at Leo. I am the one who wants to destroy something. My own thunderous footsteps charge forward. In that moment Leo senses it and his face changes. His stupid smile drops and he takes a step backwards. But it's too late.

30.

I'm in the principal's office and my mother is on her way.

Leo is down the hall in the nurse's room. I have been told to sit quietly until my mother arrives. It takes her one hour. It is a long hour.

Tick. Tick. Tick.

60:00.

The soundtrack is solemn and slow. Like a funeral march once again. My funeral perhaps. Mum finally enters the room, still in work scrubs. She looks like she has been to the funeral and heard the march. Her face is lined. Her eyes are dark. She doesn't even look at me.

'Kia ora, Michelle, thank you for coming in. I wish it was on better terms,' the principal says, turning his face to mine.

'What happened?' I can tell her heart is beating fast. She sits in the empty chair. The same one she sat in last time.

'Would you like to tell your mother what happened, Jasper?' Mr Taumata says, looking at me.

'I don't know,' I say, looking down.

'You don't know?' he says, suspicious.

'Jesus, Jasper,' Mum says, crossing one leg over the other. Tightly. And controlled.

'Don't remember.' I look at the floor and pull my sleeves down.

'Jasper, that isn't a valid answer here. I'm sure you can remember.' Mr Taumata leans back into his chair.

I remember the start of it. Leo Fulham. The bear. I remember that. But I don't know what happened after. I remember thinking the bear was there to get me. But He disappeared. And I am still alive.

'You are suspended for five days from school, Jasper, for attacking a fellow pupil today.'

'You did what?' My mother's eyes burn into the side of my head. 'Oh my god. Are they okay?' She looks at Mr Taumata.

'The student is in the nurse's room. He is hurt. His parents are on their way. I hope you spend the next few days thinking about your choices today, Jasper.'

They both stare at me, I say nothing.

'Violence is never the answer,' Mr Taumata continues. 'You are only welcome back to this school if this kind of behaviour is NEVER seen again. Do you understand?'

'I understand.' But I still don't remember.

'Jasper! I have no words. No words,' Mum says as we walk out of the school office.

'Leo Fulham has been horrible to me for years, Mum, Leo is such a . . .'

'Stop. You have been *suspended* from school. It doesn't matter what your justification is. You have hurt someone and that's not okay. You can't behave this way.'

'He deserved it.'

She scoffs but doesn't reply. We have a quiet and awkward drive home. Once again, I'm the baddie. For finally standing up for myself. Bad. Bad. Jasper.

Five long days at home. Here I was thinking I shouldn't take time off school to hang out with my dad because school is so important. And now school is making me take time off for finally standing up to someone who has bullied me for years. I don't understand the world sometimes.

We go inside the house. Mum ignores me. I make myself a sandwich and then close my bedroom door. Close her away. I don't want to talk to her either. She goes back to work. And I wait. I wait for Him to return. Surely He will come now. I have surrendered. He will come to claim his prize.

I wait.

And I wait.

And I wait.

But He doesn't come.

It is almost disappointing. I feel numb. I'm supposed to reflect on my behaviour while on suspension. How do you do that? There was a bear, then He was gone. And Leo got hurt. Then it was just me. I'm reflecting on that.

The bear was gone.

And Leo got hurt.
I reflect on something I have probably known all along.
There is no bear.
There is only me.

WHO AM I?
I AM YOUR DARKNESS
AND YOU ARE MINE
WE ARE ONE
YOU WERE SCARED OF ME
IT WAS YOURSELF YOU NEEDED TO FEAR

31.

Day one. There is nothing to do already.

There is nothing good on television. There is nothing nice in the fridge. There is no one to talk to. This is going to be torturous.

I hate this house. I attempt a few texts to Nina but delete them. She's probably heard what happened. She won't want to talk to me. Even Mum left this morning without talking to me. I look through a cookbook, thinking maybe I will make chocolate brownie but we don't have flour in the cupboard so I play FIFA instead. I lose the penalty shootout.

The day drags slowly. At 3.45 p.m. there is a knock at the door. And it's her. It's Nina. 'Hi.' I stand at the door, realising then that I'm still in my pyjamas. 'What are you doing here?'

'Thought I'd come say hi,' she says.

'I am so bored, it's nice to see you. Come in.'

We walk down the hallway to the lounge. Nina is in my house!

'Hungry?' I look in the cupboard, even though I have looked fifty-one times already and found nothing. 'But there is no food in the house. Can of spaghetti? Water?'

'No, it's fine.' Nina opens her bag and passes me a sheet. 'Maria wanted to give you these, some drawing exercises she thought you could do. This week.'

I take the paper but don't look at it. 'So, you heard what happened?' I ask.

'I saw it,' she says, quietly. 'Actually.'

She saw it? I didn't see her there at the time. I was kind of distracted.

'I can't really remember what happened,' I say. 'I kinda blacked out, it's super-weird.'

'You were so . . . angry. You lost it. It wasn't nice.'

There is silence for a few moments.

'Do you know what happened to Leo?' I ask.

'He wasn't at school today,' she replies, putting her bag over her shoulder. 'You shouldn't have done that, Jasper.'

'I know. It's only . . . I've known Leo since primary school, and he always says stuff to me. I'd had enough. He's a horrible person.'

'You didn't look like a nice person either. I better go . . .' She heads for the door.

'Why don't you stay and hang out?' I ask, following her down the hallway.

'I have to get home.' She opens the door and leaves quickly.

'Monopoly?' I say, but she leaves without looking me in the eye.

She is scared of me.

Mum won't look me in the eye either. At dinner, she moves food around her plate with her fork.

Manly Steve is weird too. He is wanting to say something, I can tell. Finally he says it: 'That kind of behaviour is not welcome in this house.'

'What, MY house?' I knew this was coming.

'It's MY house too now, mate.'

'Please, you two . . .' Mum says, but looks out the window. 'Jasper knows that wasn't okay. It will never happen again. Will it, Jasper?'

I say nothing.

'Don't think you can mope around this house for the whole week making a mess and . . .'

'Please, Steven, can we eat our dinner?' Mum interrupts. Honestly, he can't stop himself!

So we sit in silence.

Home sweet home.

I go to my room, but I can hear Manly Steve on the phone for ages. I assume it's Elise. After he hangs up, he goes to the lounge and talks to Mum. I open my door so I can hear.

'There goes her degree and her career.'

'Is she going to stay in Wellington, do you think?' Mum asks.

'She has no idea what she's going to do because she has no idea what having a baby is like!'

'We can help her out, can't we?'

'Oh, she will be putting her hand out for money, no doubt.'

What a dickhead.

I don't get out of bed for two days. There is no point. I spend my daytime hours watching Netflix and eating peanut butter sandwiches. I'm not sure what else you are supposed to do on suspension. A few teachers email me work and I attempt to do some revision, but it's hard when you're not at school. I haven't heard from Nina either. I decide to text her.

How was your day? JRW

But she doesn't reply. She has probably deleted my number.

Time feels like it's getting slower. Five days at home is feeling like a lifetime. The weekend comes but I feel trapped inside for that too because Mum resents me so much.

On day four of the suspension, I watch so much television

that my eyes hurt and I feel like crap. I try to read a book but the words blur together.

When Mum comes home, she sits at the end of my bed.

'Good book?' she asks.

'Not really.'

'Did you get out of bed today? Did you do any schoolwork?' She looks around the room, taking in the mess.

'Yes. And all of it,' I lie.

'Good. Steven is going to fly Elise up so he can talk through her options this week, okay?'

'To persuade her not to have the baby?' I say, closing the book.

'It's not that, Jasper. She will need a lot of support.' Mum stands, walks towards the door.

'Yeah, as long as he lets her decide for herself.'

'Yes, Jasper.' She sits back down on the bed and rubs her forehead like she's trying to rub a headache away.

'What's wrong?' I ask.

'I'm tired. And to be honest, sometimes I feel stuck in the middle between you and Steven.'

'He hates me, Mum. It's obvious.'

'He does not. I'm worried about you, Jasper.'

'I'll be back at school soon.' I lie down and pull the covers over me.

'And will I be getting a call because you've been expelled? If it happens again, Jasper, you know they will expel you?'

'It won't happen again,' I say. 'It won't.'

'Are you angry that Steven lives with us now? Is this what

all this is about? Do you wish your dad and I were still together or something?'

'Sometimes. But sometimes not.'

'I get that it's sad for you, that everything changed.'

'Why were you so unhappy with Dad? Was it anything to do with me?'

'You? No, 'course not.'

I figure I must have been part of the problem somehow.

It's my last day of suspension. I finally look at the sheet Nina brought around, from Maria. It is hand-written.

> Hi Jasper
> Keep drawing this week! Here are some daily drawing exercises. Come and show me when you get back to school.
> See you soon.
> Maria

There's a list of drawing tasks for the week. I really should have looked at this earlier. I grab a sketch book from my desk and a pencil.

Exercise one: Draw something you can see out your window.

I look out the window. I see the side of the neighbour's house. But if I open my window I can see out to the front garden. I see my tree. I start sketching.

DRAW: <u>SOMETHING OUT YOUR WINDOW</u>

As I start to draw the grass, I notice Princess has already been past. There's a big pile of dog poo sitting there. Thanks, Mr Schultz. I won't draw that though. I figure I'd better do the other day's sketches too. So it looks like I did what I was told.

Exercise two: Draw an object in your room.

DRAW: <u>AN OBJECT IN YOUR ROOM</u>

Exercise three: Draw your favourite shoe.

Exercise four: Draw yourself with your non-dominant hand.

Exercise five: Draw your hand.

Manly Steve is working from home. I go out into the kitchen to get some breakfast and I'm greeted by him in a shocker of a mood.

'I left a whole heap of important documents on the table, where did you put them?'

'I didn't see them,' I reply, putting bread in the toaster.

'They were right here! You are the only person in the house, Jasper. Where are they?' He storms around moving piles of books and paper.

'I didn't put them anywhere. I've just got up.' I don't know what he is talking about and have no recollection of seeing any important documents.

'For god's sake, Jasper. They can't have disappeared on their own.'

I go to the lounge, turn on the television. He continues huffing and puffing.

'Turn that off, Jasper, I'm trying to work.'

I leave the toast and go back to my room. I put some music on.

'Turn that off, Jasper, I can't hear myself think,' I hear through my slightly open door.

I slam it shut. I hide in my room as long as possible. This is actually making school seem fun.

When my hunger takes over, I go back to get snacks. But the noise of my breathing seems to upset him.

'Can you stop clanging and banging around, Jasper?'

'Would you like me not to be here?' I say, to an open fridge.

'Beg your pardon?' He comes to stand behind me.

'I can't do anything right.' I slam the fridge shut and storm down the hallway, slamming the front door as I leave the house. MY HOUSE! Where I want to watch MY television and listen to MY music in MY room and eat MY food in MY kitchen!

I walk around the block, MY block, thinking about all MY things in MY house and how I don't even feel like it's MY home anymore. For about ten minutes I stand outside, staring at my house, my tree in the garden. The house doesn't look the same anymore.

It looked different once Dad left, when it was just Mum and me there. And now it looks different again with him here.

I sneak quietly back inside and I stay in my room, listening to music (using my earphones). Luckily I find a muesli bar in my bag from last week. I don't know how much time passes but soon Mum knocks on the door and barges in.

'Jasper, what are you doing?'

'Listening to music with these, thanks to your boyfriend,' I say, taking the earphones out of my ears.

'Steven says you have been really rude today.'

I roll my eyes. 'So has he.'

Mum launches into a big lesson on politeness but I don't listen. Then she tells me that she and Manly Steve are going to go out for dinner.

'Where? Can I come? I haven't eaten all day.'

'No, we won't be long. We have some things to talk about but there are leftovers in the fridge.'

Oh great, that sounds fair. They go out for a nice dinner and it's leftovers for me.

'I hope they spit in his dinner,' I say faintly as she walks out.

'What?'

'I said have a nice dinner.'

When they finally leave, I make my way out of my hiding place into MY house and finally eat something. Leftovers! I put some music on the highest it can go. It hurts my ears and I feel the bass right through me and I dance around the house LIKE I OWN THE PLACE, which I kind of do!

DOFF. DOFF. DOFF.

The bass is loud and thumping.

But it's not making me feel any less angry. Instead it's like an electric charge. I dance past the bathroom and catch a glance of myself in the mirror. I go in and stand in front of the mirror. I stare at myself.

I don't like what I see.

The music thuds through the floor. I have stuffed everything up. Nina is never going to forgive me. My mother hates me; so does Manly Steve. I've mucked everything up with my dad. Why bother trying not to be angry . . . when I AM!

I AM ANGRY AT EVERYONE!

I AM ANGRY AT MYSELF!

WHY DO I HAVE TO FEEL LIKE THIS?

WHEN.
WILL.
IT.
STOP?

Is this me forever? I stare at my reflection for what seems like an eternity and then I realise who I am staring at. It's not me.

It is Him.

I bare my teeth. He bares His.

I growl. He growls.

I clench my fist. He clenches His sharp, clawed paws.

I knew it was inevitable, I suppose. I knew He would come and it would be the beginning of the end, the end of me. I hadn't realised I would become Him.

WHO AM I?
I AM YOU
YOU ARE ME
YOU ARE THE DESTRUCTION
YOU ARE THE DARKNESS
IT IS TIME TO SHOW THE WORLD

32.

How dare Steve make me feel this way, like I don't belong in my own house? Like everything is my fault.

I wish he was here so I could show him how much I hate him. I want to hurt him. I want to destroy him. I want to show him how bad he makes me feel.

How can I show him how much I hate him?

I walk down the hall and I see it. I see that dumb painting. One of the first signs he was making his way into our lives and intending to stay. It does not belong here. He does not belong here. I rip the painting off the wall and throw it as hard as I can on to the floor. The wooden framing hits the ground hard, and it bends out of shape.

Destroy more, Jasper, He tells me.

I pick it up again and throw it down the hallway. This time, the wooden framing snaps. I walk to it and pull hard at the canvas to rip it from the framing. I use my claws to rip it into shreds.

Maybe now he will know how much I hate him.

Maybe now they will see how I feel. How much anger is inside me.

And I remember doing it all.

I remember.

For a moment, it feels better. I feel better. I see the broken painting and feel great. I was Him. I was angry, filled with hatred and I wanted to destroy! Who am I trying to kid? This is me and I can't hide it away. Sometimes it feels good to finally release all the rage.

For a moment.

For a short moment.

It feels good.

But as I turn away from the broken frame, I remember that look Nina gave me — the *I am scared of you* look. And I don't want to be that person anymore. I said I had changed. I thought I could change. I lied to my mother.

I failed.

I send Mum a text.

I messed up

One minute later:

What's wrong? What did you do?

I reply.

You will see

19:12.

Nineteen minutes and twelve seconds later they are home. I hear them come in the front door.

'Jasper!' Mum yells. She comes into my room, her face in fear. 'What's wrong?'

Moments later I hear Manly Steve.

'Where is he? Where the hell is he?'

Mum rushes out of my room. And I wait.

'No, Steven. No! Do not go in that room. No!'

The front door slams. The house shakes and I hear movement in the hallway, Mum is picking up the broken painting.

'No. No. No,' she says, breathless.

I hear her lean it against the wall. I step out into the hallway, which is littered with torn pieces of the painting.

Mum sits outside my room and puts her head in her hands.

'Why, Jasper? Why on earth would you do that?'

'I hate him, Mum. I hate him.'

'Don't say that, Jasper.' She can't look at me.

'I do. And I hate myself.'

'Please don't say these things.'

'I can't live like this anymore, Mum. I can't.' I collapse down next to her.

She starts to cry. Before long she can't talk, there are too many tears. I thought she was going to be angry, but she is too sad to be angry. I have left her broken. I can't bear it any longer.

I can't bear it. I can't *bear* me.

I don't see Manly Steve in the morning. My mother is at the kitchen table staring at a cup of tea. She tells me he has

gone to stay somewhere else for a bit.

I should be happy, but I feel awful. I thought that's what I wanted? Him gone.

'He is absolutely beside himself, Jasper. I don't know if you know what you've done.' She still can't look at me.

'It was a painting, Mum, he'll get over it,' I say, sitting down at the table.

'No, Jasper. No, it wasn't just a painting, it was his wife's. It was Elise's mum's. She painted it for her family before she died. It was hers.'

I see the figure standing on the clouds. Elise's mum. 'Why didn't you tell me?'

'You were sad when I told you about Elise's mother. I didn't want you to be sad every time you saw it.'

'You don't tell me anything. You think I can't handle it but then I stuff up, because I don't know things! No one talks to me about anything and now I feel like crap.' I put my head into my hands.

'You should, Jasper!' She yells across the table. 'It doesn't matter who painted it. You shouldn't have ruined it. Imagine if I did that to your art?'

I don't know what to say to that. I would be pissed, I know that. Even putting my art in the box in the garage upset me. And now Elise . . . I remember that day she told me about the jumper she wears and how she doesn't have much from her mother. She is going to hate me. I didn't know it was her mother's. I didn't. I know how I felt when Manly Steve wanted to throw Nana and Poppa's couch out and how hard that was. And now it is my turn. I hit my hand into the side of my head, again and again.

'Don't, Jasper. Stop that!'

'Mum, I'm sorry. I'm so sorry. I hate myself sometimes.'

'Please don't say that anymore, Jasper. Don't.' She comes around the table and sits down next to me.

'But it's true, Mum.'

'Okay, look.' She puts a hand on my shoulder. 'I'm sorry you feel so angry, but we can't keep doing this. Things have to change.'

I nod. It's true.

'I haven't been listening, I'm sorry, Jasper. I need to talk to you more, I need to have those big conversations.'

'It's my fault.' I put my head down onto the table.

'You asked for help last night, I want to help. Please let me help. I want us all to be a family, Jasper, I do. That's all I want for you. For us.'

Family. A family? I remember the picture I drew as a child, now in the box in the garage. My parents and me, together. I miss that.

'It's just hard, Mum,' I say, and she grabs my hand.

'Why won't you go to the school counsellor?'

'Because it won't help,' I reply.

'Maybe it will, Jasper. How will you know if you don't try?' She squeezes my hand tight.

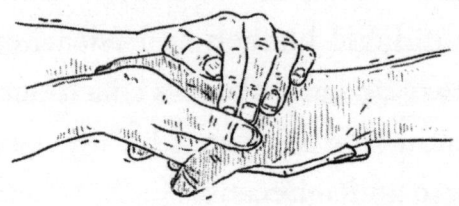

I'm back at school. And now I'm that guy: the guy who got suspended. It's a horrible feeling. Everyone is looking at me differently. People talk about me in whispers as I pass them. And Leo Fulham won't look me in the eye: that's one good thing, I suppose. Nina won't talk to me either, not like before anyway. I try to talk to her as she's walking ahead of me.

'Nina. Wait up.'

She turns around, but I can tell she doesn't want to see me.

'Oh. It's you.'

'I'm back.'

'Seems that way.' She turns away from me.

'Nina. That stuff with Leo, it won't happen again,' I say to her back.

'Won't it?' She turns around. 'I heard about Emily Molloy.'

The ball. The nose. The blood.

I walk home alone. When I get there, I'm up the tree. There is no bear to hide from now. I almost wish there was, then I wouldn't be hiding from myself. Everyone is clearly talking about me, probably saying how I have problems, I'm messed up and Nina should avoid me. Do I have problems? Am I the only one?

Maybe I can make this better, maybe I can go and talk to someone? What's to lose? I've lost so much anyway and maybe if I could go and see the school counsellor, Nina will know I want to change. Because I'm trying. She will forgive me, and everything will be okay. I hope.

I go inside. Manly Steve still isn't staying at the house, and I don't know where he is. I heard Mum talking to him on the phone last night, in her room, but she hasn't talked about him to me. I've asked where he is, but she always gives the same answer: 'He's taking some time away.'

When Mum gets home from work, I tell her. 'I'll go and see the school counsellor.'

She smiles. 'See what it's like, Jasper. See what he has to say.'

33.

I find the counsellor's email address on the school website and he emails me back with an appointment time for the next day. I can't change my mind now. It's done. My heart races at the thought of it. I'm nervous that it's going to be super-weird leaving class for the appointment, that my teacher will say: 'Jasper, it's time for your appointment because you're so messed up, so you'd better hurry up and go and try to sort your life out.'

But it's not like that at all. I pack up my stuff and the teacher nods in my direction. Students actually do this all the time, and I had no idea that's where they were going.

Callum Hughes is different to how I imagined he'd be. He is different from the other teachers at school: he talks more quietly.

As I sit down, Callum sits too and lifts his right leg over

his left. As he does, his brown pants reveal brown socks, with brown shoes. It all sort of matches his beard. I wonder if when I am an adult I will wear all shades of brown.

'Welcome, Jasper,' he says with a warm smile. 'Good to meet you.'

Nothing much happens for the first appointment. He talks through what the 'process' is and how often I will see him. He tells me the things we talk about are confidential but sometimes he talks to a supervisor about the work he does and how he might be able to help his students. He won't talk to my mother unless he is worried about my safety. He says that his job is to listen and that he won't judge me.

We'll see about that.

'Do you have any questions, Jasper?' He leans forward to grab a pair of glasses then slides them on. I can't work out how old he is. He could be mid-twenties or mid-fifties. It's impossible to tell.

I shake my head.

'Is there anything you would like to tell me about why you're here today?'

I shake my head again.

He leans forward again and rests his chin in his hand. 'This is your time, Jasper. You let me know when you do want to tell me.'

I can't see that happening, but you never know.

'Can I ask you about sleep, Jasper? How is your sleep?'

'Pretty bad . . .'

'How many hours a night are we talking?' he asks, readjusting his glasses.

'I dunno. Sometimes I don't feel like I sleep at all.'

There were those twenty-eight days. Then the nightmare.

'That's no good. We need to sort that out, Jasper. Sleep is important. When did that start? The not-sleeping?'

'A while back.' The bear. Manly Steve. Dying fish. Bear. Bear. Bear.

He gives me some tips on sleep, not using screens in the evenings and telling myself it's time for sleep, not time for thinking, or worrying.

I worry I might not be able to do that.

We finish the session. I said a total of about fifteen words. But it wasn't too bad.

'Well, we'll leave it there for now. I look forward to seeing you again soon, Jasper.' He stands and walks towards the door and smiles. 'Have a good rest of the day.'

That night, I think and think and think about not thinking. I think about not sleeping. I tell myself it's not time to worry, it's time for sleep. And then I remember the exhibition is supposed to be tomorrow night and I have no idea if we are even going to go.

Somehow, at some point, I sleep.

We haven't seen Manly Steve for three days. I'm beginning to think, *Here we go, here is another person who can't live with me. I am impossible. See?*

Mum mopes about too and hardly talks to me. Clearly, I've destroyed another of her relationships. Whenever I walk down the hallway, I see the empty hook where that painting was and my heart hurts. It hurts.

I wonder if he has told Elise. She must know. I dreamt of her the other night. She'd had her baby: it was a fish. A small fish but she held it and loved it like a real baby.

Just when I think Manly Steve is never coming back, he does.

It's the night of the exhibition.

I come out of my room, and he is sitting at the table in front of me, without words. He nods his head in my direction. I told Mum I would apologise when he came home and he's home. I just don't know how I'm supposed to do it.

I sit at the table.

'Hi,' I say.

'Hi, Jasper.'

I shuffle in my seat. 'I'm really sorry,' I say, looking down at my hands. 'I feel so awful about the painting, more than I can say. I know you hate me now.'

'I don't hate you, Jasper,' he says. He leans back into his chair and looks out the window. In a quieter voice than I'm used to he says, 'I'm upset, but I don't hate you.' His eyes move to mine. 'And I'm sorry too. You've had some big changes lately and I've been under a lot of stress. I haven't been patient with you.'

'It's okay.'

'Thanks for saying sorry.' He shuffles in his seat too and then taps his fingers on the table. 'We should get ready for your exhibition,' he says and then stands, pushing his chair in.

'Are we going?' I ask, as I stand too.

'Of course we are. Your mother is due home any minute. I want to go and see your art.'

And he leaves the room. 'Go get ready.'

I have a shower and get dressed in jeans and a vaguely nice T-shirt, even though it's been at the bottom of my drawer and smells musty. While I'm getting dressed, I think of Leo Fulham. I think one day I'm going to have to apologise to him too. And Emily Molloy.

I stare at my cap, trying to work out whether to wear it or not. I decide not to. Manly Steve will tell me off: 'Caps aren't for indoors.' We have an early dinner of hash browns and scrambled eggs.

'Okay team,' Mum says, coming out of the bathroom putting on earrings. 'Let's go!'

Manly Steve is even wearing his fancy business jacket. Maybe I should put a buttoned shirt on? Do I even own a buttoned shirt? I don't think so.

We drive to the convention centre in silence. As we approach, the crowds going inside make my heart race. I hope my art is not the worst. Inside we see rows of artwork and lots of families gathered around. Students are proudly showing their families their work. I search for mine, but I can't see it. Maybe there was some mistake and it's not here. We walk up and down the aisles.

'There is some impressive artwork, isn't there?' says Mum.

'A very high standard,' says Manly Steve.

'Mine's not here,' I say.

But then I see it. A man is standing in front of it with a glass of orange juice in his hand. He's probably thinking: 'Which weird kid drew this nonsense?'

'Oh, there it is,' I say quietly, pointing momentarily and immediately wanting to find a corner to hide.

Mum goes up close and the man moves aside. 'Sorry,' she says. 'This is my son's work.'

The man smiles at me and moves to the next piece of art. Mum puts her hand on my back. 'Jasper ...' she says, then goes silent. I don't know what this means. Is she impressed? Or mortified? Could be either. But then she says: 'It's amazing.'

'Not really. I rushed it.'

'It is incredible. Look at it, Steven.'

Manly Steve nods and smiles. 'It's really good, Jasper. Well done.'

Okay, that was unexpected. They like it.

Mum goes up even closer as if to step inside. 'But what does it mean? Who is that?' she asks, pointing to the bear. As if maybe it was meant to be her.

'Dunno.'

'That's how I felt when I was your age,' Manly Steve says,

taking a sip of his drink.

'Really?' I ask.

'Yep. You capture angry teenage boy well.'

I didn't realise that's what I was doing, but I will take the compliment.

'Is that what it's about?' Mum is confused. Desperate for her son to be explained.

'Jasper!' I turn to see Maria approaching us. She's out of her usual jeans and shirt and is wearing a bright-coloured jumpsuit which I know my mum will be jealous of. 'You made it! Isn't it fabulous?' she says to Mum and Manly Steve. 'You must be Jasper's parents.'

I interrupt. 'It's my mum and her ... Steven.'

'Hi Mum and Steven,' Maria smiles. 'I can't stop staring at this piece. I was so blown away. Jasper is extremely talented.'

'We think it's incredible,' says Mum, putting her arms around my shoulder. 'Are there many students from Havenside in the exhibition?'

'Only a few. Jasper was the only year nine though, he should be proud of himself. You should be proud. I can't wait to see what else he presents this year.' She gives me a big smile. 'Enjoy your evening.'

Mum watches her walk away.

'I wonder where she got that jumpsuit.'

Knew it.

We spend an hour at the exhibition. There are some speeches and a dude from a real estate agency gives out a few prizes. I don't win. But I'm glad because the winners have to go and get a certificate and a bunch of flowers. There is some quite impressive work on display and it turns out mine is not the weirdest at all. Turns out other teenagers *see* some crazy shit too. I keep looking out for Nina, but she's not here. I see a few faces I recognise from school, though. Manly Steve spends ages looking at some paintings.

When we get home, Mum makes us hot chocolate.

'I couldn't be prouder, Jasper,' she says. Although she probably doesn't mean it, considering I was recently suspended from school. 'What is it about?' she asks again; she can't let it go.

'Nothing much, Mum. I just drew it one day. I don't really know.'

'Well, you are very clever.'

That night I sleep well, actually sleep well. I'm relieved that no one thinks I'm totally nuts. In fact, no one asked about the bear at all, except Mum. And everyone felt proud of me and maybe I'm even a little proud of myself.

I see the counsellor again.

'Great to see you again, Jasper,' he says as I sit down. Maybe he thought I wouldn't come back.

'How's your day going?' he asks, playing with his closely shaven beard. I notice a few grey hairs on one side so maybe he isn't that young.

'Yep, good,' I reply, scratching the back of my neck even though it's not itchy. I'm just not sure what to do with my hands.

He's wearing the brown pants again but this time I can see his socks are black. He asks me if I've had any better sleep lately and I tell him I'm trying. I'm trying to sleep and not think all night.

'Things always seem worse at two a.m., don't they?' he says, watching my face for a reaction.

I give a slight laugh, nodding slightly.

'So, tell me a bit about yourself, Jasper.'

'Um . . .' I don't know what to say, there's nothing interesting about me.

'Who do you live with at home?'

I tell him about Mum, that she's a dental hygienist and I'm an only child. I tell him about Manly Steve moving in.

'How has that been for you, since he moved in? Must have been a big change.'

'I didn't want it at first, but I'm getting used to it, I suppose.' I'm not sure if this is correct but I will go with it.

'And your dad? Is he around?'

'Not much,' I reply. 'Not much at all.'

He nods, writing something down in his notebook. It feels quiet in this room with him. It's different to any other room in this school, with the teachers and the students and the expectations. Time is different here. The air smells different too, like orange essence or something, or maybe it's the little unlit candle on the table, I'm not sure.

'When do you see your dad?' he asks.

'He doesn't live in Auckland. We went away together for a few days recently though, but I hadn't seen him for ages.'

'How was that? Must have been nice?'

'Kind of . . .' Besides Han Solo, the bear and the destroyed house, it was *amazing*.

'Good to have some time with him though?'

I nod. Although it hardly felt like time with him. I hear voices as a class walks past the window on the way to the auditorium. I listen as the laughter fades, grateful for the lowered blinds.

'Tell me, what do you do to relax? What makes you feel happy?'

There it is again. That word. Happy.

I shrug. 'Why is everyone obsessed with being happy?'

He puts his pen down and looks up. 'Do you feel pressured to feel happy?'

'Dunno, I don't feel happy much.'

'When was the last time you did?' he asks. 'Or have you always struggled with that?'

I try to look back, back into my memories. School. Nana. Holidays. Road trips with Dad. I have to go so far back, so deep into those memories.

'A long time ago.' Maybe there have been moments. With Nina. With Elise. Snippets of happiness that flash for a moment. But they disappear quickly too.

'Happiness means something different to everyone,' Callum says. 'We can't feel happy all the time. It's not possible. Maybe we can feel content with our lives though?'

'I feel like everyone is happy but me. Like I'm doing something wrong, or like there's something wrong with me. Because I can't get there, you know?'

'I do know what you're saying. It sounds like it's a heavy word for you. Actually, growing up you start to realise life isn't about being happy, or sad, there's lots in between. Lots of different emotions. You're not doing anything wrong, Jasper.'

'Tell me more about living with your mother's new partner,' he says as leans back into his chair. 'It's a big adjustment for everyone I'm sure.'

'It was pretty bad for a while to be honest. We had a rough start.'

'When he moved in, is that when your sleeping got worse?' he asks, his voice soft. I notice how his manner makes me feel quiet too. Calmer. Not rushed.

'It was before that. My goldfish got sick. Now he's dead.'

DEAD.

'Oh, I'm sorry, Jasper, that was really tough, was it?'

'Yeah.' I look down at my hands and push my palms together.

'It's always hard to lose pets,' Callum says, nodding slowly.

Yes. Pets. And people.

34.

I am quietly walking on eggshells at home.

I don't want to get in any more trouble. But there is a new calm in our house. And then Elise arrives. Seeing her feels hard, something has been in the back of my mind the whole time. I know I have to apologise to her too.

I am in my room when she arrives. She knocks gently on the door. She looks different. She *is* different. 'Jasper, how are you?' She jumps into the room and sits on the bed. 'Okay if I come in?'

'You're already in.'

She laughs. At least I have cleaned my room in advance this time.

It's nice to see her again, to smell her rose-petal smell and hear her jingly jangly jewellery in the house. She must know about the painting, though, and she must hate me.

She looks around. 'No more Han Solo?'

'Yeah. No more Han Solo.'

'Sorry about that, Jasper. And I hear you got suspended.'

'Yeah . . . not good. I've been a bit of a dick lately.'

'I got suspended once,' she says, twirling her hair through her fingers. She laughs. 'For encouraging everyone at school assembly to wag and go to a protest march.'

'At assembly? Subtle.'

'No wonder I wasn't head girl.'

I laugh. I don't think I will be head boy either. Not that I want to be. There is a silence in the room, then I hear Elise breathe in sharply, then sigh.

'Elise?' I say and she looks over to me. 'Do you hate me? For the painting?'

She pulls her legs up onto the bed and sits cross-legged. 'Things have been tough, Jasper. I get it. You must wish Dad never moved in sometimes.'

'I didn't know it was your mum's painting. If I had known I would never have . . .'

She nods.

'Are there any other paintings?' I ask. 'Was that the only one?'

'There are a few in storage. Dad's going to give me some to take home with me. We talked about it.'

I sigh as a small weight lifts away.

'But that one, that was her watching over you, wasn't it? It always creeped me out.' Oh god. Why do I talk sometimes? 'Sorry. I shouldn't say that.'

'It's fine. Yeah, she painted it when she was sick. But I don't need a painting to remind me of her. I think of her every day. Like your nana and poppa, eh?' she asks, looking over to the couch. 'They kind of stay with us.'

I nod. 'Although they wouldn't like what they've seen lately. Not from me.'

'Everyone understands, Jasper. Being a teenager sucks sometimes. We all felt it when it was our turn. You've apologised, so we can move on, okay?'

How is she so nice? I don't deserve it.

'But you actually had good reason to find life hard though, with your mum,' I say. 'Why does this feel so hard for me? What's my excuse?'

'You don't need one. Feelings are just feelings. They can be overwhelming. My father can be a pain too, I know it. But you two actually might get on quite well, one day.'

'Maybe . . . How is it being pregnant?'

'I've been feeling a bit crap to be honest.' She leans back against the wall. 'I've spewed every morning this week.'

'Gross.' I have a spew-phobia. I feel like I can smell vomit.

'But I feel okay today. I can't wait to meet the baby.' She smiles, but it is a worried smile.

'Is it a boy or a girl?' I ask.

'A girl, but I haven't told Dad yet. So keep it quiet, okay? I will tell him while I'm here.'

'That's cool, Elise.'

A girl. A baby girl.

'I know.' She smiles.

I love how Elise talks to me. She doesn't talk to me as if I'm a kid. She talks to me like a friend.

Manly Steve is quiet at dinner time.

Elise eats meat, she really is different! 'It's for the baby. My iron levels. It's weird doing it though, meat is a strange texture.'

Tofu is a strange texture! But I don't bring this up.

'Jasper must be pregnant. He's been eating a lot of meat lately as well.' Mum laughs at her bad joke. 'Sorry . . .'

'A lot will change when you have a baby,' Manly Steve says. 'You just wait.'

'I know. I have thought about it all, Dad. I only want her to be healthy.' Elise looks to Manly Steve for his reaction. 'I'm going to do the best I can, okay?'

'Her?' He stops eating. 'It's too early to know that.'

'Actually, I had a weird thing happen last week. I was a bit worried so I had a scan to make sure nothing was wrong. It's a girl. They're pretty sure anyway, can't be a hundred percent. I do feel like it's a girl . . .'

Manly Steve takes a sip of wine. And gulps loudly.

'I know some girls my age aren't ready to become mothers, but Louis is doing an apprenticeship now and his parents want to help.' Elise looks at her dad again.

'We will help too,' he says.

Elise continues to watch her dad, with a burning light in her eyes. 'We are going to call her Kaia, Dad. After Mum.'

Manly Steve's hand shakes as he places his wine on the table. His eyes drop to his lap, and he squeezes his eyes shut.

He says nothing but gets up and leaves the table. I watch him turn and gaze back at Elise. She looks down to her lap and I realise how she must be missing family too.

Mum grabs Elise's hand across the table. 'That's such a lovely idea, Elise. I love the name, how special.'

After dinner, Manly Steve and Elise sit in the garden while Mum and I do the dishes.

'She's going to be a good mum, isn't she?' I say, flicking the tea towel around instead of drying dishes.

'She's going to be a lovely mum. She will need lots of support though, Jasper. Being a parent is not easy.'

'But we can help, can't we?'

'Yes, we can definitely help.'

I ask her why Manly Steve doesn't seem happy about the baby.

'Dads sometimes don't want their daughters to grow up too fast.'

What about their sons? Do dads not want their sons to grow up either?

In the morning, Manly Steve and Elise say they are going to the mall. They ask if I want to go. I have nothing else to do so I say yes.

'Is it too early to buy stuff for the baby, Dad?' Elise asks Manly Steve while we are in the car.

'I don't know. Probably.' But when we are at the mall, he buys a tiny pair of merino pyjamas. They are green with white stripes and a small owl on the front. On the way home, they are both quiet but Elise holds the pyjamas and looks at them, folding and refolding them and gently tracing the little owl with her fingers.

When we get home, Elise and I sit on the couch watching a documentary about sloths. The mother sloth carries its baby around on its chest, through the trees. Elise is quiet, still holding the pyjamas. I look over to her.

'Are you okay, Elise? Do you not like sloths?'

She squeezes her eyes shut to hold tears in. But they escape anyway. 'I love sloths.'

'So why are you crying? Shall I get your dad?'

'No, it's okay. I get teary sometimes. I hope I'm going to be a good mum.'

'You're going to be the best mum ever,' I say. This is maybe a bit over the top, but she gives me a big smile. 'Like the sloth mum.'

'Thanks, Jasper. That means a lot.'

We keep watching. Elise stares back at the little pyjamas and the tears roll down her cheeks. Mum comes in and sits down next to her.

'What's wrong, love?'

'I'm just emotional.'

Mum picks up Elise's hand and puts it on her own lap. 'We'll help you Elise, whatever you need. I will be there as much, or as little, as you want me to be, okay? And Jasper too.'

Mum looks at me and I nod. At that moment I'm so proud of my mum. I suppose families don't always look the way we expect them to.

Elise offers to make dinner. She makes a big spaghetti Bolognese. Apparently, it has something called lentils in it but I eat it anyway and it's actually really good. Manly Steve and I do the dishes and talk about *Star Wars*. He likes episode four the best. I prefer three but he says I make a good point as to why. Maybe we do have something in common.

After dinner, Elise comes and sits in my room again. I like her visits. She sits at my desk chair and looks over to me, like she has something to say.

'Everything okay?' she asks, playing with her earring.

'Yeah. Why?' I answer, sitting down on my bed.

'Oh, I wanted to say that you could talk to me about stuff, if you wanted? I think I would understand.'

'Thanks,' I say and smile, because it feels really nice to know that.

'Your mother tells me you're seeing the school counsellor.'

Thanks, Mum! Why don't you get it tattooed on my forehead while I'm asleep? 'Only a couple of times.'

Elise can tell I'm embarrassed. 'I saw one when I was your age, with all the stuff with Mum. Sometimes I still go and see her. I find it super-helpful.' She picks up my school magazine and flicks through it, but then puts it down. 'Sorry, I shouldn't look through your stuff.'

'It's all good. But thanks, that's nice to know. It's been helpful for me too. I'm just trying to get some help to stop . . . some of my thoughts.'

'Oh yeah. Thoughts. They can get out of control sometimes, can't they? Actually, one thing I've learnt is that thoughts aren't so much the problem, but what we do with them is our choice. I try not to attach too much meaning to them — thoughts are just thoughts. We can choose to ignore them. Anyway, I'm no expert or anything but if you ever wanna talk to me . . .' She writes her number down on a piece of paper on my desk. 'Here's my number. You could text. Or call. Anytime.'

Elise flies back to Wellington. I don't want her to go again. She tells me she'll be up in a few weeks and might even come and stay with us when the baby is born. With Louis, her boyfriend. Woah, a baby in the house, that would be crazy! Manly Steve seems happier since her visit. Maybe he is even a bit excited? He probably won't admit that for a while.

Once again, the house seems a lot quieter and way more boring without her in it, and her jewellery jingling.

35.

Nina still isn't talking to me.

She says hello if she's passing, but she doesn't engage in conversation. Her eyes jump away before I get a chance to say anything. And she doesn't walk home with me. She sees me and changes direction. I want to tell her I'm seeing the school counsellor, so she knows I'm doing something about . . . me. But how can I tell her if she won't talk to me? I can't yell it across the classroom or anything.

'Nina! I'm seeing the counsellor! Do you like me now?'

I could text her, I know. Or write it on a piece of a paper and hand it to her in class like they do in eighties movies. But what if someone else sees it and opens it? I don't think it's worth the risk. Plus, I don't think it's worthy of a written announcement, or even a text announcement.

At my next appointment with the counsellor, he asks me

what I enjoy doing on the weekends. I can't think of anything.

'I'm sure there's something. It's important to realise what makes us feel good, so that we can include those things in our day.'

I pick at my nails. He leans forward in his chair and asks me to keep thinking. I want to have something to say ...

I scratch the back of my head. 'Gaming. And I suppose I like to draw.'

'Draw? That's very cool.' He writes it down. 'Sketches? What kind of stuff?'

I think of the bear, yet ignore the question. 'I had something in an exhibition recently.'

'Amazing, Jasper,' he says, nodding. 'Well done, it must have felt great to share your art.'

'Nerve-wracking too,' I smile.

He laughs. 'Yes, I can imagine. We share a bit of ourselves through our art, don't we? And what do you do when you feel annoyed, or angry? Is there anything that helps? Or is that when you draw?'

'Dunno. Sometimes.' Climbing trees. Is that a valid answer?

'What have you done in the past when you were angry?'

'Punched holes in the wall.'

I have two days to finish my woodcut and it's starting to look slightly like a frog face. Maria keeps coming up beside me saying: 'Keep going. I see you under there, Jasper.'

Frog face? She sees me? Thanks!

At the end of class, she comes up to me as I'm packing my stuff away and asks: 'How did you go with the sketch exercises?'

'Oh, yeah . . . I did them.' I've been carrying them around in my school bag in case she asks. 'I have them here.' I open my bag and find the sketchbook, brushing the crumbs off it from my bag as I pass it to her. She sits down at one of the desks, opening the book, her hands still covered in paint from the day.

'Nice work, Jasper. These are excellent.'

I sit down next to her. 'Thanks, Maria. I kind of rushed them but it was good to have something to do.'

'You have such an eye for detail.' She looks at me and smiles. 'And light and shade. You are very talented. Who taught you to draw like this?'

I shrug. 'Just myself I suppose.'

She passes me back the book. 'Please keep drawing. I can give you more set exercises, if you like?'

'Thanks,' I say. 'That would be good actually.'

That night when I go to sleep, I don't see the bear. I have to fight Him away though, fight *me* away from my thoughts. Sometimes when I concentrate on good things it works. I imagine being friends with Nina again, Elise's baby girl and Maria saying I'm 'very talented'.

Then there's the counsellor. He wants to see some of my drawings, if I want to show him. I try to keep thinking of those things.

For a moment I see the bear. 'I'm not going away,' He says. But I fight back.

'Yes. Yes, you are!'

At school the next day I see Nina from a distance as I walk into the front gates. I wave at her. She quickly looks away and changes direction away from me. I swallow deeply and make my way into English class.

Halfway through I have another session with Callum Hughes.

It's not a good day to see him, I have nothing to say. We sit in silence for the entire session. It's a complete waste of time: I could have been finishing an essay in English class. He asks to see one of my drawings and I snap.

'I haven't got one.'

'Next time?'

All I can think is I don't want there to be a next time.

'Not in a talking mood, Jasper?'

'No.'

'That's okay. Is there anything you *do* want to talk about?'

'No. Can I go back to class?'

I wait for him to tell me off, but he nods. There is a gentleness to his eyes. 'Sure. I will see you next time.'

The next time I see him, I'm not really in a talking mood again but I remember why I'm there. And I stay. Callum seems to see it.

'Thanks for coming. Jasper, I'm glad you are here.'

I pick up a cushion from the couch and put it on my lap. I hear Callum take a slow breath and I slowly take one too.

'Tell me about your friends here at school,' he says.

'I don't have many,' I reply.

'What about out of school?'

'Not really, anymore.'

'That must be hard, Jasper.'

'No. It's fine.' I turn the cushion over, tracing the seam with my fingertip.

'You like it that way?' he asks.

'Yep.'

He watches me for a moment. As if trying to read me. I don't want him to say the word. But he goes and says it.

'That must be *lonely* at times, Jasper . . .'

Sometimes words feel like they hurt, worse than punches. Even worse than rocks thrown at you while you're up a tree.

And he sees that.

'Do you feel lonely sometimes?' He says it carefully.

'Sometimes. I did have a friend here, but she's not talking to me anymore . . .' My voice wavers. Dammit. 'She is scared of me.'

'Scared of you?'

'Because of how I used to be, too angry.'

'Too angry? Has she told you this?'

'I can tell.' I look out the window, then close my eyes for a moment, remembering her changes of direction. Her walking away.

'You're not angry anymore?' Callum asks. I look at him. His eyebrows are lifted.

'I'm trying not to be. She won't let me show her. She is avoiding me.'

'Can we talk about the things that make you angry, Jasper?' he asks, looking directly at me.

I shift in my seat. 'I don't really want to talk about them, it will make me angry again.'

'I get that, I do. But when we do, it helps us understand what's important to us. It will help me understand more about you,' he says. He rests his hands on his knees. 'I know these things are hard to talk about, maybe we can add that to our agenda for next time?'

'... Fine.'

I finish my woodcut. Maria was right — I was under there. I'm actually pleased with how it turned out. The whole class gathers around to admire it.

'It really looks like you,' Hannah, another girl in my class, says. Nina says nothing.

'Great work, Jasper,' Maria says and pats me on the shoulder. 'Let Jasper's work inspire the rest of you. We will start on our prints soon.'

Woah. I'm an inspiration. I try to be happy about it, but all week, all I can think about is Callum Hughes and the *agenda for next week*. What am I going to tell him? Anger has not helped me in any way and I don't want to go there. I don't want to think about those things. I've been trying to brainstorm all the plausible options. Maybe they will do? Angry with Mum, Manly Steve, my teachers? They are true. Angry about never getting to school on time? Having to tidy my room and pick up my towels? Angry about the essay I have to write on 'media stereotypes in teen films'? I didn't even watch the films I was supposed to. I mean, all these things do make me angry. It's all normal teenage stuff, isn't it? That should cover it. But they are little bits of kindling in the fire. Not the big logs that keep it burning.

My life. Burning.

36.

I hand the essay in. It's pretty terrible. I probably spelt many, many words wrong and added commas and capital letters in all the wrong places.

Nina still won't look at me, let alone talk to me. I arrive ten minutes late to my session with Callum Hughes, hoping that might mean we don't have time. But he gets out his notebook and reminds me about the 'agenda'. The what-makes-me-angry agenda. He waits, pen in hand.

I say: 'Oh that's right,' like I haven't been thinking about it all week. I tell him the plausible list of angry things. He writes them down, but he is on to me. 'Anything else?' he asks. Like he knows. He knows there is more.

'Can I ask you to think about something else? Can I ask you instead about the things that worry you?'

I pick at my nails. I pick up the candle from the table and

analyse it. I even smell it and it does smell like oranges.

'I know fears can be hard to talk about too,' he says, watching my hands move the candle around.

'I have a fear of talking to you,' I say, putting the candle down again then moving it to a new spot on the table.

He laughs. The first time I've heard him laugh. 'Fair enough. It's human to have worries, Jasper, I have lots too. Everyone does. When we begin to face them, those fears lose the power they have over us.'

There is silence for what seems like an eternity. I want the world to swallow me up. I know I'm scared — of lots of things. What doesn't scare me? This whole world scares me.

I can't tell him all those things, can I?

I start tapping on my knees, a song that doesn't exist.

'We can't always run away from what scares us. Sometimes we need to stop running, turn around and look it in the eye.'

I stop tapping. I don't know if I can do that. Can I stop

running from Him? I start to hold my breath.

Look Him in the eye? Those dark, terrifying eyes. Angry eyes.

I try really hard to keep it in, but I can't stop it. I will it to go back inside but it forces its way through, burning as it does.

A tear. In the corner of my eye. A hot, fiery tear. I push it away with my middle finger and itch my forehead to hide the fact it was there.

But he sees it. 'Are you scared, Jasper?'

'Yeah. Sometimes there are so many,' I say. 'I don't really know where . . .'

'Take your time.' A silence, then he says: 'Tell me the silliest, stupidest fears you have. The more ridiculous the better! Let's start there. I'm scared of toenails. Finding them on the bathroom floor or something. Don't get me started.'

I laugh. 'Yeah gross.'

'What about you?'

Where to start? 'Geese. Brussels sprouts. Public humiliation.' I try to laugh, but I think he knows they are actually for real. 'Feeling lonely . . . forever. Disappointing people. Losing people.' And for my father I add: 'Global warming.'

He nods. 'Those are all big and valid fears, Jasper. Losing people . . . Have you lost someone important to you?'

I nod as another fiery tear falls down my cheek. I leave this one to fall.

'My nana. And my poppa before that.'

'That's really hard, Jasper, losing your grandparents.'

I nod again.

'That grief can last a while. Maybe it will always be there, reminding you of how much they meant to you.'

'Yeah.' Tears are now a river down my cheek. It feels like I can't hide anymore, that there is no point because he can see it anyway. He can see me.

'I'm scared I'm not a good person, not good enough. That people don't want to be around me.'

He nods, his eyes telling me to keep going. 'Your dad leaving was hard, wasn't it?'

'If I was different, maybe he would have stayed. Sometimes it feels like I lost my dad too. Even though I didn't. He's still here.'

'But not really here? Not present?'

I nod.

'He's important to you. But Jasper, he didn't leave because of you. Lots of kids whose parents separate blame themselves. Or wonder if it's their fault. But it's not.'

'But he never came back. Well, hardly ever.'

'That's really tough, Jasper. And when your mother's partner moved in, did that scare you too?'

'Maybe. That I might lose my mum a little too.'

'It changes things, doesn't it? Between you and her?'

'He's always there.'

'And you still need her, don't you? And you miss your dad.'

'I hardly see him; he doesn't care about me.' It hurts to say it out loud. 'I don't want to turn into him.'

'Is that a bad thing? To be like him?'

'Yeah. We're different in lots of ways. But the same in others.'

'Okay . . . What ways are you like him?'

'The fact that I'm even here. That I even need to be here in the first place.'

I take something with me to my next session. A drawing. I keep it in my bag, in case I feel like showing him.

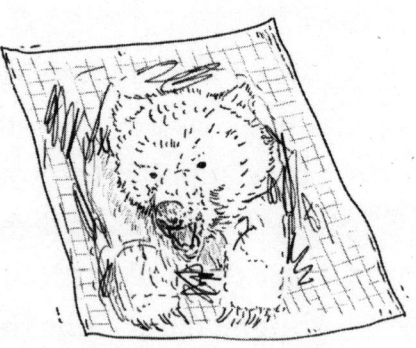

'How are you today, Jasper?' he asks as I take a seat.

'I'm okay.'

'We had a big session last time.' Callum smiles at me. 'Thank you for being so open with me. How have things been at home lately?'

'All right, I suppose. I haven't heard from my dad. And Mum's been busy.'

'And how have you been sleeping?'

'Better, I suppose.'

I open my bag and get out a drawing, tucked in the pages of my maths book. 'I drew this.' I hand it to him, and he takes the piece of paper from me. He places it on the coffee table and looks at it intently.

'Wow. You can really draw, Jasper. Tell me about this...'

I look down at the paper.

He looks back at me. The bear. His eyes burn holes into me, even from the coffee table. I say something I never thought I would tell anyone.

'This is why I can't sleep. I have this nightmare. I had it when I was a kid. And it's back.'

He picks Him up, analyses Him. 'When did it come back?'

'A couple of months ago.'

He nods. 'What was happening at the time the nightmare came back?'

'My fish got sick. Mum's boyfriend was staying a lot. I knew she wanted him to move in. I hadn't heard from Dad in ages...'

'So things were tough. And the nightmare came back.'

'Yeah.'

'When did you first have it?'

'When my parents split up. And Nana died.'

He puts the drawing down. 'So when things are hard, it's scary too... And this is who you see? I wouldn't want to meet this in my dreams, Jasper.'

'I hate it. I hate Him. I feel like He follows me around. He won't go away. He's always with me. Even in the day.'

Now he knows. Somebody knows that there is a bear in my mind. I worry I have said too much.

He knows I am not okay. My mind is not right.

> **WHO AM I?**
> **I AM YOUR END**
> **I AM YOUR DARKNESS**
> **I AM YOUR SHADOW**
> **IF YOU SHOW ME TO THE WORLD**
> **THEY WILL KNOW**
> **THE TIME HAS COME**
> **IT IS THE END**

We sit in silence. Callum continues looking at the drawing. At Him. And I wait. I wait for him to tell me that I'm not normal. That I am impossible too, like my father. There is something wrong with me. But we continue to sit in silence. My heart races.

He picks the drawing up again. 'You're such an incredible artist, Jasper. I love that you can express this. He is a scary creature, I see why He frightens you. You can be really angry, can't you?'

'Yes.'

He puts the drawing down and looks directly at me. 'Who are you so angry at, Jasper?'

'Myself. My dad. I'm so angry at him.'

'Yeah. I can see that.'

'He left me. He doesn't know who I am anymore.'

'He doesn't *know* you?'

'No. He doesn't. Are you going to ring my mum?' I ask, looking at Callum.

'Why would I ring your mother, Jasper?' He clasps his

hands together.

'Because I told you those things. About the bear.'

'I'm not going to ring your mother, unless you want me to.'

'I don't want you to . . .'

I wait. I really thought it was going to be the end of me. I thought if I told anyone about the bear, they would know that I am not okay. I thought it was only a matter of time.

'What did you think was going to happen, Jasper, when you told me about your nightmare?'

'I sometimes think there is something wrong with me, like my dad. To feel these things.'

'Like your dad?'

'Yeah.'

That's why I didn't see my father for a while when my parents split up. He disappeared for ages and we couldn't find him. He was depressed and he couldn't see me.

'He's had struggles with his mental health?' Callum asks. 'And you worry that you might too?'

'I've started to think maybe I'm like him. I figure it's only a matter of time until it happens to me.'

'What happens?'

'What happened to my dad.'

'What was that, Jasper?'

'I don't know, exactly. No one really told me, but he had to go into a hospital when I was younger. For a while. He had to have medication, I think.'

'So you're worried about something, but you don't really know all the facts about it?'

'Yeah.'

'That's a big weight to carry. But you are not your father.' He looks straight into my eyes. 'You are Jasper.'

Sad, but true.

'And you're doing your best, Jasper. We can explore some of that, about your dad, but because that happened to him doesn't mean it will *inevitably* happen to you too. It doesn't work like that. No one knows the future.'

There is something wonderful and terrifying in that fact.

'I do appreciate knowing that about your dad though. There can be a genetic link with mental health, with anxiety. Maybe you could ask a few questions?'

Do I have anxiety? Is that what he's saying? I think I know the answer to that.

'But Jasper, trust that you can handle these feelings and that you can learn skills that will help you cope. You can ask for help. And feelings can be overwhelming, but they come . . . And they go.'

As I leave the room Callum smiles again and says: 'Good work today.' I don't know what he means by that. But I smile back. 'Look after yourself, okay?' he adds. 'Maybe get some exercise, some decent sleep, eat well. It's all going to help. But some big stuff came up today, you know where to find me if you need me, yeah?'

'Yes. Thanks.' I gently close his door behind me and make

my way back to class. Back to real life. Back to Jasper at school in the world.

Exercise and nutrition have not been high on my agenda lately. And the sleep thing, well that's complicated. To be honest, I don't really know what it means to look after myself, but it sounds like it's about time I learned because I'm ready to start feeling better. I want to feel better.

As I sit back at my desk and get my books out, I remember something. I did love to run, no catching balls required. The hundred-metre sprint was one of the only times in my life I actually did well in a physical endeavour.

Not that Dad knew.

37.

I walk home fast, faster than I ever have.

I go straight inside, straight to my room and find my old sneakers. They're at the bottom of the wardrobe and I force my feet into them. They're tight but I do squeeze into them. I grab my phone and type in 'running music'. The first song starts. Fast and loud. I don't know what it is, but it will do.

I slam the front door and jump down the steps. And then I do it: I just start running. It's more of a slow jog to begin with and pretty soon my chest starts to heave and groan. But I do it, I make it around the block. My throat is dry and my legs are heavy, but I want more.

I do another lap. The pain almost feels good. It feels good to run, to feel the wind rushing into my face, my heart beating fast and after three more laps of the block and a quick sprint home I'm left exhausted, hot and sweaty but it feels good.

Everything hurts, but my heart is racing for a good reason, and I feel a rush of adrenalin: not panic, adrenalin. Or is it different? Endorphins. We learned about them in health. Chemicals released when you're exercising. They can make you  feel more positive, apparently, and I can feel them pumping through my body. I have a shower, and I feel water, sweat and more tears flow and drain away as I remember what came up with the counsellor today. Once I'm dressed, I collapse onto my bed and sigh deeply. My face is still hot from exercise; I'm still a bit sweaty and I'm absolutely exhausted, but I'm feeling something I haven't felt in so long.

I don't want to jinx it and it might not last, but since telling Callum about the nightmare and then going for a run, I feel lighter. I feel like the heaviness is beginning to shift. It's lifting away and taking with it the dark cloud that's been hanging over me. What was that word he used in one of our sessions? Content. Maybe that's it? Maybe today I am content.

When Mum gets home, she comes into my room.

'How's your day been?' she asks.

I tell her about the session with the counsellor. 'It was really good today, actually. It really helped, Mum.'

'That's so great, Jasper,' she says, smiling. 'I'm so, so pleased to hear that.'

I figure she wants to know more but she resists the urge to ask. She sits down next to me and grabs my hand instead.

'And I went for a run when I got home too,' I say. 'Four times around the block.'

'You've always been a great runner.'

She knows. Mum knows.

'Thanks. I told the counsellor something today.' I pull my pillow onto my lap and draw circles with my fingertips on the material. 'I told him how we couldn't find Dad after he left.'

Mum seems taken aback. 'I wasn't sure if you remembered all that, Jasper.'

'I do. What happened?'

'Ah, well your father had been quite low for a long time. He was depressed. He wasn't in a good place.'

I push the pillow away. 'Like how bad?'

'It was really hard for him. In the end he realised he needed help to get better. Depression is something he has struggled with on and off for a long time, Jasper. But he got that help. And that's a really good thing.'

'Does it mean I'll have it too, Mum? I mean, I think I already do.'

'Lots of people suffer from depression at some time in their lives, Jasper.'

'But does it make me more likely, Mum? Tell me. If you don't tell me about this stuff, I'm going to make up a whole story way worse in my head and worry about that. Please tell me the truth.'

It's true, I'm sick of googling things and letting my imagination run wild. I want someone to tell me the facts.

'Lots of people will need support at times of their life. I

don't know, maybe you are a little like your father. I know you worry about lots of things, but just accept this as part of your story. And you're getting help now. It does help, doesn't it? Talking to someone?'

I nod.

But can I accept it? Can I do that? Can I accept myself?

Speak of the devil. That night my dad calls, like he knew he was on my mind.

'Guess what? I have a phone number now, Jasper! A cellular phone. I have no idea how to use it, but my friend Helene is going to teach me. I'm ringing on it right now!'

I have no idea who Helene is, but he has a phone. Finally. This is good. He asks me what my mobile number is (even though I have told him many times) and he says he will send me a text so I have his number.

'I didn't think you'd ever get one. And no one calls them cellular phones, by the way.'

'I figure I need one to keep in touch with you. Seems to be the way you kids communicate.'

'And the rest of the adult population, Dad!' I laugh.

'Well, I'm finally on board. Okay, I will text you. Now. How do I hang up? Helene? Helene? Do you know how I hang up the . . .'

And the phone goes dead.

Twenty minutes later, I get a text. TWENTY MINUTES! That's how long it took him to text me!

This is your dad

I send one back. It takes me less than three seconds.

This is your son

Better late than never.

Mum comes in while I'm doing my homework. Well, it's more of a video game.

'Fancy a game of Scrabble?' she asks. 'If I can find where it is? We haven't played in so long.'

'Sure,' I say, turning the computer off. 'I know where it is.'

I open my wardrobe and find it on the top shelf. It's been up there for years, since Nana died. I pass it to Mum and follow her to the kitchen. She starts setting the board up on the dining table.

'You pick a letter first.' She holds out the bag of letters, shaking them to mix them. I pick out the letter H and she picks out N.

'You start,' she says, sitting down.

I start moving my letters around on the little letter stand. It's a tip Nana taught me. 'Move the letter tiles around and all the possibilities will reveal themselves,' she used to say.

A N H U T A J

Nothing much is jumping out. What now, Nana?

Mum watches me. 'How are you doing, Jasper?'

'Not good. No decent letters to start.'

'No, how are you *doing*, not in Scrabble?'

'Oh.' I keep moving the tiles around, wondering what to spell and what to say. 'I'm doing okay, I suppose. How are you?'

'I'm a bit sad.' She looks down at her tiles, moving them around as well. 'It was your nana's birthday today. It's June the eleventh.'

She's right. I hadn't even thought of it.

'I forgot,' I say.

We sit in silence. I place NUT down in the middle of the board.

'Nana would not be impressed with this terrible start,' I say, as Mum writes the score down. I can tell she's thinking about something else. Probably Nana. She loved birthdays. Not the presents, not the cake, but having us over — homemade cards, us all together. She just loved us.

'Mum . . .?'

'Yes, Jasper?'

'I really miss her. Sometimes I feel so gutted that she's not here, that I don't get to have a nana anymore.'

The words make Mum's shoulders collapse. She grabs my hand and holds it tightly. 'I feel the same, Jasper. I miss her every day. She was such a lovely mother and grandmother. We were lucky to have her. And Poppa too.'

I look over at the empty chair across from me and for a split second, I see Nana sitting there, smiling, about to put down a really impressive word on the triple word square. Poppa's in the background too. He's watching the cricket, yelling at the umpire. He's on Manly Steve's couch. He would have loved that couch, now I think of it.

Mum adds her letters on the board. 'All I have is TRAIN. She would not be impressed with me either. And on her birthday!'

We both laugh. Nana would certainly be appalled at this effort. She really did know how to whip our butts at Scrabble.

Mum beats me, but she doesn't celebrate. We both know there were better words in there and something, someone, was missing.

I climb into bed. My body is sore from the run and I am ready for sleep. As I drift off, I see letters on Scrabble tiles. All the words I didn't think of while playing swirl in my mind. I dream of birthdays with Nana — of cake and cards and roses and teacups.

Her birthday was two weeks before mine. She used to call us 'birthday buddies'. We are both born in June.

In two weeks it will be my birthday.

I will be fourteen.

Mum must have been thinking the same thing.

In the morning, she's looking at the calendar in the kitchen while eating her muesli.

'What shall we do for *your* birthday, Jasper?' she asks.

'Oh. Nothing. I don't really want to do anything.' I want

this year to be over. I want it done and to start afresh. Thirteen has been an unlucky number for me.

'You could ask some friends around?'

'Which friends?' I ask.

'From school? Or Finn? You haven't seen him in ages.'

I scoff. I can't see that happening. 'He's hanging out with his private-school mates.'

'Well, let me know what you want to do.'

At school, I see Nina from a distance. She's walking to school alone, wearing headphones. I can't call out, I don't want to surprise her. So I just walk behind.

I miss her.

In maths class, I sit up the front. I listen (for once). I put my hand up, I answer the teacher's questions. I want this. I want to care again. When I pass Nina in the corridor, I smile, and she smiles back. Maybe I can save this friendship.

When I see Callum Hughes again, I tell him about my conversation with Mum, about Dad being depressed when they broke up and before he left too, that he has struggled with depression throughout his life. Callum says my mum is right, many people have times in their lives when they are down, that Dad having struggles with his mental health is not a life sentence for me.

'It's nothing to be embarrassed about, or scared of; however, it does mean it's important to look after yourself. We all need to do that,' he says. 'Every time we have a period of being a bit low, we learn something about what we need to help keep us happy. Sorry . . . I know you don't like that word.'

I nod. Maybe that word is getting easier to hear? I do feel like I'm learning stuff through this, about how I work, how my brain works and what those logs are that keep my fire burning.

'You're not broken, and you don't need to be fixed, okay?' he says. 'You are learning about your thoughts and feelings and trying to understand yourself better and that's a good thing.'

I nod and repeat that to myself. *I'm not broken.*

He gets out the drawing of the bear. He'd asked to keep it until our next session. As he puts it on the coffee table, I take a deep breath. I figured he wasn't going to leave that one, but there's no point trying to hide anything from him, I know this. And I suppose I trust him now. His questions don't scare me as much. He doesn't scare me.

'I find it interesting he's a bear. Do you?' he asks.

'I haven't really thought about it.'

'What do you associate bears with?' He turns the drawing around on the table so it's facing me. I look down and He looks back at me.

'Destruction. Anger. It's like I feel Him, when I'm angry. I feel like I turn into Him. And He destroys things. In the house.'

'*He* destroys things?'

I think about Him. I think about the painting broken on the floor, the books, the plates at Lizzie's. I think about what I saw when I looked in the mirror that day. It's Him. It's me. It's both of us.

'I do.' It comes out before I've had a chance to think about it. A release. 'I destroy things. I break things.'

'So when you feel angry, you feel like an angry bear? Does it scare you, that you can be so angry?'

'Yes. I think it's me. It's me I'm scared of.'

He leans forward towards me. 'You can learn to control it, Jasper, to express it without it being so terrifying. But there are a few rules with anger. We can feel it, tell people when we feel it, but we can't damage property, or hurt people. Or ourselves. Can you promise me that?'

I want to be able to promise him those things. I want to. I really do. I nod. I think of Nina. And how I never want her to feel scared of me again.

'Find the things that help to calm you,' he continues. 'Go for a run, draw, watch something on television. Find whatever works for you.' He puts his notebook down and looks at me. 'Do you know something else about bears? I thought about it after you left last time.'

'What's that?' I ask.

'Bear cubs never know their fathers.'

'What do you mean?' I ask, looking down at the drawing.

'They're solitary animals. Once they've mated, the male leaves. The female bear raises the cub on her own.'

The bear looks back at me, a fatherless cub.

'What would you say to your dad, if you could tell him anything?' Callum asks.

I take a big breath in, feel the weight of that question. Anything... 'I wish it was different.'

That seems enough. Because there's so much.

I see my father's face. From when we were driving along the motorway that day. I know that every time he tells me how tall I'm getting, it's salt in the wound. It shows how long it's been since he's seen me, and he doesn't seem to see it. If I could, I would tell him that Elise must be devastated having lost her mother, but it's also really hard losing a father when he chooses not to be with you. That is devastating too.

I would tell him that I wish it was different between us.

I would tell him that I miss him.

38.

'Jasper? . . . Wait up!'

I turn and see Nina behind me as I approach the school gate.

'Hi?' I'm surprised to hear her voice; to see her walking towards me. 'How are you?'

'I'm okay,' she says. 'Are you okay?'

'Yeah, I'm good actually,' I say, smiling. And I am.

'You seem different.'

This makes me happy, that she can see it. Here is my chance.

Did I say that makes me 'happy'?

Don't stuff this up, Jasper.

'I've been seeing the school counsellor actually, it's helping.' I have no idea how she is going to respond but it's worth the risk.

She smiles. 'That's good, Jasper. And it's really helping?'

I nod. 'Yeah, it is.'

There is a relief for me now, that she knows I'm trying. Not that I needed the counsellor just to prove something to her. I needed it for me, I know that now.

We start walking together, like we used to.

'I was in a bit of a bad place before, about a lot of things, Mum's boyfriend moving in, angry with my dad. But hey, guess what?'

'What?'

'My mum's boyfriend has a daughter, right? I told you about her...'

'Elise?'

'Yeah! She's having a baby. A girl. Her dad's freaking out about it.'

'So, you're going to be a kind of an uncle?'

Yeah. I suppose she's right!

As we approach the corner, I have that same feeling that I used to have, that I don't want to say goodbye. At that moment, I know what I want to do for my birthday.

'Hey, Nina. It's my birthday next weekend. Would it be totally weird if you came to a family dinner? I'm going to ask Elise if she can come up too and I really want you to meet her.'

She doesn't say anything for what feels like ages, and I think she's probably trying to think of an excuse, trying to find a reason not to come. I feel like a dick for even asking. But then she says: 'Yeah, sure. That sounds nice.'

When I get home, Manly Steve is on his computer in the office.

As I walk down the hallway, I notice there is a new piece of art up: the picture hook on the wall isn't empty anymore. I feel a huge sense of relief to see the blank space filled. There is another bare hook next to it.

'How was your day, Jasper?' he calls out to me and I stand in the doorway.

'It was good, thanks. How was yours?'

He turns around on his chair. 'Not bad. Thanks for asking.'

I tell him about my birthday and ask if he thinks Elise could come up for a family dinner.

'I'm going to cook something vegetarian. My friend Nina is going to come and if it's okay I might ask my dad too. He might not be able to come up, but I'll ask.'

'That sounds like a great idea. I'll let Elise know. I'm sure she would love to come if she can.'

'Actually, I have her number. I can text her,' I say, getting my phone out of my pocket.

'Tell her I'll pay for the flight,' he smiles and turns back to his computer.

'Thank you, Steve. Thanks a lot.'

I go into my room and throw my bag on my bed. I text Elise the details. She replies: *Wouldn't miss it for the world, especially if Dad's paying*

I call my dad but it goes to voicemail. 'Hello this is David Woods. I'm not sure how to check the messages on this thing yet. So maybe don't leave one. Cheerio.'

Ha. I send him a text.

It's my birthday soon. I'm cooking dinner. Saturday June 25, 7 p.m. Can you make it?

I figure he might not get the text, but a few minutes later I get a reply.

I will try to be there.

My heart jumps. This is good. This is what I want to do for my birthday. It feels right. I go into the lounge and grab a pile of Mum's recipe books and start looking through them for inspiration. I immediately regret saying I would cook. Everything looks impossible and I don't really know what sauté, julienne or garnishes are. Maybe it's going to have to be pizza.

Mum arrives home and sees me looking through the books.

'Are you cooking?' she asks.

'Not tonight.' But I tell her about my birthday plans and that I may or may not attempt to cook something for everyone.

'Oh, that sounds great, Jasper.'

'Nina, from school, is going to come too,' I say, trying not to make a big deal out of it.

'Really?' she says with a smile. 'And who is Nina?'

'A friend,' I say.

The next day I sit with Nina in art class.

I tell her how Mum thinks I'm cooking my birthday dinner but now I'm freaking out. Elise is a half-vegetarian and there are going to be six people there and all I know how to cook is eggs, scrambled or poached, but that probably won't cut it.

'I make a really good risotto thing. Pumpkin and parmesan cheese. Lots of herbs. Maybe we could make it together?' she says.

'Are you serious? You'd help me?'

'Yeah, it will be fun!' She smiles. 'I'll come over in the afternoon.'

'Awesome. Thanks, Nina.'

A feeling rushes through my body, I feel like this might be the best birthday ever. Maria comes over to our table and hands me a package.

W-WHAT ARE YOU GONNA DO TO ME?

'Hang this somewhere special, okay?'

'Thanks,' I say, taking the envelope. It's a framed copy of my artwork. I place it by my bag at my feet.

Maria smiles and looks over to Nina. 'I kinda want it for my house. But I suppose I'd better let him keep it.'

'Oh. Can I see it?' Nina moves her chair closer. And my heart sinks.

'It's weird.'

'I like weird,' she says, blushing a little.

My heart races as I bring the envelope back onto the table, slowly unwrapping the tissue paper.

'You're going to think it's really dark. Don't judge me.'

'Hurry up and show me.'

I take the last of the tissue away and show her. The bear. I look around for something to look at instead of her face.

'Cool. That is amazing, Jasper. Like better than amazing. I absolutely love it.'

'An angry-looking bear is going to eat me and you are like I love it.' I wrap it up again. Hoping we can move on.

'I do though. I love it. But I don't want him to eat you. I would be sad if he did.'

Sad? Okay... Is that a compliment?

The bell rings and I place the art back in the envelope.

'I need your signature now because you're going to be famous one day,' Nina says as she packs her things into her bag.

I laugh. 'Don't know about that.'

Nina gets up to leave. 'Bye, Robinson-Woods,' she says with a wave.

'Later, Frankton-Forbes,' I reply.

I have another session with Callum Hughes. I tell him about my birthday plans, and he smiles. 'It sounds like it's going to be a great day.'

I can't help but smile too. I nearly invite him, but that

would be super-weird and probably very inappropriate.

He leans back into his chair and watches me. 'You seem in a good space at the moment, Jasper?'

'I suppose I am.' I smile.

'It's great to see you like this.'

I nod. It does feel good too. I think back to the Jasper who sat in this room not that long ago. I wish I could have told him he was going to feel very different soon.

'Every time we have a tough patch, it sends us a message about what we need in the future,' Callum says, placing his chin into his hand. 'I'm curious: what have you learned about yourself lately, Jasper?'

I fiddle with the zip on my jacket. It makes the sound like the zip of a tent, slowly opening.

I imagine poking my head out of the tent in the early morning.

'I think . . . I was lonely. I suppose I've learned I need to talk to people, because my thoughts get a bit out of control otherwise.'

'Yes. For sure. Talking can definitely help when you are holding a lot in.' He continues to watch me, encouraging me to keep thinking.

'I was in a bad place. I didn't like myself. But things feel quite different now. And I'm not so worried about the what-ifs.'

'Yeah, nice work. The what-ifs aren't helpful, are they? We can worry ourselves around in circles with those.'

I bring my hands together. One thumb traces small circles

into the palm of my hand. I know that's what I do. Up that tree. How much time I spend worrying about all the potential disasters. And what if the what-ifs aren't true? What if the what-ifs don't happen? What a waste of my time.

'If we only have negative thoughts, it's hard for positive things to happen,' Callum says, as if he sees me up that tree. 'That's what we can do for ourselves. We can gain back that power over our thoughts. The way we *feel* comes from how we *think* and you're a deep thinker, Jasper. Sometimes it helps to ask: Are these thoughts helpful? Are they making me feel good? If the answer is no, choose to think of something else, something more helpful.'

'My thoughts can turn into monsters,' I say, remembering the bear like a shadow behind me.

'Yeah. So tell that monster thought to get lost. It's spoiling all the fun.'

When I get home, I put my artwork in my cupboard. I'm not sure what I'll do with it. Maybe Maria should have kept it?

I sit on the bed and find myself grabbing my phone and googling *do father bears know their cubs?*

Callum was right. Not only do father bears leave, but they've also been known to eat cubs! Even their own! Holy crap. Turns out there are some really shit fathers in the animal kingdom. To balance all that out, I read the list of good dads in the animal world. Red fox dads, marmosets, emperor penguins, ostriches — they all do very well. And dad seahorses actually give birth to their young. Male giant African bullfrogs too, they carry like six-thousand eggs in their vocal sac and throw them up releasing baby tadpoles. Gross — but what good dads!

My birthday approaches quickly. Before I know it, it's the weekend.

Elise arrives on Friday night. She has a small baby bump that she proudly shows off. We sit on the front steps while Mum and Steve plant some flowers in the front garden.

'I can even feel little kicks, Jasper. It is the craziest thing ever!' She places her hand over her stomach and smiles.

'That must be weird,' I say, imagining an alien inside me.

'Weird. And amazing.' We watch as Steve hands my mum a punnet of yellow flowers, kissing her cheek as he does.

'Did you know African bullfrog dads carry heaps of eggs

in their vocal sac and throw them up?'

'Um. No. I didn't! But eww.' Elise laughs and hits me on the leg. 'You're hilarious, Jasper.'

'Sorry, been learning about that . . . at school.'

'So . . . tell me everything.' Elise turns to face me and looks me in the eye with a smile.

'Everything?'

'Yes, tell me why you seem so chirpy? Is it because you are about to be fourteen tomorrow?'

I laugh, trying to wipe a mark off my shoe. 'Yeah and other stuff too.'

'Yes! Oh to be fourteen.' She stands up, balancing her hand on my shoulder to help herself up. 'Let's go inside, I need water.' I follow her down the hallway and midway, she stops. She looks at her mum's painting, the new one hanging, then notices the bare picture hook. 'What's that one for?'

'I dunno,' I shrug. 'Your dad left it empty.'

That night we watch a movie together and have dinner on our knees: normally we're not allowed to do that but Mum says it's fine. I try really hard to not spill dinner on the fancy couch. Elise sits next to me, Mum on the other side and Manly Steve next to her. All four of us on the big goddam comfortable couch that I thought would ruin my life. Turns out it didn't. In fact, we needed the extra room.

Out of the corner of my eye, I find myself watching the people sitting next to me, instead of the movie.

Once I'm in bed, I don't sleep.

I don't sleep because I'm excited about tomorrow.

37.

I am fourteen years old.

Mum comes in around 9 a.m. to wake me.

'It's your birthday, sleepy-head. Time to get up!' She opens my curtains and bright light fills the room.

I get changed quickly and go out into the kitchen. Everyone else is up, waiting for my arrival.

'Happy birthday, my darling,' Mum says, hugging me. Elise comes and hugs me too.

'Happy birthday Jas.' Or is it Jazz? I still haven't decided.

Manly Steve just says: 'Happy birthday, mate.' No hug. I'm good with that.

Mum hands me an envelope. I open the card, it says: *With love from Mum and Steven.* My first birthday card from them both. Inside is a one hundred dollar note.

'Woah, that's awesome, Mum, thank you. And thank you

too,' I say to Manly Steve, who pats me on the shoulder. 'Happy birthday, mate.' (Again.)

'We thought this way, you can decide what you want to do with it. Another fish maybe?'

'Ah no. Definitely not,' I say. That will NOT be happening!

'Well, whatever you choose.'

Manly Steve has made pancakes again and this time he gives me the best one, first one out of the fry pan. He doesn't even say anything when I drown the pancakes in loads of maple syrup.

After breakfast I go to my room and give it a tidy, in case Nina comes in here later. The thought makes my heart race. I throw my stinky running shoes under the bed and seeing them helps me realise I know what I want to buy with the birthday money: some decent running shoes. A good pair. I want to run more, like I used to. Not to run away. But to run towards.

As I'm making my bed, Manly Steve appears at the doorway.

'Hi. Can I come in?'

'Sure,' I say, pushing dirty socks under the bed.

'I wanted to check something — are you happy if I put your art up in the hallway? The piece from the exhibition?'

'Oh,' I wasn't expecting that. 'It's not too ... dark?'

'What? No, it's great. You should be so proud of it. We certainly are.'

'Sure, then I will find it.'

Manly Steve watches as I open my cupboard. The package is there, still wrapped. I take it out of the envelope and tissue and pass it to him. I dunno how I feel about Him in the hallway. The Bear. But I will see, I suppose. Maybe it will be okay? Manly Steve smiles. 'I'll put it up now.'

'Thanks.'

Maybe he's not that bad.

'Your room smells like socks, Jasper. And put those dishes in the dishwasher.' He points to the six mugs on my desk before leaving the room.

And there it is . . . He's back! Dick knob.

I hear a beep on my phone, and I open the window. It is from Nina.

Happy B.Day Robinson-Woods. List for dinner: Vege Stock, Onion, Garlic, Olive Oil, Arborio rice, Pumpkin, Parmesan cheese, Salad stuff? If we want, on the side? And bread? I'll bring herbs from Dad's garden.

I read the text twice. I think I know what most of those things are. I have never heard of an Arborio. And salad stuff? That could mean lots of things. Can't she be more specific?

I reply.

Thanks Chef. I'm on it, see you 4ish

I feel really stressed about the whole thing but I'm trying to not freak out. What's the worst that can happen? We order pizza. It will be fine. Mum gives me her EFTPOS card and Elise says she can come with me to help. She will know what an Arborio is. Steve gives Elise his car keys.

She looks shocked. 'He's never let me drive his car before.'

'Can you even drive?' I ask as we walk to the driveway.

'Yes. I have my full licence. But Dad has never let me drive his fancy car before. This is a big step in our relationship, Jasper!'

'Don't mess it up then, Elise!' I say, scuffing dirt off the soles of my sneakers quickly before I get in.

'I can't wait to eat your delicious food, Jasper,' Elise says as she starts the car.

'It might be very bad. Don't expect too much.'

She does know what Arborio is. A type of rice, apparently, for risottos. She helps me find everything we need at the supermarket. She even chooses the salad stuff and adds a few extra things into the trolley 'for the baby'. Peanut butter, gherkins and cheese . . . ? Apparently, she likes to eat them on toast? Strange.

'This kid has an unusual taste in food. I'm gonna call her Gherkin. Well, maybe that'll be her middle name.' She chuckles then looks at me with a smirk as we wait in the checkout queue. 'So, you got a crush on this Nina, or what?' She leans against the trolley.

'Nah . . . She's cool. Just because she's a girl doesn't mean it's a crush. Boys and girls can be friends.'

She gives me a cheeky smile. 'Oh totally. I have loads of male friends.' She is on to me. 'But you seem like you have a little crush.'

'What's your boyfriend like?' I ask, starting to put the groceries on the counter.

'He's really nice. You'll meet him next time. But don't change the subject, you have a crush, eh?'

I go bright red and even the checkout guy smiles.

Nina arrives at 4 p.m. on the dot. She knocks on the front door quietly. I rush to answer it so a stranger doesn't greet her.

'Hello,' I say, trying to hide the shock that she has actually turned up.

'Happy birthday!'

I usher her inside. She looks nervous and I hope she didn't feel like she had to come to this weird birthday dinner. Out of sympathy for me.

'Have you had a good day?' she asks as she gives me a hug. I have the electric shock feeling again, the one when our elbows touched in art class.

'Yeah, I did.'

And it has been nice. It was a quiet day, tidying the house, hanging with Elise, and a bit of gardening with Mum and Steve.

Nina follows me into the lounge and Mum, Steve and Elise all stand up formally and in unison and it feels so ridiculous. I introduce them.

'Nina, this is my mother Michelle; and this is Steven and Elise. And this is Nina.'

'Welcome, Nina. Lovely to meet you,' Mum says.

Elise waves.

Nina has two presents in her hands, which I have not yet acknowledged. Am I supposed to? I'm not sure of the etiquette. She does though.

'Oh, I have presents! Um, this one's for you,' she says, handing me a small box. 'And I got this one for you too,' she says, handing the other one to Elise.

'What?' Elise says, looking surprised. 'Me?'

'It's only little.'

'You didn't need to bring anything . . . Should we open them now?' I ask, wondering if I should have got her a present too? Would that have been weird? I'm that grateful she has turned up.

'If you want,' she says. 'Go ahead.'

I open mine first, awkwardly. I find present-opening particularly stressful: everyone staring at me. The present has blue-and-white-striped wrapping. Inside is a really fancy set of artists' pencils in a carved wooden box.

'The lady in the art shop says these are good for sketching,' Nina says, nervously. 'Wasn't sure if you had any.'

They are amazing. And I love them. 'Wow, thank you, that is so nice of you. I haven't got fancy ones like these.' I feel my cheeks warm from blushing again. 'Your turn,' I say to Elise so that everyone can look away from me.

Elise smiles at Nina. 'It's so sweet of you. You really didn't have to get ME anything?'

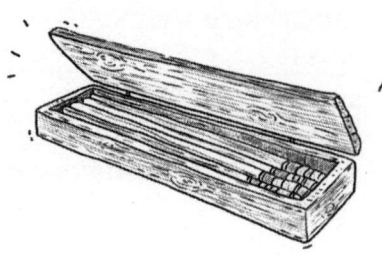

'It's more for your baby really,

Jasper told me you're having one.'

Elise smiles as she opens the box, pulling out a tan-coloured teddy bear.

'Oh. It's so adorable, Nina.' She hugs the bear close. 'I love him. It's her first teddy. Look at it, Jas.' She passes me the bear. It's got a cute, stitched nose and smile and little button eyes. It's wearing a green ribbon. It's super cute.

Nina smiles. 'I know how much Jasper loves bears.'

I laugh. She doesn't know what she is saying.

But maybe I feel differently about them now. Every time I see Him in my mind, I don't see an angry bear, but a lost bear, lonely, wondering where his dad is. I feel like the shadow the bear cast on me has gone.

'Well, we should get started, I suppose,' I say, keen to get away from the awkward present-opening ceremony. Nina follows me to the kitchen.

'You bring presents. And now you're going to help cook dinner. I think my mum will want to trade me in for an upgrade.'

She laughs. But I'm being serious. 'So this is the kitchen,' I say, pointing out what is clearly a kitchen. 'Apparently there are pots in here somewhere, I suppose we need one?' I point to random cupboards.

'Are you serious, you don't even know where the pots are?'

'I'm kidding. I actually cook a bit . . . mostly eggs. And toast. Does toast count?'

'Well, you don't need a pot for it. We have this thing called a toaster.'

She opens cupboards, looking for a chopping board. I tell her I know where it is but then can't find it. Dammit. Someone has moved it to make me look bad. Probably Manly Steve . . .

Mum comes into the kitchen. 'We're going to go for a walk, leave you to it,' she says, putting on her jacket. 'Need anything?'

A chopping board. 'No, we're fine,' I say, waving her away.

'I'm staying here,' says Elise, lying on the couch. 'But I like setting tables. I'll do that once I've had a lie-down.'

Before Mum leaves she comes up to me and quietly says: 'What time is your dad coming?'

I still haven't heard from him today. Maybe he will turn up, maybe he won't? I'm not sure yet how I feel about that but I'm trying not to think about it.

'Probably six-ish,' I shrug. But that's a guess.

Nina gives me the job of cutting onions and garlic. I pretend to know what I'm doing, but she comes and finishes the job, cutting the onion into much smaller pieces.

I watch her as she does it.

'My nana says good meals always start with onion and garlic,' she says, throwing the onion skins into the food waste bin.

'What? So does my nana. Well, she did.'

'Oh . . .' She smiles. 'Funny.'

Nina is a good cook. Well, she knows how to cut way

smaller than I do, anyway. It's quite obvious I don't do much chopping.

'Where are the wooden spoons?' she asks, looking around the kitchen again.

'Next to ... the metal ones?'

'Which are ..?'

'Where all good spoons are kept,' I say searching the drawers but having no luck.

She works out it's best just to open all the drawers and eventually she finds things. She adds her 'secret herbs and spices' and the kitchen starts to smell delicious. I'm shocked I had anything to do with it — though I have mostly dropped things on the floor.

'Right, now cut the pumpkin. But don't lose a finger,' she says, handing me a knife. 'You do not want to spend your birthday at the hospital.'

Oh. God. Is this when disaster strikes? I knew today was going too well. Am I going to end up in A&E? I actually manage to survive the challenge, although pumpkin-piece sizes vary drastically.

Elise puts a nice tablecloth on the table and arranges some candles down the middle. She goes into the garden and picks some roses from Mum's rose bush and puts them in a vase.

'Is this too much for you, Jas?' she asks.

'No. I like it.' It reminds me of my nana, she loved roses and always had little bunches on the table. For a moment I feel a little sad, but there she is on the table. In a vase.

Mum and Steve return from their walk. There is still no

sign of my dad. But I'm okay. I am okay.

'Nina, this looks incredible,' Mum says as Nina puts the risotto down on the table. 'We could smell our house from down the road.'

'I helped,' I say, wanting some credit.

'He did . . . You did!' Nina says reassuringly. 'And you can teach me how to make a poached egg next because I suck at those.'

'And the table. Beautiful, Elise. No sign of your father, Jasper?' Mum asks, looking around as if he might pop up from behind the couch.

'Nope.'

'Call him and see where he is. Or shall I?' she asks.

'You can if you want.' I take a seat at the table. 'Whatever.'

But when she does, his new cell phone is switched off. 'I'm sorry, Jasper. His phone is off. Shall we wait?'

'No,' I reply. 'Sit down. Dinner is ready, we should eat.'

Mum looks sympathetic, but I am not prepared to wait for him. We all know it would probably be a long wait.

'It's fine, Mum. I am fine. I honestly don't care.'

And I actually don't tonight.

'We need music!' Elise says, and puts a playlist of her favourite Wellington bands on the stereo and everyone else sits down at the table. There is one empty chair for Dad, but then I look around.

I have everything here that I wanted, right here. This is as it was meant to be.

I stand and start to serve out the risotto, like I had

something to do with it.

'Who taught you to cook like this, Nina?' Mum asks, as I put some down on her plate.

'My dad. He's a really good cook,' she replies. 'And we eat this one quite a lot.'

I grab my fork and try some. The risotto is amazing. It's creamy and flavourful and full of herbs. I could eat vegetarian food for life if it all tastes like this. Elise eats four helpings 'for the baby' before I've even finished my first.

'I need this recipe, Nina!' she says, looking like she's considering a fifth helping.

There are no awkward silences at the table. Everyone asks Nina lots of questions about her family, and she handles it pretty well, telling us all about their summer holiday in the South Island and all her hobbies.

'I was born in Wellington, actually,' she tells us. 'But we moved here last year for Dad's work.'

'Oh, I live in Wellington,' Elise pipes up.

'Jasper told me,' Nina smiles at me.

Elise tells us all about her favourite theatre shows and what her boyfriend Louis is like. I sit pretty quietly and absorb it all. At one stage Manly Steve looks over to me and smiles. I think he's even enjoying it too. At one stage he grabs Mum's hands across the table and it doesn't even gross me out.

Mum doesn't offer me a glass of wine, but it does feel different from all the birthdays I've had before.

There is still no sign of my dad.

Once everyone is finished, Mum and Steve offer to do

the clean-up since we were the cooks. Elise says she needs another lie-down because she's eaten too much, so Nina and I go and sit on the front deck. I can hear Mum and Manly Steve putting on some cheesy music and singing along as they tidy up.

'Sorry,' I say, embarrassed.

'My parents do that.'

The house feels alive. The sun is starting to set, and the sky is a warm yellow colour. There is a chill in the evening air.

'Your stepdad seems nice,' Nina says.

'Yeah, he's not too bad,' I reply. I'm getting used to him being around.

'And Elise is super-cool.'

'She is,' I agree. It's been so nice having her here tonight.

'So,' says Nina, pulling her hair up into a ponytail. 'I have a strange question, Jasper.'

'Okay . . .' I say.

'When I first came to your house, to drop the invite off for the exhibition? Were you . . . in that tree?'

My heart sinks.

'Tree? What? Which one?'

'That one.' She points to my tree. I look up as if I've never even noticed a tree in my front garden before. 'I turned back at one point and thought I saw something jumping down from it. Something that looked like you.'

My brain races. Imaginary cat? I don't know if that's going to work here. Do I lie? Do I try to be cool? Or do I admit defeat and just laugh? I'm going with that.

'Okay, fine. I still climb trees sometimes, okay? It's dumb, I know.'

She smiles but looks down. 'So you *were* hiding from me?'

'No! Not from you. No way.' I look over to the tree and remember that day. I'd just come home from the trip with Dad. 'Hiding from other things, but not you. I did jump down. I tried to come after you, but you had gone.'

'I thought you were trying to keep away from me. I felt a bit gutted.'

'Is that why you didn't talk to me the next day in art class?'

'I felt a bit stupid.' She plays with the hem of her shirt. 'Like I shouldn't have come.'

'Oh man, I wasn't dodging you. I was a bit messed up that day. Sometimes I hide up there. I feel like such a dick. I wanted to talk to you. I really did.'

She looks back to the tree. 'Is it a good hiding spot? Show me.' And with that, she jumps off the steps and starts making her way to the tree. She lifts herself up onto the first branch and puts her hand down to pull me up.

'You're good at this.' I take her hand and climb into the tree as well.

'I've done some tree climbing in my day,' she says, climbing another branch higher.

I follow her and then we sit next to each other, swinging our legs below us. It's not that comfortable but there we are, both of us, perched precariously in my poor tree.

'I think I can understand the appeal,' she says, looking around. She leans her head back into the trunk of the tree.

'I'm sorry, Nina. I'm sorry I didn't jump down that day when you were here. I was really, I am . . . really shy and I didn't know what to do. I know I'm weird.'

'Jasper, we're all a little weird,' she says, picking a leaf from a branch and blowing it into my face. 'You're not the only one.'

40.

Nina looks around the tree and rests her hands on the trunk where I carved into it with angry, deep grooves.

'Thanks for asking me to dinner,' she says. 'It's been really nice.'

'Thank *you* for coming. And cooking dinner. This has been my favourite birthday yet.' I smile. And it really has.

'I'm sorry your dad didn't turn up,' she says, looking up to the night sky through the leaves.

'His loss,' I reply. 'He missed out on "Nina's Magnificent Pumpkin Risotto". What a dick.'

She laughs. There is a moment of awkward silence, which is broken by Mr Schultz and Princess walking along the road. We both watch as Princess does her daily poo on our front lawn. Oh god. Timing.

'Gross,' says Nina. But her face soon turns to shock and

disgust as Mr Schultz looks around and moves on. 'No, no, no. He's not picking it up!'

'That's Mr Schultz ... Every day without fail that dog does a poo on our lawn.'

'That is so not cool, you should say something. Go on!'

'Nah, it's okay.'

'No. It's not. Go on!' Her elbow digs into the side of my ribs. 'Say something.'

'No.' I shake my head and readjust on the branch, starting to feel uncomfortable.

'Jasper!' She looks at me. Eyebrows raised.

And I surprise myself. I close my eyes and yell out in a voice I didn't know I had: 'We can see you! Pick up your dog poo ... Please.'

Mr Schultz looks around confused over where the voice is coming from. But he swiftly returns to the pile of poo and scoops it up with a plastic bag, looking embarrassed. So he does have some of those doggie poo bags, he's just lazy. He yanks Princess in the direction of home and they scuttle off.

I put my hand over my mouth, surprised at myself. We both silently laugh, like tree-ninjas. Nina looks at me and I realise I've been kidding myself lately. Is she a friend? Do I have a crush? I watch her lips curl in a shy smile: this is definitely a crush. I like her a lot. Nina Frankton-Forbes. In all her double-barrelled glory.

'I should have done that ages ago,' I say. 'Hey and thanks for the pencils again. They are great.' More blushing. Obvious blushing.

'Glad you like them. Will you draw me something?'

'Yes. I will.'

Another silence. We sit, listening to the bad singing from inside the house, the sounds of the city and the rustling of leaves. And my mind exploding with things I want to draw, for her.

'He's missing out, you know?' Nina says, looking out onto the street.

'Who? Mr Schultz?'

'No. Your dad,' she says then looks to me. 'He is missing out, not having you in his life. You are pretty cool, Jasper, and very talented. Even if you don't see it.'

The blushing intensifies.

'He will regret it one day, I think.' She continues to look up to the darkening sky. Now her face is harder to make out in the diminishing light.

I sit with that, not sure how to respond, but she might just be right. And did she say I was pretty cool?

'Thank you,' I say quietly.

Then something happens that I'm not expecting, not in the tree, nor today on my fourteenth birthday. Nina leans towards me, balancing precariously on the branch and kisses me, once on the cheek. My red, hot cheek. 'Happy birthday, Jasper.'

I don't know what I'm supposed to do. She stays there for a short moment: just enough for me to feel her warm breath on my skin right where the kiss landed. Briefly, I think I imagined it, but the warm spot stays.

We both smile and then look away. Okay, now this is officially my favourite birthday in the history of all birthdays.

'Thanks,' I say, again. 'You're cool too.' And this time I say it right at the right time.

'CAKE!' I hear from inside and it really is perfect timing.

'Let's go back inside,' Nina says, climbing down.

'Sure,' I reply. Cool. Cool as a cucumber, while inside a fire ignites.

I jump down the tree and before I get to the top step, there is a beep from my phone inside my pocket.

It's my dad.

Happy birthday Jasper. Sorry I didn't make it. I will make it up to you.

I don't reply. I walk inside. Maybe one day, I will be brave and tell him that he let me down, that he is missing out, that if I ever become a dad, I won't do that to my kid. I won't walk away, I won't disappear. I will know my kid.

And that's how I am different from my dad. While there are parts of me like him, this way I can decide to be very, very different.

In the kitchen, the lights are off and a huge chocolate cake sits on the table, candles lit.

'Happy birthday!' Mum says, pulling me towards her.

Everyone sings 'Happy Birthday' and I look around awkwardly; I've never known what to do while this is happening either. But sometimes you have to sit and let things happen. Be awkward. Be uncomfortable. But be brave. And it might actually be okay. I blow out the candles and I make a wish. I'm sorry: this one is just for me to know, but even thinking it makes me smile. The future does have some unknowns and while that is scary, it's exciting too. All those possibilities.

I look around me, at Elise, Nina, Mum and Manly Steve. They are smiling too. I feel . . . content. A few months ago, I felt like I had nothing to look forward to. I didn't want to be Jasper Robinson-Woods most days.

I had no idea how different I could feel.

I honestly didn't know this was possible. I am surrounded by people I care about, people who turned up for me today and I am excited about what's ahead, a future I want, with people I want to share it with.

I don't feel lonely anymore.

I, Jasper Robinson-Woods, might be okay. I'm not perfect, I'm still shy, worrying, blushing, bad at keeping fish alive and always late for school. But I'm here, trying my best and perfectly okay.

This whole time, I thought it was nearly the end of me and now I see . . . this is the beginning.

I want to be here.

I want to be here for all of it.

HELLO
I'VE BEEN ASKING WHO YOU ARE
BUT I KNOW
YOU ARE NOT MY ENEMY
YOU ARE ONLY MY FEAR
AND I NO LONGER FEAR YOU
YOU ARE MY ANGER
AND I ACCEPT YOU
YOU ARE POWERFUL IF I GIVE YOU POWER
AND I CHOOSE NOT TO
YOU DO NOT DEFINE ME

I DEFINE MYSELF

ACKNOWLEDGEMENTS

To my daughter Sylvie, the very first reader of *Bear*, thank you for giving me the confidence to share this story. The next person I asked was my friend Sally Sutton; I'm so grateful for your encouragement. Thanks also to Rosa Shiels for your valuable feedback. Peter Salmon, thank you for being my biggest cheerleader in writing and in life, and for bringing Morgana O'Reilly into my life — an amazing friend and supporter.

Most of this book was written at the kitchen tables of my fellow writer friends. Anna Harding, Emma Vere-Jones, Kirstin Marcon and other members of our wonderful writing group, thank you for the cups of tea, laughter and helpful chats.

A huge thank you to Storylines Trust and Tessa Duder. Winning the Storylines Tessa Duder Award for *Bear* was such a privilege. Allen & Unwin New Zealand, thank you for believing in this book and for the warm welcome you gave me. What an amazing team you are! A special mention to Jenny Hellen and Leonie Freeman; it's been such a dream working with you. Thank you for choosing Emma Neale to support me in the editing process. Emma, your insightful feedback and thoughtful questions were so helpful.

Pippa Keel Situ, you are such a talent. A heartfelt thanks for helping me create this world for Jasper with your clever illustrations. I love them! Thank you also to Kate Barraclough the designer, who brought it all together.

I'm also grateful to the New Zealand Society of Authors and Creative NZ for time with Michelle Elvy as part of their CompleteMS Manuscript Assessment Programme; it was incredibly valuable. I will carry these gems of knowledge with me into future writing.

I want to acknowledge all the blended and single-parent families out there. I faced this as a child and as an adult. I know there are challenges, but there can be magic. I feel so grateful for my big family now, although it can be a little difficult explaining how we're all connected. Thank you to my children, Sylvie, Lenny and Leia, you inspire me to write. To my partner Damon, thank you for your support and for how hard you work for us. Much love to my parents, Rose and Robin, for gifting me a curiosity about people and their stories. To my siblings, Ben and Anahera, I dedicate this book to you. You exist here in Jasper's world.

And to the reader, thank you (and extra points for reading

the acknowledgements). I thought of you the whole way. I wanted this story to resonate with you. As writers, we are often asked where our ideas come from. For *Bear*, it was a feeling, or rather, an overwhelming number of feelings. I hope I've done those feelings justice. If you can relate to them, I encourage you to seek support, and if you don't find help the first time, keep trying until you do — whether from a counsellor, a parent, an extended family member or a phone counselling line. I was a counsellor for Youthline NZ for many years, and they do amazing work. Have courage in this world, and please be kind to yourself.

ABOUT THE AUTHOR

Kiri Lightfoot is a New Zealand-based author and actor. She has worked as a scriptwriter in children's television and as an actor both for theatre and screen. Kiri worked for many years as a telephone counsellor with Youthline and as a volunteer mentor in an alternative education school. Kiri has three school-aged children and lives in central Auckland. She has previously published two picture books: *Ming's Iceberg* and *Every Second Friday*. *Bear* is her first novel.